MOUTH OF THE TYNE

A Novel by Anna Heslop

There are too many people to mention them all. I love you all, but especially you, Mam.

Be kind.

Mouth of the Tyne, Anna Heslop

Chapter One

Mia Moore heaved the last back-straining box up to her stomach level and climbed the two flights to her new, shared apartment. She was twenty-one years old, tall, blonde, clumsy and sick of unloading boxes. Poor Fred, male best friend number one, had been sent home early after a ridiculous accident that resulted in most of her underwear flying down the street towards the River Tyne. It was nineteen degrees outside; the sky above the sea was a fine blue. Mia wore a thin pink strap top, since heat and manual labour do not tend to mix well. Tynemouth, in the North East of England, was where Mia and her best friend, Steph, had managed to find a little flat, which happened to be perfect for them. It was close to work and close, but not too close, to their families.

Their rented flat was a second floor three-bed maisonette and was technically sea view through the trees opposite. In the living room, there was a huge bay window, facing North, which looked towards the old Priory Castle and all its tourists. The previous owner, an elderly gentleman, had suffered a stroke so needed full time assistance in a care home. To pay the fees his family had needed to rent the flat as soon as possible, which meant the rent price was set extremely low.

The cardboard weight fell from Mia's hands when she finally conquered the torturous stairs and straightened up, staring around her new home. On the first floor, the living room and the smallest bedroom, which Mia was taking, were to the right, with the kitchen off to the left. The stairs wound up from the small entrance hall to the second-floor landing, which lead off to the other two bedrooms, the bathroom and a small second toilet. It had previously been beautifully done out, so somehow it did not feel right filling it with their mismatched furniture and miscellaneous junk. As it stood, the layout of the living room consisted of an old sofa, an even older armchair, which had once belonged to Mia's Grandma, and mounds of boxes. It could probably have done with some TLC, but that did not matter, it was theirs.

They were both too tired to do anything more than exchange a few comments on the weather as Steph settled her OCD by cleaning and organizing and Mia bustled around, trying to look busy but not actually doing anything helpful. It was too easy for her to get distracted as they unpacked. Packing had been a nightmare. Her Grandma and sister had desperately tried to throw things out, but Mia hoarded too much and was distracted by items she had not seen for years.

"Come on, lazy bones," Steph nudged Mia from her trance. "I'd like to have a bed to sleep in tonight. Get emptying the boxes so I can make mine up!"

"Sorry." Mia shook herself but still did not move very quickly.

Ripping some sellotape off the nearest box and finding kitchen utensils, she dawdled through to the kitchen and hung them along the moss coloured, tiled wall. Steph began humming the tune to 'I'm on top of the world' and it developed into a round when Mia joined in too.

Leaving many of the boxes in piles in the living room, Mia carried three through to her new bedroom. Forgetting they could have breakables in them, she dropped them rather heavily on her bed, cringing when a crunch was heard. The room was North facing, like the living room, and had doors that opened in-over to create a balcony, meaning a refreshing sea breeze could pass through the room. Between the flat and the Priory was a huge field called Prior's Park, frequented by cricket players and dog walkers. It would have been the perfect place to run, if Mia had been a runner. She left that pastime behind in high school.

Although Mia's room was small, she liked to think of it more as cosy. An excess of green, grey and gold seemed to swarm the apartment, including the bedrooms. Mia's bedroom was mainly grey – the walls, the curtains and even the radiator, all except the gold dado rail, gold plug sockets and a hideous golden chandelier style lampshade. If she could ever afford to, she was determined to re-decorate, and to buy a wardrobe. None of the rooms had wardrobes. Instead, a large communal 'dressing room' with a walk-in wardrobe was attached to the far side of the bathroom. It was a small price to pay for such a lovely flat, they would have to share where they hung their clothes.

Though she knew it would be hell to find anything in a hurry, she tipped the boxes labelled 'clothes' onto her bed and stuffed them into the drawers without any kind of order. She would sort them another time. Her double bed was in, with a small chest of drawers, her new lamp, her keyboard, surfboard and mounds of boxes. With only the one task left in her for the night, she picked up the instruction manual for her new lamp and set about completing it to feel a small sense of accomplishment.

*   *   *   *

As was usual when sleeping in an unfamiliar place, Mia spent most of the night tossing and turning, occasionally pressing her phone screen to check the time. At half seven, she decided it was an acceptable time to rise and stirred to sneak into the kitchen. Her socks slipped on the wooden floor when she swung her legs off the bed, but she luckily managed to steady herself. Stepping very carefully so not to slip again, she snuck upstairs, quietly passed Steph's bedroom, then to the kitchen for breakfast, settling for one of the only food products they owned – a mini box of cereal. They had no milk and no bowls or cutlery unpacked so she crept through to the living room, flopped into the armchair and ate it straight out of the box.

With no television set up, Mia settled into the chair and opened *Netflix* on her phone. Unfortunately, it was still linked to Steph's speaker from the day before and blasted out the *Friends* theme song from the floor above. Mia winced, trying to look innocent as Steph immerged, messy and angered.

"Sorry, man." Mia threw her an apologetic look and dug back into her cereal box, while Steph got a box for herself. Her brunette hair was scraped back into a bun and her dressing gown drowned her.

It was a beautiful morning; ships passed each other out at sea and the resident cricketers were already out, ready to make the most of the morning sun.

"Why are you up at this ungodly hour?" Steph said, gruffly. "I'll have to find two new flat-mates if you do this every morning."

"I said I was sorry." Mia muttered, swallowing a mouthful. "And you love me really."

Steph grunted a reply.

They had been friends for three years, meeting on the first day of University. Placed together in student halls, they had held each other's hands through Fresher's Week and still lived to tell the tale. With them both studying on the same campus, they practically lived in each other's pockets for three years, supporting each other through deadlines, suffering through hangovers and drowning sorrows together. At the end of September, they were both starting their new jobs, with different employers, and the divorce from part of each other's lives would be ugly. They had laughed about it many times. Even their work in the meantime was at the same place.

"Try and stay quiet for once and wake me if I sleep till one." Steph ordered as she carried her cereal box and glass upstairs, shuffling her slippers on the wood.

"OK." Mia agreed with a confused frown. "Any particular reason?"

"We're out for Zoe's birthday tonight." Steph raised one eyebrow as she reminded her.

"Oh, yeah," Mia remembered, it had been a long day yesterday. She was supposed to meet her older sister, Molly, for a wedding dress fitting first. *Joy*, she thought.

"Wake me up then."

"Will do."

Mia heard Steph flop heavily onto her bed through the thin walls and snuggled further into her armchair, too comfortable and lazy to find the bin bags for her rubbish. She spent the morning lounging and trying not to feel too fat as she sat munching through another box of cereal. She was reasonably thin and athletic when she had the motivation but enjoyed her food and could easily work her way through an extra-large 'Digestives' packet. Luckily, there was not too much food in the house for her to work her way through.

Eventually, she made herself move to recover some papers and notes from one of her boxes. To keep Steph happy, she dug out the bin bags and cleared her rubbish. She made a mental note to buy a proper kitchen bin.

Sinking back into her Grandma's chair, she smoothed out the battered script on her knee. She scraped her long blonde hair back and tucked her feet underneath her, ready to learn some more of her lines for *Wicked*. In September, she was starring in an amateur production of the musical. She kept stressing quite a lot though everything was currently going according to plan.

Steph emerged at half two, looking slightly less sleep deprived and clutching her dressing gown to her.

"You look like Oliver Twist but smaller." Mia smirked.

"What time is it?" Steph asked, stretching into a yawn while choosing to ignore her. Mia looked at her phone and realized she had not woken her up like she promised - she had been too distracted.

"Oops! Erm, It's twenty-five to three." Mia answered sheepishly.

"Twenty-five to three?! Zoe's party is in, like, three hours!" Steph yelled and rushed back upstairs to their moderately sized bathroom.

Mia heaved herself off the chair and crawled into her room to see what she had to work with. With no mirror downstairs, she settled for temporarily using her phone camera. There was no noticeable parting left and her hair needed a good brush, probably a wash too. She envied Steph and her brown hair as it never looked greasy, on a blonde it always felt obvious. She gave up and trekked up to the vacated bathroom, too.

"Out, please, I need a shower." Steph said, hitting Mia on the shoulder. Mia turned to face her friend.

"Well, I need one too." Mia replied. "And I'm going out first."

They mimicked a cowboy show down, hands on hips, wearing stubborn expressions.

"But I said it first." Steph argued.

"Rock, paper, scissors?" Steph nodded in agreement, cast a playful grin across her face and lowered her stance to battle.

"Ha, Ha!" Mia laughed, triumphantly as she claimed victory over 'Rock' with 'Paper.' "Bye." Steph sighed and graciously left the bathroom to Mia who had to follow her out anyway to find a towel.

The main bathroom was the easily the nicest room in the flat; one wall was all exposed brick, with an arch layering it across the middle. A stand-alone bathtub took centre stage beneath the arch, with the shower, toilet and sink pushed to the end of the room under a slanted roof window.

Disappointingly, the shower turned out to be nothing more than a mere trickle of water so after fifteen minutes, Mia had only managed to wash her hair, never mind shave her legs. She decided to take baths going forward.

"Is it a nice shower, then? You've been in ages." Steph asked when Mia emerged after twenty-five minutes, quite flustered.

"Yes." Mia replied, robotically and sarcastically. "It was wondrous, magical, the best shower I've ever been in."

"It can't have been that bad." Steph replied.

Mia stepped back smiling and bowed to Steph, gesturing to the bathroom. "Be my guest."

Steph took even longer in the shower, by which time Mia had dried and straightened her hair, painted her face with make-up and was standing in her underwear trying to choose an outfit. Unsurprisingly, all her clothes were creased. It was a difficult decision as her Grandma would be seeing her first at Molly's dress fitting so it could not be too revealing yet, she did not fancy looking like a nun on a night out in Newcastle. Eventually, she gave up and packed a bag with a second outfit in it. That would save the lecture occurring.

"I'm off, see you at seven." Mia shouted from the doorway.

"You aren't coming to town like that, are you?" Steph looked her outfit up and down with slight disgust.

"Don't worry." Mia wiggled her bag at Steph. "I've got another outfit with me."

"Thank God, I don't think you'd get in anywhere like that." Steph replied and Mia turned to leave. "Say hi to Molly for me."

"Will do." Mia shouted back as the door swung shut behind her.

She trotted down the stairs, along the street and hopped on the metro, en route to seeing her sister. Her phone pinged as soon as the doors closed.

[Molls] Fitting cancelled but let's still have lunch. Get off at Chillingham Road and I'll meet you at The Busy Bean. Love you x

[Mia] Okies. See you soon. Love you too x

There were seven years between the two sisters and Molly had always 'babied' her. Being a dentist, Molly always had excess money to spend on her little sister, and Mia would never turn down the free food. With blonde hair, similar features and the same dorky smile, it was easy to tell they were siblings. Mia texted her as she hopped off the metro and headed up the ramp.

[Mia] Be there in 5 x

The Busy Bean was living up to its name, but the food was reasonably priced, and the portions were big. It had a large stone oven and the displays were full of delicious cakes to choose from. As Mia stepped into the café, she spotted Molly near the back, sitting alone and waving, enthusiastically. She could have worn her 'second' outfit after all; Grandma was not there. The smell of pizza was prominent, and her stomach rumbled as she waltzed through the sea of tables to join her. Though she was supposed to be the 'big sister,' Molly was at least four inches shorter, even in heels, and she had to stretch upwards to hug her 'little' sister.

"Have you not stopped growing yet?" Molly asked, pulling Mia into a hug. Their blonde hair matched perfectly.

"Hello to you too, my darling sister." Mia laughed and sat down opposite her sibling who she adored so much. "How're you doing?"

"I'm not too bad thanks, wedding plans are driving me crazy, yourself?" Molly sighed. *'The planning did seem to be going on forever.*' Mia thought. "Enjoying life without Grandma as your cleaner?"

"It's been one whole day, Molls. I think I'm managing." Mia laughed, picking up the menu.

"One whole day though, I'm pleased you're still alive, Mi." She smiled. "I've ordered for you, by the way, I hope that's ok?"

"I think I trust you to have ordered what I like." Mia replied, putting the menu back down.

"True." Molly laughed. "Anyway, I want to get straight to the point of why I brought you here."

"What's up?" Mia asked, scratching her forehead.

"I booked the car the other day and it's a Rolls Royce, a proper Cruella De Vil car. But I need a Maid of Honour to ride in it with me, and I wondered if you wanted to be that person?"

"Of course - I will." Mia replied, swallowing a lump in her throat.

Trying to hold back the tears of happiness failed and before long they had tears creeping down their cheeks.

"Of course, I'd love to." They hugged again and let the worried waitress deliver their drinks.

"Thanks." They chimed together.

Though Mia was not really interested in wedding plans, she found she was once it came to her sister. They talked weddings, dresses, hen plans, colour schemes and cake until the napkins could take no more scribbled plans and their plates were scraped clean. Most decisions had been made already, with the wedding only two months away, but Molly repeatedly went over the plans, checking that everything would go smoothly. Mia spent most of the time nodding, smiling and saying 'ooh' at the right times.

"Have you actually eaten since you left home? I barely saw your pizza." Molly asked, eyeing her empty plate.

"I've missed Grandma's well-stocked fridge." Mia chuckled, finishing the last mouthful. "I eat too much to have no money."

"Hey, I've not lived there for seven years and *I* miss Grandma's fridge."

As per usual, Molly performed the beautiful art of paying and Mia agreed to do some of her Maid of Honour duties over the coming weeks in the form of dress shopping. Molly gave her some post-it notes in case she had any further ideas for the hen party and drove her to town to meet the girls.

"Can you keep my spare bag?" Mia asked. "I don't really want to lug it round town tonight."

"Yeah, of course. Just drop it in the back." Molly replied. "I'll drop it off at some point when I'm passing yours. I'll come for a nosey round too."

"Love you, Moll, thank you, see you on Friday." Mia hugged her, hopped out of the car and pulled the bottom of her dress to make sure she was covered; she had changed in the car.

"Love you too, have a nice night." Molly drove off like a maniac, Mia thought she was a bit of a crazy driver, but it was a free lift – she just put her seatbelt on and hoped for the best.

Mia wandered up and down the street, so she looked like she was heading somewhere rather than standing alone. The 'girlies' did not take long to show up. Sian's voice echoed across the street and Mia smiled, knowing the rest would not be far behind.

Waving and trotting carefully, Mia crossed the street to meet up with them.

Chapter Two

As the second to last to join, Mia brought the group total up to six. When she reached them, Fred, tall, dark and handsome, scooped her up in his arms. Sian and Steph were there as well, with Maria and Zoe, the birthday girl. They had developed their mismatched group during Mia's time at University. Fred, Mia and Steph had formed the initial core of the group; they adopted people from there. After a University trip to Boardmasters Festival in Cornwall, they had all bonded.

"Hey, Mimi." Fred grinned, squeezing her in a bear hug.

"Hey, Freddie." Mia strained, struggling for breath.

When he let her go, Mia made a beeline for Zoe to wish her 'happy birthday,' before greeting the rest. With them both being so clumsy, she and Zoe managed to knock heads with an almighty clunk.

"We aren't even drunk yet." Mia winced and rubbed the sore patch. It hurt a lot more than she let on.

"Come on, we need to change that!" Zoe, a small, spritely, Cockney girl with a cute face and dimples, linked Mia's arm and began marching her down the street. It resulted in a chain of bodies being pulled along by an eager Londoner.

Newcastle exploded with life as they bustled along the streets towards 'The Gate,' a huge building full of restaurants, clubs and people. Its large front was made up solely of huge clear windows and so a variety of different colours burst from within onto the streets. Many other partygoers already lined the streets and wore very little though it was barely three degrees, exceptionally cool for a summer's eve. Some clubs were making the road vibrate to the beat of the music inside them while other clubs sat quietly, waiting for people to enter before releasing the fun. Drunkards swarmed in and out of pubs looking as though alcohol had been sustained since hours before. Mia compared herself to the rest of her group. They had been at pre-drinks since 8:30pm; Mia felt far too sober for 11pm.

"Where are we going?" Mia asked, Zoe seemed on a mission to be somewhere.

"To find Holly." Zoe replied. "She's working till 12 so can get us cheap drinks till then. She's coming out afterwards."

"Bonus!"

Turning along a small alleyway, the group darted through a fire exit to escape the poignant smell of urine and booze. The main entrance to the club had extremely picky bouncers and the queue was always very long, but Holly had shown them the sneaky way in a long time ago. The event on that evening was aptly named 'Naked' and Holly was one of the dancers, most of whom were dangling from balconies, high above the rest of the clubbers. Inside, everything was rather extravagant. Some of the dancers had spark guns to light up the ceiling every few minutes. During these intervals, the strobe lighting would emerge from its cave and fake fire would ignite the walls. Mia and Zoe tried to push each other towards 'The Dentist's Chair.' Maria and Steph prioritised drinks while Fred and Sian drooled over the same dancing girl.

"You two are about as subtle as a punch in the face." Steph laughed, turning around to physically close their jaws.

Before long, Holly ran out from a dressing room behind the bar counter, still rosy-cheeked. She led them through crowds of gormless men to the exit and out into the street.

"How can you work there?" Zoe squeaked.

"It's not that bad, it can be a good laugh." Holly replied with a shrug. "Plus, the money's great!"

Mia had to agree – Holly was paid well and never seemed to worry about money. She shook herself to stop thinking about money; it was Zoe's night and Mia could eat pasta for the rest of the month if necessary.

"Here first?" Sian asked, stopping in front of a rather quiet, boring looking club. They had continued down the street, away from 'The Gate' and onto 'The Diamond Strip.' Low bluesy music drifted from a bar across the building and Mia thought the club that Sian had chosen was the least appealing.

"Don't give me that face." Sian scolded. "I've been in before and it's good. Trust me."

Sian grabbed Fred's hand and dragged him through the double doors. The others trotted after them through the corridors of the strangely arranged club to the heart of it. As it turned out, the boring exterior did not reflect what was inside. The floor simmered when lights hit loose confetti that lined it. People squashed together though the main room was very large with a high ceiling and added stage. Its black walls gave the huge space a cosy feel and made the lights and the entertainment the main attractions.

Sian, Zoe and Mia rushed off to the bar, trying not to fall over on the dance floor. Sian leaned over the counter to catch the attention of the barman and Zoe laughed with Mia as they caught a group of lads checking out Sian's backside. When she, too, noticed, she gave the lads a grin and dispersed the drinks. It was amusing to think they would never get anything more from her than a fleeting look.

The girls raised their glasses in a circle to wish Zoe a 'Happy Birthday' with a cheer and Steph pulled a 'Birthday' sash out of her bag to hang around Zoe.

"So, Zo, tonight there is only one rule." Holly began, with her glass still in the air. "To get you royally and beautifully mortal."

The girls cheered and others around them looked over. Maria and Holly were the best dancers and quickly attracted male attention but decided to play 'rejection by staring.' Whereby, if you are trying to have a girls' night or do not like the person 'hitting on you,' the best plan is to face them, make a hideous face and stay perfectly still until they move. The girls and even Fred, at times, used this technique on several occasions.

After inhaling a fair few drinks, most of them kindly donated by eager men at the bar, the party left to go to a much smaller club at the end of the street. In the basement, where the bar was, there were two pole dancing poles. Fishbowls were cheap and the karaoke was always entertaining on the big stage. Sian wrapped herself around one immediately and pulled an embarrassed Zoe on to the other one. It was Mia's favourite club as she liked a good drunken sing and it always played 90's music.

Mia and Steph tried to cross the path of the waitress giving out free shots as much as possible. Being on a budget, it was the cheapest way for the girls to get Zoe as drunk as necessary on her birthday. Newcastle had to be one of the best places in Europe to achieve that. Mia tucked into a fishbowl, trying to drink it quicker than Sian and Maria who drank from the other straws. She could feel her legs getting slightly wobbly and really needed the toilet. But, if she went, she knew she would go every half an hour from then on.

Steph and Zoe bobbed to the bar and returned with another fishbowl ready to inhale, courtesy of the happy men at the counter and their wallets. Mia laughed at their techniques; they were too good at manipulation. Maria was doing an excellent job of catching people every so often when they fell towards her.

Holly was trying to get friendly with the bartender and Sian had been missing for a while, but the girls had not really noticed. 'Girls just want to have fun' came on over the speakers so Mia, Zoe, and Maria danced in a little triangle with their drinks.

"Where's Sian?" Mia had to shout over the brilliantly loud music.

"I haven't seen her!" Steph shouted back and stretched her little frame taller, to see over the tall crowd.

"I suppose you can't see much down there, my darling Stevie." Mia replied. The pair were often compared to the comedy pair, 'Miranda and Stevie,' they embraced the idea and loved it.

"You look over, I'll burrow through. Ready?"

"Split." They wiggled through the crowds until Mia heard a faint 'Mia!' floating through the bodies. Steph had found Sian tangled with a woman in the corner of the club and, like children, she and Mia decided to annoy them.

"Look at the state of the walls, she'll get her back dirty." Steph tutted.

"Think of the germs!"

Sian continued but gestured them away crudely.

"Wow, she's not very polite, is she?" Steph said to Mia.

Stepping back from her lady friend, Sian turned to her friends to give them a warning look. Steph and Mia giggled and ran off.

Mia's shoes stuck to the floor and she was not drunk enough to ignore it.

When the karaoke started, Holly was more than willing to get up and make an absolute fool of herself. Mia climbed onto the stage with her to duet to 'Play that funky music' by Wild Cherry. It was far from beautiful, but Mia and Holly had a good laugh. The crowd was steadily growing and sung along with them as they provided entertainment. Being such a lightweight, Holly could barely stand let alone sing so Mia supported her and was surprised to hear such an enthusiastic cheer. Mia thought it may have been because the torture of their eardrums was over, or maybe it was because Holly had started a strip show en route off stage.

A group of lads climbed onto the stage to take the microphone and the one who took it from Mia strongly caught her attention. Zoe and Steph helped Holly off the stage. It took Mia a few seconds to realise that she was staring at the man she was supposed to be doing a simple exchange of the microphone with. His eyes were blue, his skin was tanned, and his brunette hair flopped in all directions.

"Sorry." Mia let go of the microphone quickly and hoped her hands had not made the handle sweaty. Concentrating more on the microphone, the guy and the thought of sweat being left behind, Mia managed to trip over her feet and tumble off the stage into Fred's arms.

"Nice of you to drop by." He laughed.

"Thanks, Freddie!" Mia laughed and was lowered to the floor.

Steph managed to pry Sian off the lips of her 'friend' and enticed Mia out of the club with the promise of a foam party at the O2 Academy – a smaller performance hall a few streets away. The Nordic God had dismounted the stage and left the club with his 'crew of lads.' Not being confident enough to follow and intercept, Mia left, too, with the girls for the Academy, not watching where he went.

They were all slightly tipsy when they left the karaoke central of the North East. Fred had a small rip in his trousers from violent 'slut-dropping' and Maria quickly managed to pull Holly away from a pile of sick on the floor. Sian decided to wrap herself around a lamppost singing her own version of 'All That Jazz.' Mia wondered how she had managed to get so drunk as she did not seem to stop kissing her woman to drink during the last half an hour at least. Maybe it was passive?

Mia did not realise how drunk she was herself until she had to try and walk in a straight line passed some policemen. Once they had passed them, Zoe and Mia skipped hand-in-hand downhill towards the O2 Academy with its exciting 'Foam Party' sign. Soppy, wet clothes such as jackets and t shirts hung over the railings standing outside, obviously some people had risked leaving them to dry as they continued to party. Bubbles floated out the doors in gangs, bringing music and laughter with them. Steph expressed her worry about Zoe's safety because of her clumsy tendencies and the risk with a wet floor but Zoe was anything but reluctant to go in, leading the group. The O2 Academy was a huge, corner building that resembled an old-fashioned movie theatre. The bouncer, with his quadruple chin wobbling, shook his head disapprovingly at Zoe's eagerness so the group snuck past, pretending to be ashamed by her.

The room was filled with blinding lights, tons of people, mountains of foam. People in shorts, bikinis and swim shorts with inflatable's bobbing around. A rogue beach ball jumped around the room in a never-ending game of volleyball with whomever. Mia assumed that all the games of 'Where's Miranda?' had given her such a good 'eagle-eye' as she spotted 'boy' and his friends almost immediately in the tangle of bodies. She made a mental note to target him. Grabbing Fred's hand, Mia headed forward into the mess. Maria swanned over to the bar with Sian to buy her round of drinks, carefully stepping so not to fall on the slippery tiles. Foam built up in higher piles as it was forced into the room. It covered benches, faces, chairs, arms, legs, plastic palm trees, dresses, speakers and the entire floor.

"You're a woman on a mission." Fred shouted over the noise.

Getting extremely excited, Zoe cut across their path, sprinting through the bubbles to be near the towering palm trees where the largest collection of the frothy substance seemed to have gathered. She disappeared into the white and emerged looking like 'The Abominable Snowman.'

"Ho, ho, ho. Merry Christmas!" Zoe chuckled and Fred raised an eyebrow.

"Hey, Santa!" Mia through her arms around Zoe's neck and lifted one leg to mimic sitting on her knee. "So, I've been really good this year, and I want a pony, and a puppy…"

"Get off." Zoe laughed and skidded Mia across the floor. Mia wobbled slightly when she tried to stand so balanced on Fred.

"Well, that was rude." Mia scoffed then, jokingly, turned to storm off but bumped into another body. "Sorry."

It was The Guy from Karaoke. He simply smiled and walked off to the bar.

"Smooth." Fred lightly punched Mia's shoulder. She slapped her palm to her forehead in comical annoyance at herself. Strangers danced like friends and Mia was constantly checking out of the corner of her eye, hoping to catch a glimpse of the man who had so easily caught her attention.

The floor vibrated beneath their feet as they jumped around to the ear splittingly loud music. The atmosphere was vibrant, pulsing and great.

Maria and Sian returned with drinks for the group, though one was spilt on the way over. In the ever-changing light, it was hard to keep track of who was who, but Mia managed to stumble across Zoe, dancing a few meters from where she had originally 'left her' and they decided to search for a bathroom. Finding it was not the difficult task however, trying to perch on the toilet after consuming large amounts of alcohol was an extremely difficult mission. Her mirror image blurred as she tried to focus, and she ended up punching the hand dryer in attempt to get it temporarily 'un-out of order.'

Zoe collapsed into the door heading out, so Mia crouched down for a minute, desperate to relax her feet from the pressure of heels for even a short time but was still not drunk enough to sit on the sticky ground. Zoe's head flopped onto Mia's shoulder, which she found hilarious.

The night was becoming more disjointed as it went on. Before long, Mia was back dancing again, although she had lost Zoe altogether and could not remember getting from the toilets back to the dance floor. Another skip ahead in time and, through the darkness, she noticed The Guy from Karaoke was dancing near her, then next to her, then very near her. The alcohol had shut off any nerves or embarrassment she had.

Snaking her hand around his neck, she pulled him in for a kiss. It was slightly sloppy and overly aggressive on both sides, but neither cared, it was fun.

Suddenly, Mia felt very exposed. They no longer had darkness to hide under or loud music surrounding them. It was only 1am, but the flood lights were on and disgruntled guests were being ushered towards the exits. Stepping away from him, Mia looked around for anyone she recognised and, unfortunately, spotted Zoe through the wave of people's legs. She was on the floor with streams of clubbers avoiding her.

"I've got to go." Mia said, beginning to weave through the crowd away from her nameless man. "Add me on Insta. OhMiMiOhMy."

When she reached Zoe, a Police Officer and two paramedics were already by her side. Two men were being escorted out of the building by a second police officer, who held the pair in handcuffs. Most of the other guests had cleared, probably flooded out to other clubs, and the music had died, but some of the lights still flickered from red to green to blue.

"It would be you, wouldn't it?" Holly laughed, as she staggered onto the scene.

"What happened?" Mia asked Fred, who looked quite distressed.

"Some guys started fighting, crashed into Zo and knocked her to the floor. They think she's broken something."

"Can you move it?" One of the paramedics asked.

"No." Zoe groaned, twisting her face in pain and frustration. At the same time, she tried to pull her dress lower down her leg with one hand.

"I'm afraid it may be broken, I think you'd better come with us in the ambulance, is that alright?" He said in a clear yet serious tone.

Holly tried to follow Zoe's stretcher, but Maria and Sian held her back, the last thing the paramedics needed was another person to control, especially a highly intoxicated one; Fred piled into the ambulance with Zoe.

"You said I've had too much to drink." Holly laughed. "But I'm not in an ambulance."

"Come on, missus, let's get you home." Maria said, clapping her hand on Holly's back. "Bye, guys."

They watched them stumble together out of the club then Sian and Mia stood in silence for a moment.

Steph had disappeared off the face of the earth, Fred had gone with Zoe in the ambulance and Maria had taken Holly home. Only Sian and Mia remained, internally debating whether they, too, should call it a night.

"I'm not done, are you?" Sian whispered, leaning towards Mia.

"Nope." Mia replied, watching the ambulance drive away with the birthday girl. "Not even close."

"Next bar?"

"Lead the way."

Mouth of the Tyne, Anna Heslop

Chapter Three

From the floor came a clink of many, many bottles as Sian turned in her sleep on the floor. Evidently, she has tried to make a blanket out of the glass. She was not even awake yet and she looked as rough as Mia felt. That hangover was going to hurt, probably as much as Zoe's broken leg. *How much had they drunk last night?* Mia thought. It had started off so well yet, somehow, she had ended up asleep on the kitchen seat with Sian at her feet.

"Alright, bud?" Mia asked, as Sian emerged from her bottle blanket; she could taste the alcohol sticking to the edges of her tongue and tried unsuccessfully to scrape it away with her teeth. Everything was too noisy and too bright.

"I feel like someone drove a lawn mower over me," Sian croaked, pressing her palms into her face. "And then decided to experiment with waterboarding."

"Oh, Christ, that is bad." Mia rubbed her tired skin and made a pitiful move towards the kettle. This may have taken several minutes as her body creaked like a robot in need of oiling. "Tea?"

"You, beauty." Sian hauled herself up and rolled into Mia's freshly vacated spot. "You'll make a great wife one day."

"First of all, that was so graceful." Mia said, and Sian pretended to bow with one arm. "Second, you're a scxist pig."

"You know I don't mean it really." Sian replied. "Like someone would ever marry you in the first place."

Mia hit her with the oven gloves.

After clicking the kettle into life, Mia drew the curtains slightly to stop the sunlight from causing too much pain. People on the street looked even more lively than usual. As the kettle boiled away in the background, she tried not to let her hangover take hold any more than it already had. She clutched her head, almost believing that she could squeeze the hangover out and walked to the sink for water. Even the sound of the tap dripping was painful to listen to, each drop was like a firework exploding only centimetres away. As she shuffled around, she narrowly avoided a collision between her toe and the central bench.

"Oi, Oi! Good morning, stud." Sian hollered, still croaking, pushing herself up on her elbows, as they heard Steph creep in through the front door. "Busy night?"

"Of course, you guys are up." Steph growled; she was clearly suffering too. "Can you maybe save the slating for later on, when I feel less like slowly dying in the dark?"

"Hmm." Sian and Mia both pretended to think for a minute before shaking their heads at each other. "Nah." They both leaned in expectantly, waiting for Steph to fill them in on her whereabouts.

Steph paused a little too long.

"Tell you what, I'll nip out and get some milk while you compose yourself and you can spill the beans when I'm back. How does that sound?" Mia suggested, remembering there was not a single drop of milk in the flat.

"You're not going to drop it 'till I tell you, are you?" Steph replied.

"Nope." Sian and Mia said together.

"Ok, then I suppose we have a reluctant deal."

"Great." Mia said, rising to leave. "I'll be back soon."

Tynemouth Front Street was a five-minute walk away from the flat and was the main street of Tynemouth Village. A Co-op sat a third of the way up and was dangerously handy. Mia bought bread and milk and was thankful for the small amount of people there to witness her in such a state. Sandeep and Aanya, the shop owners, looked sympathetic, as she crawled around their store.

By the time Mia had ventured to the shop and climbed back up to the apartment, Sian had started cooking bacon and eggs; the smell was intoxicating. Sian was a wonderful breakfast chef. Mia trotted over to the kitchen, feeling like a dog searching for scraps.

"Have I missed something? I thought you weren't moving in until the end of the month?" Mia said, peering over her shoulder to spy on the food.

"My lease isn't up till the end of the month, but I'd rather take the hit and pay two rents this month than stay in that place a moment longer." Sian replied. "I'm so excited to be in a flat where slugs don't live in the sink."

"Yeah, I'm not surprised. I don't know how you've stayed in that place so long." Mia replied, dropping her shopping on the beach. After forgetting her Bag for Life, she had refused to buy a bag. "Where did the food come from, by the way?"

"I bought it yesterday when I did the beer run for pres." Sian said, turning the bacon.

"Ah, that makes sense." Mia replied, opening the bread for Sian to use. "I really need to do a proper shop at some point."

"Do you want your bacon with fat or without?" Sian asked.

"Ooh, without please." Mia replied. She started digging around in the boxes to find some plates.

Steph shuffled back into the living room, still as sheepish as when she first entered the apartment, the only difference being she was now wrapped up in her big fluffy dressing gown.

"So, you look happy with yourself." Sian smirked from the kitchen. Steph was the easiest person in the whole world to wind up and Sian loved doing it. "Come on, what did you do? Who did you do?"

Collapsing into the armchair, Steph let out another sigh. "I did something stupid."

"No way," Mia said, sarcastically, dropping the milk in the fridge.

"We were kind of counting on that." Sian continued.

"Who was it?" Mia asked, eyeing the empty fridge shelves with sadness.

"Did he cook your breakfast? Because there's not much bacon..." Said Sian.

"Are you two gonna shut up and let me talk?" Steph scowled. Mia and Sian exchanged smirks.

"Sorry." They both replied. Steph looked to the ceiling before continuing.

"I was at Robbo's. I bumped into him in the last place. Before I knew it, we were getting food, then we were in a taxi, then we were at his..."

Both Sian and Mia looked like they had been slapped. Robbo was Steph's ex-boyfriend. Robbo was meant to be in the past. Robbo was a tool.

"Robbo?" Mia asked, a look of disgust on her face. "Robbo?"

"As in, *the* David Robson?" Sian asked.

"The one who tore out your heart?" Mia asked.

"And stomped all over it?" Sian continued.

"The very same." Steph replied.

"But, he's-"

"He's awful!"

"I know."

"And he treats you like dirt!"

"I know."

"But why do you go back?"

"I don't know, it just happens." Steph shrugged.

"Dude, no." Mia said, falling back into the chair. "Bad, Steph."

"Last time, I promise." Steph said, drawing an invisible cross on her chest with her finger.

"Pretty sure you've said that before." Sian said, under her breath and Steph pretended not to hear her.

After the revelations and with a glass of water that was not quite big enough, Mia crawled to bed. To reach it, she had to weave through some of the remaining boxes left to unpack. The usual warm imprint from her body was missing as she wiggled back into the sheets. She felt like hibernating for a whole winter and pulled the duvet in close around her shoulders, checking her phone before she dropped back off to sleep.

[Grandma] Are you settling in alright? I miss having you here x

She sighed; she loved her Grandma dearly but was pleased to have her own space again. Absence definitely made the heart grow fonder when it came to their relationship. Mia tapped out a quick reply then mushed her tired face into the pillow to sleep.

At half past one Mia woke again, feeling slightly more refreshed and awake. She drifted across to the bathroom and scrubbed all the remaining make up off her grubby face, deciding on a shower when she still looked half-asleep. It was still as pitiful as she remembered from the day before and she scolded herself for forgetting.

"Oi!" She shouted downstairs when the shower turned icy cold. "Stop running water!"

"Sorry!" Steph called up from the kitchen. Evidently, she had taken to doing the dishes at that moment. Once she stopped, the water ran warm once again. Mia let the water warm her through again, before stepping out, wrapping one towel around her body and the other around her head. She trudged back downstairs to her room and tried to get in the mindset ready for work.

Both Steph and Mia worked at a small, yet popular café named *Josie's*, that sat down on the beach at Tynemouth Longsands. When the tide swept in, it lapped against the decks of the café and allowed children to paddle in the shallow rock pools that formed. They worked in a rota of six days one week and four days the next; the café was always closed on Mondays. For a waitressing job, it paid reasonably well, and it was an enjoyable place to work, especially in the summer, when the business was packed with happy, sun-kissed beach goers. Some days, Mia would take her surfboard down and nip in during her lunch break or after work; the beach was their office.

After the arduous task of drying her thick hair, Mia twisted it carefully into a bun then threw on her uniform. It was all black, which sometimes made working outside in the heat of the summer rather uncomfortable.

She stepped into the living room to find Sian scrunched up on the sofa, fast asleep and blissfully unaware of the other two girls abandoning her for work. Mia was jealous of her being able to sleep off her hangover. Unable to find paper or a pen, Mia scribbled a note to her on a piece of kitchen roll with an old eye liner. Steph buttered some toast and slung her bag over her shoulder; Mia pulled on her shoes and the two girls ran down the stairs to the street.

It was only a short walk to *Josie's,* down the street, right turn, then a straight line to the sand. Tables were full, the deck was packed, and children piled in the pool. Surfers waded in the sea with their boards while others zoomed quickly back and forth passed the French doors as the waves crashed.

Mia and Steph took orders, cleaned benches, filled water bowls for dogs and made drinks for the following hours. They waited on sunbathers, deck loungers and visitors sitting around the tables indoors.

"I'll let you serve that one." Steph nodded her head to a man and woman sitting on one of the far tables.

"No, Steph, I-" Mia started to argue but it was no use, Steph had already scuttled into the kitchen, still wearing a devious smirk.

Letting a small growl and an eye roll escape her, Mia straightened her apron, took a deep breath and walked over to them.

"Hello," Mia chimed, holding out her notepad. "What can I get for you?"

"Hey." Nameless man from Karaoke replied, scanning her quickly with his eyes. Mia stared at him. "Can I have a cappuccino and a blueberry muffin, please?"

"Yep, no worries at all." She replied. "And what can I get you, Ma'am?"

"Sorry?" The woman looked up at her in confusion. Nameless man took her hand.

"She asked what you want to eat, Grandma."

"Oh." The lady shouted, then turned to her grandson. "What do I want, Jakey?"

"She'll have a cappuccino and a muffin, too, please."

"Is that everything?" Mia asked. They both nodded and she turned on her heel to place their order.

"Oh my God." she said, moving quickly towards Steph.

"You're welcome. I could feel the chemistry." Steph said. "He's so cute."

"I got with him last night!"

"You what?" Steph said, leaning around Mia to get a better look. "I stand by what I said, he's cute."

"Can you finish serving him?" Mia replied, untying her apron. "It's time for my break."

"What a coincidence." Steph laughed. "Go on, I'm sure I can manage."

Mia smiled and escaped through the back door.

At 7pm, Bill, the owner, left, leaving Steph and Mia to lock up. An hour before closing, Mia and Steph were behind the bar and their side of the counter was the crowded side. Most of their daytime guests had filed out to their houses. Only a handful of couples still dotted across the beach. Mia heard the bells on the door chime together calmly, closely followed by a bar stool scraping across the floor as it was pulled out. She spun around, staring at the glass she was in process of cleaning.

"Hi, what can I get you-" She stared into the face that was quickly becoming familiar. "-You're back."

"I am, indeed." Jake replied, leaning his elbows on the bar. Mia turned around but Steph had magically disappeared; she then took a slow breath and turned back to face him.

"Are you going to run away again?" he asked.

She smirked slightly at his confidence. "It was time for my break, I didn't run away." Mia defended herself.

"Mmmhmm." He nodded, with a half-smile.

There was a pause where Mia continued to clean the glass and Jake looked up threw his eyelashes for effect.

"So, Mia, what time do you finish?"

"Wow, straight in there." Mia laughed.

"I'm here till closing and I'm in really early tomorrow morning for a long day."

"Ah, that's too bad."

"Sorry." Mia shrugged with a half-smile.

"We are closed on Monday though." Steph contributed, as she walked by with a crate of glasses.

"Great, how does Monday sound, then? 6 O' Clock at Ralph's." He tapped his hand on the counter and turned to leave. "See you then."

When he was safely out the door, Mia turned to glare at Steph.

"And for the second time today," Steph said. "You're welcome."

<u>Chapter Four</u>

A harsh onshore wind buffeted the coast that day, with heavy rain and angry skies. It was typical that the weather was atrocious for her morning off; Mia had hoped to try the new kayaking place that had opened on the sea front or to get in the sea for a surf. Instead, she hibernated inside most of the day, wondering how she could manage to do all the things she wanted to do in life, without any money, and anxiously awaited the arrival of her Dad.

As the time drew near, Mia shuffled in her seat and danced her fingers on her knee. She had already cleaned the kitchen counters four times, refilled the kettle and straightened the rug multiple times. The toilet bowls had been filled with Domestos every time someone had used them throughout the course of the day. It would only be a short visit, but undoubtably an impactful one. They heard him long before they saw him, the roar of his Lexus outside alerted them to his arrival, followed by the sound of his heavy footsteps climbing the stairs.

"Helloooo!" Ian Moore burst into the living room. "Where's my youngest? Where is she?"

Even though she was clear to see in the armchair, Mia stood up to make herself more visible and to embrace him. It was like a tornado had entered the flat.

"Hey, Dad." Mia smiled, as she was squashed into his chest.

Ian was in his late fifties, easily six foot four, with a full head of slightly greying hair and large shoulders. After letting go of Mia, he turned to Steph, then Sian for similar greetings.

"Can I get you a drink, Mr Moore?" Steph asked, moving towards the kitchen, but Ian waved her down.

"No, don't worry yourself, love." He patted his large coat, as though searching for something. "I brought my own, though I will need a glass."

Pulling a large bottle of red wine from his coat, he uncorked it easily with his hands.

"I'm afraid I can only offer you a mug or a champagne flute." Steph replied.

"I'll take the mug, thanks, love." he said.

Steph obliged, walking back and forth to the kitchen, passing Ian a mug and taking a seat once again. Mia was simply waiting for the fanfare to begin. Once the mug was in his hand, Ian poured his poison, leaned back into the sofa and crossed his feet on the low table in front of him. Mia saw Steph shuffle in the armchair, as her OCD screamed.

"So!" Ian said, at a volume far too loud for the size of the room, gesturing Mia to shuffle closer into a one-armed hug. She felt nervous and uncomfortable as she moved in, though felt an odd feeling of reassurance and comfort once settled. He squeezed her shoulder and rested his chin on her head for a moment. Steph felt she was intruding on a private family moment but did not want to break into the silence of it by leaving the room, instead she sat and appreciated their juncture.

"So." He repeated, slightly quieter this time. "What have you got for me? Fill me in."

Sitting upright again, though still in the confines of his arm, Mia took a breath as she thought. "Nothing much, Dad, to be honest. Everything is ticking over pretty nicely here."

"Nice place you managed to get sorted here!" He said, downing the first mug full in one swig. "Does it go upstairs too?"

"Yeah, Dad." Mia replied. "It's just-"

"I had a place like this once." He interrupted, pouring himself another glass and unintentionally stomping over to the window. He looked like an advert for North Face, a real mountain man head to toe in adventure gear. "In Kailua, overlooking the bay. We were out there for six months filming mantarays. One of my favourite places. You've got a hell of a view from here too."

The girls sat silently waiting for his next contribution.

"Have you found yourself a man, yet?" He asked bluntly. Usually, both Sian and Steph would have seized the opportunity to throw Mia under the bus about a man, but not now. She did not even need a warning look.

"No, no, I haven't." Mia looked at her feet.

"Hm. That's a shame." Ian scratched his cheek. "I'd quite like to walk at least *one* of my daughters down the aisle."

Mia looked at her feet again, she had not expected to reach the subject so quickly.

"I even set up an Instagram account," Ian said, staring into space and taking another swig from his mug. "But she's blocked me on that too."

Mia patted his hand and Steph took the opportunity to slide out of the room.

***

As she watched her father's Lexus draw away from her and around the corner, she could only wish she had tried harder to take his keys from him.

She had two unopened messages from Molly and the unwavering feeling that she was stuck between a rock and a hard place within her own family.

"You ok?" Steph asked, when Mia skulked back into the flat; Mia nodded.

"Do you want to go and find that geocache?" Steph asked and Mia could not help but grin and nod.

They had started geo-caching a few years earlier, during their Duke of Edinburgh award, going loopy on their Gold hike. They did sometimes sigh at how tragic they felt playing but who could dislike a giant, worldwide game of hide and seek, really? It usually led to some ridiculous scenarios and some even more adventures.

"What you up to today?" Mia asked Sian, as she waited for Steph in the living room.

"Well, I brought the first load of stuff in my car, so I suppose I'd better move it inside." Sian replied. "Not that anyone would want to steal any of it. It's just a board and a few boxes."

"Fancy coming with us first?" Mia asked Sian as they crossed paths in the hallway.

"I can't believe you're still geocaching. You guys are so weird. No, I'll just trek down to the car in a bit instead." Sian shook her head and waved them off. "Have fun."

"We always do." Steph said, jumping onto Mia's back. "Onward, MiMi!"

Ten minutes later, Mia was scrambling up the grassy sand dune, huddled under her umbrella. It had stopped raining so heavily, but the ground was still wet. From her vantage point, Steph was yelling instructions, not wanting to wade through the wet grass.

"Mi, can you hear me?" Steph shouted up, while flicking through the guidance on her phone.

"Yeah!" Mia yelled back, searching in the area the cache was supposed to be in.

"I was thinking last night."

"Dangerous." Mia said quietly, but loud enough for Steph to hear.

"Should we get a pet?" Steph asked.

"Bit random." Mia responded, shuffling uncomfortably. The wind was trying hard to steal her umbrella. "Were you thinking like a goldfish or something?"

"I was thinking more like a cat."

"We aren't becoming cat people. At least go for a cool animal. What about a dog?"

Mia asked and received no reply. "Steph?" Still no reply.

She turned around to see if Steph had trekked back up to her vantage point, but she was nowhere to be seen.

"Steph?" Mia shouted a little louder and leapt forward to look for her. It was too late for her to be inconspicuous and she was immediately noticed by the woman Steph was talking to. Unfortunately, it looked like she had snuck up the dune for a wee.

"Hi, Sam." Mia smiled and did a little wave awkwardly from the bank.

With a quizzical look, Sam waved back and continued her conversation with Steph. Sam was in the local amateur dramatics' society with Mia. Her shorts, trainers and headphones suggested she was out for a run and had been intercepted by Steph. Her bright, blonde hairline glistened slightly with beads of sweat and rain. Mia stepped carefully and climbed down to join them like a normal person, trying to act as though wading through the tall, wet grass on a steep dune was what every did with their spare time.

"Hey, Mi." Sam smiled, waving with a fist that clenched a headphone. "What were you doing up the dune?"

"Erm, bird watching." Mia stuttered.

"What were you watching, seagulls?"

"Yeah, they're fascinating creatures, you know."

Steph stared at Mia – half in disbelief, half waiting for her to finish.

"Anyway," Steph interjected. "We better be going; we have to get to work."

"No worries." Sam replied, tucking her headphones back in. "See you later."

"See you tonight!" Mia shouted after her and Sam conducted a skilled spin in her run to salute; Mia smiled to herself.

"You can be such a tit sometimes, you know that, right?" Steph said, shaking her head at Mia.

"I know, let's move past it." Mia laughed, and pushed Steph in the direction of the café.

Before long they were tied into their aprons and weaving between tables at work. With the radio on in the kitchen, Mia picked up a new song to hum every time she went in.

"You're in a good mood." Jubeda or 'Jay', their work friend, smiled, as they crossed paths.

"What can I say, Jay, it's a miserable day?" Mia sang back.

"I do love how weird you are sometimes." Jay laughed, as Mia danced into the kitchen.

"Did you just see Sian's message in the group?" Steph asked, squeezing past Mia.

"No?" Mia said, digging for her phone.

With her phone on silent, Mia was delayed with her social media updates. Checking carefully around for signs of Bill first, she whipped out her phone when it seemed clear. Although he was one of the nicest people ever, he was strangely strict when it came to phones, believing they were rotting the brains of the youth.

[Sian] Movie Night, anyone?

[Zoe] I'm in. Someone will need to help me up the stairs though!

[Holly] I'll put you over my shoulder, Zo, I'm so in. I'll always go for Netflix and chill.

[Sian] Maybe slow down a little, Holls, I'm not taking you to the clinic again.

[Carol] I wish I was home!

[Zoe] Thanks babe.

[Holly] Need a trip to the clinic, do you, Carol?

[Maria] I'm working from nine. ☹

[Carol] Ha! It's been a long time since I needed a trip to the clinic! Poor Don.

[Fred] As long as we don't have to watch *Mean Girls,* again.

[Sian] @Fred, shut up. @Steph, buy popcorn. @Mia, don't be too late. And Carol, we all know Don is a lucky man ☐

"I love how we're the last people invited to the party in our own house." Mia laughed, stuffing her phone in her pocket as Bill appeared.

*

An hour and twenty-five minutes later, Mia stood outside The People's Theatre, staring up at the huge, new poster advertising *Wicked.* She could not have been more terrified. Seeing it up on the board like that made it all real. It was only a small community theatre, but it had a rather large, loyal following. When she first joined the amateur company, they had produced *Legally Blonde,* which had sold out within a week. As a new member, her role was to slot in with the chorus and smile. The following year, when they took on *The Lion King,* she earned a main role, but felt shielded slightly from nerves with a huge lion costume on. This time, only green paint would stand in the way of Mia and the audience, which did not seem like enough protection.

"You coming?" Sam appeared at her side. "Or are you bird watching again?"

"I'm coming!" Mia said. Sam linked her arm and they walked in together.

"Is tonight the night I finally get you out for a drink?" Sam begged, tugging lightly on Mia's arm. "You've not come out with us since the *Lion King* afterparty."

"Noo." Mia replied. "Steph has invited our entire clan round for movie night."

Sam looked a little crestfallen.

"You can come if you want?" Mia offered.

"I'd love to, but I promised the guys I'd go with them for a drink after rehearsal." Sam said. "Next time though."

They were both quite early; Angelika, the show's pianist, was yet to arrive. Most of the set was still scattered across the stage, with the outlines half painted. Together, they trotted down the steps towards the stage.

"Hello? Anyone here?" Sam called to no human response, just an echo. She wandered down to the piano and let her fingers run across the keys. "You can play, right?"

"I can, but nowhere near as well as Angelika!" Mia replied.

"Fancy a warm-up?" Sam asked, pulling a *Wicked* music book out of her bag and setting it down on the stand.

"Yeah-sure." Mia replied, taking a seat; Sam hopped up to sit on the edge of the stage. "Don't you need to see the words?"

"I know I haven't sung the songs a lot, but I've heard them about three thousand times. I think I'll be okay." Sam chuckled.

"Are you happy to try 'For Good?'" Mia asked, flicking to the right page.

"Let's give it a try."

Slowly, Mia began to play the intro but made a mistake, choosing to start again. The second time, she made it far enough for Sam to start singing and got such a shock at her voice; she had to restart a third time.

"Third time's a charm." Sam smiled and Mia began to play.

As her fingers danced across the keys, Sam swayed slowly and began to sing the part of Glinda first. When Mia joined in, their voices tangled together harmoniously. It was Mia's favorite song from the whole musical, it was so sweet. When they finished, a small group, including Angelika, applauded them from the back of the theatre.

"That was beautiful." Angelika grinned and Sam did an overzealous bow to her.

Before long, cast members were being fitted into their, in some cases, complicated, costumes. Sets were getting licked with new coats of paint and the flying monkeys were practicing their acrobatics.

"I just don't get how to make the horns stay on!" Mia heard the shout come from backstage and had to laugh.

"Right, Mia, you ready?" Angelika shouted up.

Mia nodded. Even after all the hours she had spent on stage, she still got nervous, especially during rehearsals; there were no blinding lights to shield her from seeing who was watching.

"Mia?" Sam shouted from backstage. Mia held up a 'one second' finger to Angelika and followed the voice to find Sam.

"Yeah?" Mia left the stage and ran to see what she wanted.

"I've managed to hook up four microphones, can I just test yours?" Sam asked.

"Yeah, of course." Mia agreed. "I'm just about to practice *Defying Gravity.*"

"Perfect timing." Sam said, battling to untangle the wires in her hands.

Sam fiddled more with the portable microphone before grabbing the neck of Mia's t-shirt and pushing the main box down it.

"Sorry, we'll need to wiggle it passed your boobs." Sam said.

Mia blushed.

"Test, Test, Test. 1-2-3." Sam said into the microphone. "Great, you're good to go."

Mia turned back to the stage and Sam smacked her on the backside with a 'good luck.'

Out she stepped, ready to sing.

**

At nine, they were all thoroughly ready to call it a night, worn out with rehearsing. Sam and some of the cast and crew made a beeline for the Surf café, after one last attempt to get Mia to go with them.

"Next time!" She promised, climbing into Angelika's car for a lazy person's lift home.

"Cheers, Angelika. See you next week." Mia thanked her, closed the door and waved as she drove away.

The sun was lowering in the sky, but it was still relatively warm; the windows of the flat were all open on the street side and Mia could hear laughter billowing out.

"Honey, I'm home!" Mia sang, bursting into the flat.

"Ey!" The gang all cheered; some lifted their drinks.

"Finally." Sian laughed. "We were beginning to think you'd been kidnapped."

"I nearly was." Mia replied, kicking her shoes into the shoe spot. "I turned down a trip to the Surf café for you lot."

"Wow. We feel so honored." Zoe grinned; her leg was propped up on the sofa.

"You should." Mia pulled her hoodie over her head and hung it up on the hooks under the stairs.

All the sleeping bags were already unpacked and scattered across the living room. Pizzas were en route.

"Anyway, that's enough talking, what are we going to watch?" Sian asked.

"*Mean girls*?" Steph suggested.

"Absolutely not." Fred moaned. "How about *Die Hard*?"

"It's not on Netflix." Sian replied.

"I'm sure we could find it somewhere!" he retorted.

"What wrong with *Mean Girls*?"

"I am *not* sitting through that again."

"Oh my God, wait, go back, go back. *The Boat that Rocked*, have you guys seen it?" Mia practically bounced on the spot.

"No." The room echoed.

"It's *sooo* good, watch the trailer." Mia demanded, pointing at the screen.

"It's Netflix, there's no trailer." Sian said. "Once sec."

After Sian pulled it up on her iPad for them to watch, they were sold. The delivery guy arrived just in time for the film to begin.

"I don't want any pizza on the carpet mind!" Steph warned, thrusting a duvet towards Holly and Fred before carefully passing drinks to Sian. Zoe readjusted her cast on a cushion and Mia scooped up her first slice of pizza. A very British looking street popped onto their screens as their movie night began and they were transported back to 1966.

Mouth of the Tyne, Anna Heslop

Chapter Five

Keeping her promise of not playing the keyboard before 10am, Mia waited until the hand hit twelve to start playing some of the soundtrack songs from *The Boat That Rocked*. She had been itching to try some of them since the night before, when the film had caused her to dance in her seat for 135 minutes. With the window slightly ajar, a light, sea breeze drifted through her room as she began to play.

"I know I wasn't a fan at first, but it really is a nice way to wake up in the morning." Sian smiled, leaning on the doorframe of Mia's bedroom. Wearing her iconic red and white polka dot dressing gown and matching slippers, she looked extra cosy.

Mia smiled, without turning around, and carried on playing '*Lazy Sunday*,' by Small Faces.

"You've got your date tonight, right?" Sian asked and that stopped Mia.

"Yeah. I'm actually pretty nervous." Mia confessed.

"How come?" Sian asked, shuffling into Mia's room and clambering onto her bed.

"I dunno." Mia spun round on the stool towards her, puffed her cheeks and exhaled. "I just hate first dates. They're always so awkward."

"First dates are great!" Sian exclaimed with a grin.

"Of course, you would say that. When's the last time you had a first date that didn't end in sex?" Mia laughed.

"That one a couple of weeks' ago where I took her to Harry's." Sian defended herself.

"Yeah, but that doesn't count!" Mia replied, shaking her head.

"It does!" Sian argued.

"No, it doesn't. She wasn't even gay! She was a student doing research into lesbian dating." Mia said.

"I've never heard anything gayer." Sian rolled onto her stomach and propped her head on her hands. "Are you saying that, if a date goes well, you wouldn't bring them back here, just because it's a *first* date?"

Mia furrowed her eyebrows and lightly scratched her cheek. "I don't know. It depends."

"Depends on what?" Sian asked, cocking her head, awaiting the answer.

"How long I'd known them." Mia talked with her hands as she listed. "If I'd been friends with them for a little while before dating then maybe, but if I'd met them online, I don't think I'd trust them enough after one date."

"It's not about trust, it's about alcohol consumption and how hot they are." Sian replied, nonchalantly.

"Wow, a true romantic, right there." Mia laughed at her friend.

By 11am, Steph had given them a shopping list and kicked them out of the flat so she could clean. Initially, they had tried to protest being thrown out of their own flat, but they caved when they realised if Steph did the cleaning, they would not have to. In Morrisons, Sian kept dropping unwanted items into the trolley, starting with razors, then condoms, then strawberry flavoured lubricant.

"You're so mature." Mia rolled her eyes when she found a cock ring hiding under the bananas.

"You never know, you might need it." Sian shrugged, but Mia left it to the side for some poor old dear to find later when she picked up her '*Women's Weekly.*'

They shared out their bags and started home, planning every second of Mia's night on the way.

"Next time, make sure your car is empty." Mia said. The bags were becoming increasingly heavy. "I feel like a donkey."

"The exercise is good for you."

**

Not one to be fashionably late, Mia stood outside Ralph's at 6 o'clock precisely, though she was too nervous to go in. The girls and Fred had discussed the upcoming date at length with her the night before, but she still did not feel prepared. They told her to play it cool, stay no longer than three hours, and meet them at the Surf café afterwards for the full debrief. She had opted for a smart casual look, mainly black with a light brown overcoat and had tamed her hair with straighteners. Although she was tall, he was much taller, so she was happy meeting him in heels. Some men hated being towered over.

Ralph's was a small Italian on the seafront, overlooking Cullercoats Bay, just over a mile north of the flat. Mia hopped on the metro for one stop to avoid turning up wind swept and, potentially, sandy. Thanks to the large front windows, she could see Jake already seated at their table, looking as Viking as ever. Unfortunately, that also meant that she was spotted, hovering outside, rather quickly. He waved at her. She waved back, took a deep breath and let herself in.

"Good evening, bella!" The overenthusiastic waiter greeted her with open arms. "You are with the young gentleman, no?"

She nodded her head and smiled in Jake's direction; he grinned back.

"You two have a lovely evening." The waiter smiled, handed them menus and backed away.

"Hey," He got up to give her a slightly awkward hug hello.

"Hey." She smiled again, wanting to swat the butterflies caged in her body. "Sorry, have you been waiting long?"

"No, no." He dismissed her with the wave of a hand, a *huge* hand. "I've only been here, like, an hour, trying not to seem to eager."

He showed his perfectly white teeth and she laughed, looking down at her the table. He really was very handsome, so she readjusted the cutlery in front of her and straightened a napkin on her knee.

"Can I get you anything to drink?" The waiter asked, appearing at their table. Jake offered for Mia to order first.

"Can I have a lemonade, please?" She was keen to try and behave herself a little; Jake ordered the beer on tap.

The waiter gave a little nod and hopped away to the bar. Other than an elderly couple sitting in the window, they were the only customers in there.

"You're not a drinker?" Jake asked, cocking his head like a dog.

"No, no, I drink." Mia replied, with furrowed eyebrows. "Just not all the time."

"Why? You're not a part timer, are you?" he asked, with a half-smile.

Mia laughed and looked at her lap again. "Noo. It's just once I'm on it, I am *on* it."

Jake smiled at her and shrugged his shoulders. "Doesn't sound like a bad thing to me."

"It is when you can't get out of bed for work the next day!" Mia pointed out.

"Fair enough." He laughed and they had a short pause. "Do you live nearby?"

"Yeah, just along the seafront. Well, about a twenty-minute walk away. Do you?"

"I'm about two miles that way." He pointed West then wrapped his hand round the pint glass placed in front of him. "Cheers?"

"Cheers." They clinked their glasses.

For over an hour, they talked. There were very few awkward pauses, some delicious courses and a laugh or two. Mia liked to think it was going well.

"So, you know where I work, what do you do for a living?" Mia asked, as he gently scrubbed his knuckles on his short beard.

"I'm a primary school PE teacher." he replied, nodding.

"That is adorable." Mia said. "Do you enjoy it?"

"Most of the time. I love getting paid to teach rugby, but I'd prefer coaching adults, then you don't feel so bad for shouting at them. I do a bit of surf coaching with adults; my dream would be to own one of the surf schools down here."

"Oh my gosh, same." Mia said. "That would be such an amazing job. I always get so jealous watching them from the café."

"Do you surf?" Jake asked, raising his eyebrows.

"Yeah, but not well!" Mia replied. "You should see my Dad. He grew up in South Africa and he is *amazing*. Probably the best surfer I've ever seen."

"Ooh, bold claim!" Jake said. "You haven't seen me yet."

After almost two hours, the date ended with a debate over the bill.

"Put your card away," Jake said, waving her purse away. "I'll pay."

"No, I insist that we split it." Mia replied, pulling her card out.

"Are you sure?" Jake looked sceptical.

"100%." Mia replied. "I don't understand how it's fair that you pay."

"Fair enough!"

They split the bill, left a tip then left the restaurant.

"Can I walk you home?" Jake asked.

Mia did not want to tell him that she was going to meet her friends at the Surf cafe, so let him walk her to the door. It was a beautiful evening for a walk along and they took the beach route, kicking off their shoes when they reached the sand and giving *Josie's* a wide berth, so tongues did not start wagging at work. At the far end of the beach, they wandered back onto the path and followed it round to the old priory ruins, along Front Street and round to Mia's. Three fishing trawlers were heading home, inbound for the River Tyne; a pilot vessel was darting out to one of the awaiting cargo ships.

"Just up here." Mia directed, diverting them back towards the sea.

"You live here?" Jake asked the rhetorical question. "It's gorgeous."

"It's not too shabby, is it?" Mia smiled. "It hasn't sunk in yet just how lucky we are."

"I'd kill to live this close to the sea." he replied, admiring the surroundings.

"I'll warn my flatmates, then, in case I disappear." Mia said.

"Don't worry, I'm not that sick of you, yet." he grinned.

"Charming." Mia replied with a smile.

He flashed her his set of brilliant teeth and kissed her on the cheek for a goodbye. She waved him off, briefly went inside and waited in the entrance hall till he walked far enough away before letting herself back out.

At the top of the Tynemouth Longsands dunes, looking very out of place, sat a row of buildings overlooking the sea. Beside them had once stood a grand plaza building that had been devastated by fire in 1996. The row of low buildings were the only survivors. At the northern end sat a small surf shop with a café attached, both were very popular. Though technically a café, it also acted as a pub in the evenings. If they were able to get a seat, Sian, Steph and Mia loved to head along, especially for open mic night. Because Sian worked there, they only needed to wangle two seats, if she was on shift. With Steph being a decent guitar player and Mia loving to sing, they made quite the duo to a small, and therefore less intimidating audience. They knew most of the local faces anyway.

[Mia] On the way.

She texted Steph and started towards the Surf café. Jake had texted her already, 'I had fun tonight, let's do it again.'

As she walked up the dark street, she was aware of someone not far behind her. It made her uncomfortable enough that she started walking faster, gripping her keys in her pocket, just in case. She was relieved when she walked through the door of the pub, the warmth of the place washing away her discomfort; the man had continued up the street.

"MiMi!" Mia heard Steph's voice carry across the room and turned to see her overenthusiastically waving. Carol and Sian were seated at the same table. "Hurry up!"

Carol Boon was one of their dearest friends. Some may call it an unusual relationship; some did. While they were at University, Carol was also studying, but as a mature student. She was fifty-three, with grey hair, a husband and two children roughly the same age as Mia, Sian and Steph. Her husband, Don, was a highly successful lawyer, one of the best in the country. Together, they had five properties in four different countries, and she was residing in the Newcastle home for the weekend.

"Hey, Carol." Mia pulled her into a hug. "It's so good to see you!"

"You too!" Carol smiled that brilliant smile.

"There's enough time for niceties later!" Steph whined. "You've got a date to tell us about."

One of the bartenders brought a plate of nachos to the table. Even though Mia had just finished a huge meal, they looked too irresistible.

"Put your tongue away." Mia nudged Sian as the bartender walked away, but then had a sneaky look herself.

"I swear, you accuse me of way more than I'm actually doing." Sian replied.

"No, I just notice more than you want me to." Mia retorted, with a grin.

"*Anyway...*" Steph pressed. "How did it go?"

They discussed the date at length. As always, Sian lowered the tone, Steph asked the invasive questions and Carol kept them civilised.

"So, when are you going to go out with him again?" Carol asked.

"We didn't sort out a second date." Mia replied with a shrug of her shoulders. "He did text me though saying it would be nice to do it again."

"And what did you say?" Steph said, with excited eyes.

"I haven't replied yet." Mia said with gritted teeth.

"Give me your phone." Sian demanded.

"No." Said Mia.

"Why not?" Sian asked.

"I just want to think about it a bit more." Mia defended.

"Did you get the goods and realise you're not interested anymore?" Sian asked.

"No." Mia said.

"Come on, mate, you were gone a while. Do you expect us to believe he walked you home and you didn't creep upstairs for a bit before coming here?"

"We didn't!"

"Is he small?" Said Steph.

"No-"

"Is that actually a thing, size matters?" Sian asked.

"Oh, don't panic, *you* can buy a new one if you need it." Steph patted her hand.

"Yeah, but you guys can't." Sian replied.

"Will you two give over?" Carol interjected.

"Sorry." Steph and Sian apologised together.

"Sorry. Anyway, why might you not want to date him again? I thought he was lovely. Not to mention he is gorgeous." Steph leaned in to hear the answer.

"I don't know." Mia shrugged.

"You've only known him two minutes. Give him a chance! You can't expect him to win you over that fast."

"Well, he managed to get into her pants quick enough." Sian laughed.

"I didn't sleep with him." Mia said, defiantly. "And even if I had, says you, we've already covered this, have you ever waited until a second date before?"

"What's a date?" Sian smirked and Steph, jokingly, rolled her eyes.

"You're such an animal." Steph continued. "Anyway, I think you should give him a chance. If it didn't feel right, it was probably because you don't know each other well enough yet."

"You're probably right. If he asks, he is lovely. And yes, he's gorgeous too." Mia trailed off.

At that moment, a large, black, angry cat skulked underneath the table and Mia watched it cautiously before bringing herself back into conversation.

***

Before work on Tuesday, Mia had two *very* separate appointments with her family. Her Dad and Molly could still not be in the same room together, so she was meeting Molly and her Grandma first, followed by her Dad in the evening. It had only been a few days, but her Grandma was already experiencing withdrawal from not having her youngest granddaughter in the house. She arrived at the dress fitting with a bag full of goodies for Mia to take home – milk, bread, biscuits, chocolates, kitchen roll and home-made fairy cakes.

"Thanks, Grandma!" Mia said, kissing her on the cheek and gratefully taking the bag. With the weight of it, she hoped Molly would drop her home afterwards.

Molly was trying on the seventeenth dress of the day. With the wedding fast approaching, time was running out to get everything organised. The bridesmaid dresses had been sorted within a matter of days, but Molly could not find a dress anywhere that, in her words, 'made her heart skip.'

"That one's nice, sweetheart." Grandma smiled. Mia was pleased she was there to give the upmost attention to Molly as she had drifted off after dress number seven that day.

"I like it except for the neckline." Molly sighed. "I wish I could take the train off this one and the neckline off the last one."

It was slightly awkward when she needed to leave at a certain time. When she mentioned who she was meeting, Molly went cold, and Grandma tried to dispel the tension with an offer of cake. The argument would not happen again, but the difference of opinion was palpable, and the atmosphere continued right up until Molly dropped her off at home.

"Do you want to come in and look around?" Mia asked, extending the olive branch.

"No, thank you. I wouldn't want to intrude on your other *guests'* time." Molly said, gruffly, gripping the steering wheel as Mia stepped out. "Don't forget your bag."

Mia grabbed her bag, smiled meekly at her sister and waved her off, still twisting uncomfortably at her family dramas.

"How was dress shopping?" Steph asked, as Mia let herself into the flat.

"I made the mistake of saying Dad was coming this afternoon." Mia replied, glumly.

"Oh God, I bet that went down like a shit in a bath." Steph said, pulling a face.

"I would have preferred a shit in a bath." Mia groaned.

Less than an hour later, a six-year-old, black, cocker spaniel with the energy of a puppy came bounding into the kitchen. He was jet black, all for a white fleck on his chest, and was closely followed by Ian. This time, as well as his own wine, he had also brought his own glass, learning from his last experience.

"Hello, darling." he said, pulling Mia into a hug. "Do you want a drink?"

"No, thanks, Dad." she replied, ruffling Charlie's ears. He had already made himself comfortable on her knee.

Ian made himself at home in the kitchen, exploring the contents of the cupboards, fridge and freezer. He had a bad habit of snooping, so Mia was always cautious of which room she took him into.

"So, I need you to take Charlie for a few weeks." Ian said, nonchalantly.

"Why?" Mia said. She had never been asked to care for him before. "Where are you going? Doesn't he normally go to that lady, Brenda, from next door to you?"

"She's dead. Massive heart attack a couple of days ago. Pity, she was a nice lady, good with Charlie." Ian said, in a matter of fact way, still searching through the empty cupboards. "And I booked another trip to South Africa. Shark diving again. Maybe some kite surfing."

"Wait, when do you go?"

"Two days' time. I brought all his stuff." he said, gesturing to a 'bag for life' by the door. "There's an envelope of cash in there too in case he needs anything.

"Dad!" Mia shook her head. "You can't just dump a dog with us with no warning!"

"Oh, don't be daft!" Ian replied, standing to leave. He patted Charlie hard on the head. "He's as good as a teacher's pet. Have fun with him."

And, as quick as he had arrived, he left. They had a dog.

Chapter Six

Sian was thrilled with the new flat addition and rang the landlord herself to check it was okay for him to stay; Steph was not so pleased. Charlie's presence messed with her dream of having the perfect show home. Initially, she had tried to argue that it looked bad for them, asking to have a pet less than a week after moving in, but neither Sian nor Mia would listen, and Charlie was staying. He already had an allocated corner for his bed and toys and his own hook for his lead by the door.

"Fine, but he's not allowed upstairs!" Steph said, adamantly.

"Deal." Sian and Mia chimed, though they knew Charlie would sneak up as soon as he was able.

"Why couldn't he leave a kitten with us? They don't smell this bad." Steph moaned, lifting her legs onto the sofa as Charlie scuttled by.

"He doesn't smell that bad." Sian protested, tapping her knees and calling to him; he obliged and bounded over.

"He smells pretty bad, Sian." Steph replied. "No, not on the furniture! Down!"

Charlie had made himself comfortable in the armchair beside Sian and was staring Steph down. As she drew closer to him, he rolled on his back, asking for a belly rub.

"Oh, look at that cutie!" Sian cooed, leaving the full chair to him and dropping to her knees to scratch his fur.

"Look at that folks, the first and last time you'll see Sian Holiday drop to her knees for a man." Mia laughed. Sian was too besotted to care.

"Let's take him for a walk!" Sian said, jumping to her feet. "I bet he'll love the beach."

"Yeah, and I bet he'll love getting sand all over the sofa when he gets home." Steph said, miserably.

"Hang on, if you wait, like, ten minutes, I'll get ready for work then we can walk along together." Mia replied, pushing herself up and darting to her room.

"But you don't start for ages?" Sian said.

"I know, but we'll have to walk him to the far end because of the dog ban." Mia shouted through.

"Damn, what a stupid rule."

Sian waited like an impatient child and Steph reluctantly agreed to go too when Mia was ready.

It was another beautiful day at the coast. The tide was at its lowest, revealing the large expanse of white sand. A cluster of rocks with pools sat in the middle and an old, disused swimming pool lay dormant at the far end of the sand near *Josie's*. Much to Mia's dismay, the sea was flat calm, so her surfboard would need to sit patiently for a little while longer.

"Bloody hell, he's strong for a little dog!" Sian said, as she was pulled ahead of them towards the sand.

They walked to the far end of Tynemouth Longsands, as the sun beat down on them. The car parks were full, and others were still battling to find spaces. Dogs barked excitedly and children cried if they were denied ice cream. Footprints and paw prints zigzagged across the sand, before waves washed and wiped the slate clean.

"Do you think he'll be okay to let off the lead?" Sian asked, struggling to stay upright as he pulled her down the stairs.

"Give it a go." Mia replied with a shrug. "Dad never mentioned about keeping him on."

Pulling him close, Sian bit the bullet and let him free. Immediately, he darted off towards the sea, then to another dog on the beach.

"Charlie, come back!" Sian shouted, running after him. Steph and Mia looked at each other, deciding they should probably run after him too.

But he ignored them, he was far too interested in the other dog, whose owner grabbed Charlie while he had the chance. The girls caught up with him, severely out of breath.

"Thanks for catching him." Mia panted, putting her hands on her knees after the sprint. She felt far too unfit. *I need to take up running again,* Mia thought, as stars appeared in the corners of her eyes. There was burning in her chest.

"No worries." The man fawned over Charlie, who lapped it up. "He's gorgeous, how old is he?"

"He's six." Steph said, edging to the front of the group, elbowing Sian out of the way in the process. Mia could not remember the last time she had seen Steph so heart eyed.

"I bet he's spoiled rotten, right?" The man asked, still crouched down stroking Charlie.

"Yeah. He is - he's great. I love him to bits." Steph replied; Mia and Sian looked at each other again.

"He's gorgeous." Steph said, pointing to the man's dog.

"*She.*" he corrected, lightly, ruffling his dogs' ears. "This is Bailey. She's the lady of my life."

"Awww!" Steph cooed.

"She's crazy though." he said, looking up at Steph, then pulling himself to human level, holding out his hand. '*Hell, he's tall,*' Mia thought. He was at least six foot three, if not taller. "I'm Dimitri."

"Steph. I'm Steph. And-and this is Mia and Sian." Steph said, pointing to the friends she wished would disappear.

"Hey." Mia waved, awkwardly. "We've got to go to work, but nice to meet you." She tugged at Sian's shoulder. "See you later, Steph."

Mia turned towards the café but spun back briefly to watch as Steph and Dimitri walked back down the beach together with the dogs.

"And what am I meant to do now without a house key?" Sian asked, looking at Mia expectantly. "Break in?"

"Why didn't you bring a key?" Mia asked.

"Because Steph had hers!"

"Well, I don't have one. We only have the two of them." Mia replied, patting her pockets in case one had magically materialised.

"We really need to get some more cut." Sian sighed.

"Job for you then bud." Mia clapped her on the back. "Nicely volunteered."

"Volun-told, more like."

Sian, reluctantly, followed Mia into work, setting up camp at the bar.

"Coffee?" Mia asked, tying her apron.

"Please." Sian replied, flicking through her phone. Mia checked herself in, flicked the coffee machine to life and started reading the to-do-list.

"Are you on Tinder, again?" Mia asked, watching Sian swipe left and right, gormlessly. "You must have dated half of Newcastle by now."

"I don't date." Sian replied. "How many times?"

"Sorry," Mia corrected. "You must have *seduced* half of Newcastle by now."

"That's better. And not yet, new fish keep popping up to fry."

Mia rolled her eyes and placed a coffee in front of her.

"I thought I heard your voice." Jubeda sang, waltzing through from the kitchen.

"Hey, Jay, how are you?"

"All the better now you're here." Jay was far too happy for Mia's good.

"Tell me everything!" Jay dashed forward, grabbed both her hands and pulled her towards the bar.

"Jay, I don't even have my apron on yet!" Mia laughed; peeling Jay off her.

"Come on! I need to live vicariously through you!"

Mia rolled her eyes and tied her apron.

"How was it? I want every dirty, little detail."

Jubeda 'Jay' Aktur was possibly the nosiest person in Mia's life. She was a devout Muslim, always wore the most beautiful headscarves and had a wicked sense of humour. As soon as Mia went near a boy, Jay wanted to know *everything,* and she meant *everything.* If it was possible, Jay would even want to know the exact number of hairs on their head and how many freckles they had crossing the bridge of their nose.

"There aren't any dirty details! Not from the second date." Mia replied, stacking the trays together.

"Don't give me that 'first date' crap, what about Liam?" Jay said, hands on hips.

"Liam was different. It didn't feel like a first date." Mia said, rolling her eyes.

"Yeah, whatever." Jay nodded, accusingly. "Anyway, when are you going to have his babies? I think I've been waiting long enough to become an Aunty."

"Jay!" Mia scolded.

"Have you had sex with him yet?" she asked.

"No." Mia replied.

"Why don't I believe you?" Jay asked, tapping a finger on her chin.

Mia looked at her suspiciously. "What are you not telling me?"

"We had a delivery for you this morning." she replied, swinging her torso from side to side. "Came about just before twelve."

"A delivery?" Mia genuinely did not know what it could be.

Jay dug under the counter and lifted a marvellous bouquet of yellow, white and pink flowers. The card read: To Mia, I had a great time last night. J x

Mia was mortified; the blood was rushing to her cheeks. She could already feel the smile on Sian's face behind her.

"I knew you slept with him!" Sian roared, aggressively punching the air. "Guys don't send flowers to girls after the first date unless something happened!"

"Shh!" Mia hissed; acutely aware she was at work. "Nothing happened."

"I don't believe you for a second." Sian replied. "I knew you were gone a while."

"Seriously, nothing happened!"

"Whatever." Jay and Sian said together.

Despite the promise of more teasing later, Sian, kindly, took the flowers home for her, to avoid more questions throughout the day. It turned out that *nobody* thought a man sent a woman flowers after the first date unless something had happened. Mia made a mental note to kill Jake if they went for a second date. Their flat group chat pinged not long after Sian left:

[Sian] I'm working tonight. You both better get your arses to the SC later.

[Steph] I'm keen but, why?

[Sian] I need too much information from you both to wait until home time.

Mia was on shift 3pm-9pm and Sian was working till 11pm, meaning Mia had time to run home, get changed and still be sitting in the Surf café by 9:30pm.

"I wish they did pizza and a pint night in here on a Tuesday." Mia said, thoughtfully.

"Well, we don't, so what can I get you?" Sian asked, leaning on the counter.

"Er, two pints of Amstel and a sharing Nachos, no jalapenos." Mia replied, blowing Sian a kiss.

Sian tapped her fingers on the bench and shuffled over to pour the pints. The beauty of the Surf café was it was so small and intimate, that Sian could sit with them at the table unless someone needed to be served.

"Who's going first, then?" Sian looked between the two of them.

"Wait, what does Mi have to say? I thought we heard it all last night?" Steph asked.

"She left out some key details." Sian replied, looking unimpressed.

"She did, did she?" Steph's eyes glistened.

"She didn't." Mia replied.

"Jake sent her flowers this morning – to work." Sian said.

"He what?" Steph gasped with a smile, grabbing Mia's wrist.

"I am not going over this again." Mia replied, huffing slightly. "I *didn't* sleep with him, can we move onto Steph now, please?"

"Boys don't send flowers to girls after a first date unless something happened." Steph said.

"That's what I said!" Sian replied.

Mia was starting to feel like a huffy teenager. "I'm not talking about this anymore." Mia put her foot down and they knew they had pushed as far as they could.

"Right, Steph, your turn." Sian said.

Steph's dog walk had turned into an impromptu date with Dimitri – the tall, handsome, fire-fighting identical twin from the Ukraine. They had walked North, towards Cullercoats, stopping outside for a drink at the far end of Tynemouth Longsands. Charlie had taken to Bailey a little too much, but it had broken any potential tension.

"I just don't get how you happen across these people?" Sian said.

"Says you? You've got so many notches on your bed post, it's fallen down." Mia replied.

"No, but you know what I mean. How you just happen across these perfectly chiselled people as soon as you step out of the front door? I have to trawl through all the weirdos online and most of the ones I pick are still weirdos." Sian grumbled.

"I stand by my theory that you attract weirdos." Steph said, making a motion. "Give me your phone."

As Sian stood up to serve a customer, she slipped her phone out of her pocket and onto Steph's lap. They all had each other's phone passwords memorised.

"Listen to this." Steph said, opening Tinder to Sian's profile. "Sian, 21, coffee enthusiast, biology grad (winky face). Ironically, let's get something straight here. I'm on Tinder and my first picture is one of me in a bikini, I'm not looking for a friend or a relationship."

"Wow." Mia smiled. "That girl, just wow. I don't know whether to be impressed or not."

"Can we make changes or not?" Steph asked, as Sian came back within earshot.

"Go for it." Sian shrugged. "Just don't save anything until I've had a look."

Between the two of them, Mia and Steph made Sian's profile appear more wholesome.

"You've made me look like a nun!" Sian protested, reviewing the changes they had made.

"I thought you wanted to attract nicer people?" Steph frowned.

"Nicer, yes, but I don't want a Sunday school teacher!" Sian groaned.

Steph rolled her eyes. "You're never happy."

"I would be if you were actually helpful." Sian said, then pointed to the empty stage. "Anyway, are you guys singing tonight?"

Mia looked at Steph. "Fancy it?"

"Yeah, can do." Steph shrugged. They always enjoyed playing together. "What do you fancy singing?"

They decided on Toploader's 'Dancing in the Moonlight.' The song held fond memories for Mia. Her fondest memory being from a Barbados evening when she was five years old. On the dimly lit beach, with a restaurant nearby, she had been twirled around to the song by her Dad. He was away a lot, especially when they were children, so she clung to the memories.

When they left for home, Mia had a message from Jake:

[Jake] Sorry about the flowers. I thought they'd be a good idea.

[Mia] They were lovely, thank you. I was mortified they came to work though!

[Jake] Yeah, maybe an error in judgement, but I had a good time.

**

On Wednesday night, Mia was walking home after her shift when Holly dropped her an invitation that she could not resist.

[Holly] Cheeky Nando's?

[Mia] So keen, when?

[Holly] I'll pick you up in twenty minutes.

With both Steph and Sian at work, Mia took Charlie with her and they got a takeaway.

"Woah! It's not as warm as I thought it was gonna be!" Holly shivered, stepping out of her car. "Here's me thinking we'd have a lush picnic in the sun!"

They had driven down to the Royal Quays, on the bank of the River Tyne, to eat their dinner in picnic form. A cool breeze whipped across the river, dropping the temperature enough for jumpers to be necessary. They sheltered slightly behind an old watchtower, feeding Charlie the occasional chip, as the DFDS ferry left its berth, bound for Amsterdam. Passengers waved to them from the decks and they waved back, enthusiastically. As it rounded the bend in the river, its horn sounded across Tyneside.

"We should go on that one day." Mia sighed, watching it draw further away from them. "We could do another interrailing trip."

"It would be nice to go on one where I remember more than 50% of it." Holly laughed, so did Mia.

"Yeah, I'm surprised our livers survived the last one." Mia replied, unwrapping more food. "How're things with you, anyway? I feel like you've been elusive recently."

"Yeah, things aren't too bad, really. I feel like I've become nocturnal though, working so many hours in the club. It's actually weird to be outside with the sun." Holly said, shielding her eyes from the light. "What's happening with you? Didn't you have a date the other day? How did it go?"

"It was nice." Mia nodded.

"Uh, oh. That doesn't sound amazing." Holly said, smearing lemon and herb sauce on her wrap.

"No, no, he was lovely. It was just nice. Like, he's funny and he's hot, I just always find first dates a little awkward, it's hard to tell if there's a proper spark there, you know?" Mia said.

"Are you going out with him again?" Holly asked, taking a messy bite of her food.

"He hasn't asked me." Mia replied. "I suppose I could ask him, you know, modern world and all that."

"Yeah, you could, but then you wouldn't know if he really wants to see you or not."

"True." Mia stretched back and lay on the grass. "I don't know. I don't know whether I'm just not letting anyone in, at the moment."

"How do you mean?" Holly lay back too.

"I think part of me wants to meet someone and be all happy and loved up, then the other part of me just wants to stay single and free and run off to travel the world."

"Hey, if you're running off and travelling anywhere, give me the heads up, because I'm definitely coming with."

"I suppose I'd allow you." Mia laughed. "Do you know what I mean though?"

"Yeah, I get you." Holly replied. "But you've been on one date with this guy. It doesn't mean you have to marry him. You're not Molly."

"No, I'm not." Mia said. "You're right there."

"Although, if you go in the opposite direction and *do* decide to get married and have lots of babies, I am so bagsying maid of honour *and* godmother."

"You can battle that one out with Steph."

"She's like four-foot-tall, those titles are mine." Holly said, stuffing four chips in her mouth at once.

Mia laughed.

**

On Thursday night, Fred turned up with a very Fred assortment of items. His family owned an incredible bakery on Tynemouth Front Street – 'Norman Family Bakery.' Occasionally, his Grandpa would pack a basket full of pastry goodness for the girls and send it along with Fred, who was, that night, laden with a full basket and a box.

"I love your Gramps." Mia smiled, accepting the food gifts. "Give him a big cuddle from me."

"Give him one yourself." Fred replied, squeezing through the front door. "He's always saying you need to visit more."

Fred and Mia had been friends since they were born. With birthdays one day apart and grandparents who were close friends, they had grown up together. His family felt like hers and vice versa. They were always welcome in each other's homes.

The 'Norman Family Bakery' was famous in the North East. Their café, which was attached to the bakery, was legendary. It had such a good reputation that a celebration was not up to scratch unless the cake came from Norman's. Even the shop itself was like something out of 'Home Alone.' A working train set snaked its way around the food, passing the people who gawped through the window. The smells drifting from within were intoxicating, luring crowds in off the streets. Fred's Grandpa was a skilled sculptor too, a skill he had passed on to Fred, and elegant marzipan creatures and creations decorated the shelves. Mia's personal favourite had been the year they made an entire snow-coated gingerbread village for Christmas.

"What's in the box, boy?" Mia asked, as they settled in the living room.

"Our task for the evening." He shook the box and what sounded like hundreds of tiny pieces rattled together. "Now, like every year, you are sworn to secrecy."

Mia giggled like a little kid. She knew what was coming. "What's the theme?"

"Do you need to take the oath again?" Fred asked.

"Come on, Freddie, what's the theme?" Mia whined, impatiently.

Slowly opening the box to build suspense, Fred pulled another box out of the first, revealing it to be: The Lego Knight Bus from Harry Potter and the Prisoner of Azkaban.

"Oh my God! You guys are doing Harry Potter! That's amazing!!" Mia squealed with delight.

"Yep, Ciara, finally got her way." He smiled, referring to his little sister.

Every year, the bakery would set up a new display for Christmas, hence the Gingerbread houses a few years back. It took months to put together and hours-worth of work from all family members to get it ready.

"This is your Thursday night for the foreseeable future." Fred said. "I hope you're ready."

"That's fine by me." Mia smiled. Fred tore open the box and they set to work on the magic, purple bus. The previous year's theme had been 'Christmas in the Capital.' The final addition, Lego Buckingham Palace, they had stayed up until 2am on the launch day creating.

"Do you know what I realised the other day?" Fred asked, as he assembled the driver's cab.

"What?" Mia asked, searching for the pieces to make the final sliding bed.

"That we live on the wrong side of Hadrian's Wall."

"What are you on about?" Mia asked, pulling a face.

"Think about it, if the wall was still up, we'd be on the wrong side of it."

"No, we wouldn't."

"Yeah, we would." Fred argued.

"No, we wouldn't." Mia argued back. "Hang on a second, what do you class as the 'wrong side?"

"We'd be on the Scottish side."

"Ah!" Mia replied. "See, to me, that's the right side."

"See you in battle then!" Fred laughed.

They continued, generally chatting nonsense, until they had a fully functioning Lego knight bus.

"Well, that wasn't too painful." Mia said, proud of their first model.

"I think he started us off lightly." Fred replied, getting to his feet to find his shoes, pulling them on without undoing the laces when he found them. "Just wait until we have the whole of Hogwarts Castle to do."

"As long as A) I don't have to pay for them and B) I don't have to store them for you, I am happy to help in manufacture."

"Deal." Fred leaned in to give her a brief hug, opening the front door. "Oh, and Mam wants to buy, like, twenty-seven thousand tickets for your show so don't be surprised if she hunts you down."

"Great, more people to embarrass myself in front of!" Mia said, with nervous laughter.

"Don't worry, I'm sure you've done far worse in the past or will do far worse in the future!" Fred laughed, waved and started down the stairs, empty basket and new creation in tow.

Mouth of the Tyne, Anna Heslop

Chapter Seven

Made up of an Anglo-Saxon monastery, a royal castle and an old defence station, Tynemouth Priory dominated the coastline, with the ruins overlooking the sea. Once a year, in July, a festival was held with the priory at its heart. Throughout the week, the girls had faintly been able to hear some of the acts preparing for the weekend ahead. Tynemouth Front street was decorated with bunting of red, white and blue; the road was closed to all cars and cafes brought their tables and chairs out into the streets for the festivities. Food vans pulled onto the grass verge near the sea front and people spilled out of the pubs full of good food and beer. The event organisers had lucked out with the weather that year and it was perfect – no wind, no clouds and luscious warmth. By Saturday lunchtime, many event attendees were already sunburned and plenty of people were enjoying the beach and sea.

The closest beach to the priory was a small bay nestled amongst the cliffs called King Edward's Bay, named after Edward II. A long stairway wound its way down from the cliff top on one side and met the opposing ramp at the bottom promenade. Only two buildings neighboured the sand – a well-used lifeguard hut and a revamped shack named '*Kay's Plaice*,' whose owner had scattered fire pits and deck chairs on the beach for the event. The local trawlers supplied the fresh fish, straight from the North Sea and all the beers on tap were from small start-up microbreweries in the region.

It was a rare Saturday evening where Steph, Sian and Mia all had the same night off work. They lined a backpack with tin foil, placed a reusable freeze block in it and stocked it with plenty of beer, plus a stray bottle of water for Charlie. Mia dug the camping chairs out from under her bed and, once they were ready for evening, they set off along the street. The festival mainly took place on a dog ban beach, but the rules seemed to relax around the festival, if the dogs were on leads.

The group chat was pinging as they walked:

[Holly] Where are you guys?

[Steph] Walking along now. Be there in 5.

[Maria] Why don't you meet me at the metro? I'm pulling into the station in about 2 mins.

[Holly] Will do. I'm such a loner right now.

[Zoe] I haven't left yet so I'll be a little late! Sorry!

[Carol] Do you want me to pick you up? I'm leaving soon in the car.

[Zoe] Yes, please, you gem!

[Carol] I'll be round soon.

[Fred] Can you pick me up too, Carol? Please! I'm up near Morrisons.

[Carol] Will do.

They approached down the ramp and wound down until they reached the minefield of people. The free spot they got was, unfortunately, nowhere near a fire pit but it was too warm for them to mind anyway. Sian splayed a picnic blanket on the ground as Steph and Mia propped the camping chairs in the sand.

"Right, I'll tie Charlie to this chair but it's going to have to be manned at all times." Mia said, taking the first watch. Sian had been walking him a few days before when he tore off down the beach and stole a whole chicken from a stranger's BBQ. Rather than apologise, she had run in the other direction.

When Carol arrived with Zoe and Fred, she brought a full kitchen – salad, cocktail sausages, sandwiches, biscuits, fruit and wine. Even though Fred was a well-built man, he was struggling to carry her cooler bag across the beach due to the weight, while supporting Zoe, who had bin-bagged her broken leg. Holly and Maria appeared not long after.

"I don't know if I know any songs from the band on tonight." Steph said, looking up to the priory. The audience within the walls were starting to murmur louder as the band prepared themselves.

"Of course, you do!" Mia said and started singing an old banger.

"Oh, I didn't know that was them!"

"Wine anyone?" Carol offered. Mia had given up her chair to Carol, who seemed to lord over them from there. She had decided to abandon her car for the evening. Her chair was highest on the slight sand bank so she could oversee the rabble beneath her. Other than the three on the chairs, everyone else was tangled in a heap on the picnic rug. Sian was furiously adding to her Instagram story; Holly was debating whether she could justify a cigarette after only one beer and still blame the alcohol.

"Oh, hey!" Steph jumped up so quickly off her camping chair, she sent it flying backwards, spilling one of the beers in the sand and freeing Charlie at the same time. Sian managed to catch him as well as her beer. "Sit down, please, just find a space. Do you want a beer?"

"Thank you." Dimitri replied in his deep voice. "I hope it is ok, I brought my two friends. This is Peter and this is Jake."

Mia smiled at the man she was yet to arrange a second date with. Of course, Jake and Dimitri were friends, the world was just that kind.

"Hey." Jake smiled at Mia; Steph looked between the two of them with awkward eyebrows.

"Hey." Mia smiled, meekly, back and he sat down next to her on the far edge of the group.

"I was starting to think you'd dropped off the end of the earth." he said, waiting for an answer.

"No, sorry, it's just been a busy week." Mia replied. Jake had been texting but had not officially asked her to go out again, so her replies had been poor, even for her normal standards.

With a glass of wine in her hand and a smug grin on her face, Sian leaned back ready to watch the show. Although, she was more attentive to her phone than usual.

"How do you know Dimitri?" Mia asked, trying to ignore the rest of her crowd subtly, but not subtly, watching them.

"I live with Peter and they work together." Jake replied, quietly, as though saying something offensive, but loud enough for Holly to hear.

"Oh, you're a firefighter as well?" Holly wasted no time; she was straight in there, extending a hand out to Peter. "I'm Holly."

Mia scoffed, smiled and rolled her eyes.

"Anyone want to play frisbee?" Fred asked, jumping to his feet, sensing the awkward air.

By the time the music started, they had begun a game of frisbee on the beach, which had become quite competitive. Zoe, Carol and Charlie were the refereeing panel at the side. Fred, Peter, Mia, Maria and Sian were on one team with Steph, Dimitri, Holly and Jake on the other. They drew the lines in the sand for end zones and quickly introduced rugby tackling as an effective way of gaining possession. As most families and groups of friends huddled around fires to relax and listen to the music above, they wrestled each other to the floor and sprayed sand everywhere. Luckily, the tide was out so they had plenty of room to keep away from other people.

"Of course, you're winning, you've got more players than us!" Steph shouted; her face was glowing red. Competitive Steph was scary Steph.

"Yeah, but we've got Maria – no offense – so it's pretty fair." Sian argued back.

"None taken!" Maria said, lifting her hands in acceptance.

Until she saw Maria play, Mia thought she was bad at frisbee. But Maria was terrible. On one occasion, when play was stopped, Maria was throwing the frisbee in the air to herself and dropped it – she could not even catch it playing on her own let alone when anyone else threw it to her. She was better at throwing, though usually over compensated and threw it too hard.

Mia was sprinting for the frisbee, after one of Maria's throws, and could hear Jake hot on her heels. As she caught it, he barrelled into her. But, instead of knocking her to the ground, he picked her up and spun her to face him. She could not remember the last time she had been picked up, especially so easily, it stunned her. Jake cracked a half smile and lowered her towards him, as though to kiss her. She could feel her heartbeat in her ears, and it pounded hard in her chest.

When he was no more than a few centimetres away, his half smile turned to a full one and he whipped the frisbee out of her hand. He lightly plopped her onto the sand, kissed her forehead, turned and bolted, throwing it ahead of him as he did so.

Mia scolded herself.

"Dammit." Sian appeared, clipping her on the back of the head. "Stop chasing cock and get your head in the game."

"Says you," Mia replied, rubbing her head. "Since when are you so glued to your phone? Are we keeping you from another one-nighter?"

"Never you mind." Sian snapped. "Put your thoughts on the game, not my virtual social life."

Mia grinned and ran back into the game. Although it was close, Mia's team ended up winning. They collapsed back onto the sand to crack open another beer.

"We definitely would have won if it had been five on five." Mia heard Steph and Sian arguing behind her as she unzipped the backpack.

"Are you free tomorrow night?" Jake asked, flopping onto the sand beside her.

"Erm, yeah, I am." Mia replied, choking slightly on her gulp.

"Am I allowed to steal you for another night?" he asked.

"I suppose one more night couldn't hurt." she replied, cringing at her own attempt at flirting.

Jake smiled and allowed Dimitri to draw him into conversation.

"And who is hogging all of your attention?" Steph asked, ripping the phone from Sian's hand.

Sian turned in the sand so quickly she sprayed it everywhere. Holly leapt up to pin her down.

"Woah, woah, woah, watch the beer!" Mia protested, holding the bottle high above her head.

"Who's Amy, Sian?" Steph asked, still playing keep away with her phone.

Peter's eyes nearly popped out of his head as he watched the girls wrestle each other. Looking between her friends, Mia had to laugh. To her right, there was a violent play fight with the words 'no biting!' being hissed. To her left, Zoe and Carol were sharing a homemade cheese plate while they drank their wine. She loved her misfits. Maria pulled her into a hug from behind, so she leaned back to appreciate the human cushion and the last of the night's music.

**

On Sunday night, six days after their first date, Mia was preparing for her second date with Jake. Jay had talked her ear off all day at work about it and had made her more nervous than she already was. Although the first date had been nice, Mia had opted for something a bit more active for the second one, when Jake asked her what she fancied doing. Instead of something typical like the cinema or drinks, they were heading rock-climbing.

"And where are you off to?" Mia asked, as Sian fought her for the bathroom.

"I have a date as well." Sian replied.

"Let me guess, The Botanist and the Metro Game?" Mia said, pulling a face to apply her mascara.

Sian had her 'dating but not dating' game down to a T. She always took her dates to the same place for drinks, somewhere impressive enough but with plenty of escape routes just in case. If the night went well, she would 'accidentally' miss the last Metro home and end up with an invite to theirs for the night.

"Actually, she picked. We're going down to the Fish Quay." Sian replied, fighting to straighten her naturally curly, brown hair.

"Oh, isn't that a bit too close for comfort?" Mia asked.

The Fish Quay was situated just down the bank from Tynemouth village, towards the river. It surrounded the Fish market and was where most fishing trawlers docked. In the past, it had solely been a working port; now it was a thriving scene for nightlife with new bars opening monthly.

"You don't normally ask them what they want to do, why now?" Mia asked, scooting over slightly to allow Sian some more mirror room.

"I thought I'd mix things up a little." Sian said. "Don't want to go stale now do I?"

"Fair enough."

They left the flat together, wished each other luck and went their separate ways. Sian wandered along the path that led down to the Quay and Mia made for the metro, just missing one as she arrived at the station. A group of young teenage lads were playing chicken on the line. When an older man told them off, they took to practicing parkour on the bike sheds instead.

The nearest metro station to the climbing centre was Byker. As she walked out of the station, Mia kept her head down and walked fast. Although there were some great facilities in the area, it was notoriously rough and could be quite a scary part of the North East. She walked fast until she reached the climbing centre and met up with Jake. The centre was built inside an old church. When Mia was younger, it had been a soft play centre that she had attended for friends' parties. It had been the coolest venue when they were eight.

Although they originally intended to go rock climbing with ropes, that activity required extra payment for an instructor, so they decided to go into the bouldering room instead. The walls were smaller but there were no ropes to catch you if you fell, only thin crash mats.

"Ready?" Jake said, looking as though he was on a starting block.

"What?" Mia laughed. "I'm not racing you."

"Why not?" he asked, straightening up from his prepared stance.

"I want to see what I'm up against first." Mia said, folding her arms.

"Prepare to be amazed." Jake said, rolling his shoulders and flexing his fingers.

As he climbed up the rocky wall, Mia could not help but admire him from behind. He was just so muscly, a bit of a man mountain, but not particularly graceful.

"If you come back down, I'm happy to race you, now." Mia called, teasing.

"Actually, I quite like it up here." Jake called down, slightly out of breath. He had clearly climbed as fast as he could to impress. "Why don't you join me, I mean, if you can get this high."

Mia dropped her jaw with a laugh. "Watch me." She summoned every ounce of determination and athleticism in her body and shot up the wall as fast as her body would carry her, trying extremely hard not to look down at the drop she was praying she would not experience.

"Well, you've shut me up." Jake laughed, clearly impressed at her vertical dash.

Mia laughed and began plotting her exit strategy.

"Mia?" A voice called from below.

Mia looked down to determine the source of the voice, trying not to vomit in the process.

"Hey, Sam!" she called, with a slight nervous quiver in her voice.

Don't fall. Don't fall. Don't fall. She thought, as her fingers started to ache from gripping. Slowly but surely, she began lowering herself down. It was so much harder than just bouncing down the wall on a rope.

"I didn't know you were a climber." Sam said.

"Er, I'm not really." Mia said, as she tried to find a good foothold. Jake was a lot better at heading down the wall than climbing up and was almost at the bottom. "I'm just here with – this is Jake." She nodded in his vague direction.

"Hi," Jake said, landing at Sam's feet and holding out his hand. "I'm Jake."

"Sam." Mia heard her say. "Nice to meet you."

"You too." Jake replied. Mia guessed he was smiling.

"Anyway, Mi, nice to see you both. I'll leave you guys to it, see you tomorrow." Sam said, and slunk two wall segments away; the bouldering area was not large. Mia wondered who she was with.

"Anytime today, Mia, would be nice." Jake laughed, with his hands on his hips. "Though I don't mind this angle."

"Oh, shut up." Mia called down, wondering how she could contort herself into a more flattering angle as she descended.

When Mia touched back on to solid ground again, she breathed an audible sigh of relief and warned herself not to climb so high next time.

"She seems nice," Jake said, eyeing up his next route up the wall. "How do you guys know each other?"

Mia released a breath and dusted some chalk off her hands. "We're in the same operatic society."

"You're in the same what?" Jake asked, turning his gaze from the wall to Mia.

"Operatic society – like musical theatre." Mia replied, hesitantly.

"Oh – cool." Jake said, racking his brains to see if he knew that already. "Are you doing anything at the moment?"

"Yeah, we're getting ready to do *Wicked* in September." Mia replied.

"How did this not come up on our first date?" Jake asked, turning his body to face her.

"It's not exactly the coolest hobby to have." Mia rolled her eyes; Molly had always teased her about loving musical theatre.

"It's still a hobby of yours though." Jake replied with a shrug. "I've never actually seen *Wicked,* is it the one that's like The Wizard of Oz?"

"Yeah, it's just told from the perspective of the witches." Mia replied.

"Does this mean you can sing and dance?" Jake asked, starting on his next route.

"Oh, god, I can't dance to save my life." Mia laughed, clambering up the neighbouring route. "Think Bambi on ice but drunk and with three legs."

"What an image." Jake laughed. "You didn't say anything about singing though. Does that mean you can sing?"

Mia squirmed. "I'm *okay,* I suppose. I could be a lot better."

"I wonder if Sam would say different." Jake said, turning his head in Sam's direction. "Should I ask her? I might need to shout?"

"Don't you dare." Mia warned.

"Hey, Sam!" Jake shouted over to her.

"Pack it in!" Mia hissed, with an embarrassed laugh.

"What?" Sam called back.

"Can Mia sing?" Jake asked, as Sam hung off her wall. Mia inched closer to Jake.

"Can she sing?" Sam said. "Of course, she can sing, she's the star of our show."

"The star?" Jake said, his eyes alight as he flicked his head back to Mia. "That's interesting to know."

Mia glowed red.

"Thanks, Sam!" Jake shouted over.

Attempting to storm away from a wall was a lot harder than Mia thought it would be. Missing her second foot hold, she slipped and fell approximately three metres on to one of the crash mats to a chorus of 'ooooh!' When she landed, the wind was completely knocked out of her and she gasped for breath, trying hard not to panic.

"Mia? You alright?" Both Jake and Sam, alongside other onlookers, rushed over as she desperately gasped for air.

When the first breath came, it was a relief. Her breathing slowed and gradually returned to normal. Even though she insisted she was fine, she still had to sit with the seventeen-year-old first aider for the allotted half an hour. He stared at his watch in terror the entire time.

"Fancy a drink?" Jake asked, looking sympathetic, when her imprisonment was over.

"Yeah." Mia nodded, keen to get away from her babysitter.

"Are you going for a proper drink this time or are you still behaving yourself?" Jake teased.

"You know, I might have one. But, actually one." Mia laughed.

Jake drove them down to the Fish Quay, abandoning the car at one of the car parks facing the river. The Ship's Cat overlooked the river too but was slightly raised and slightly further back. They made a beeline for it. With its outdoor picnic tables, street food shack and fairy lights, it drew people in like flies to an electric light. Unfortunately, the outdoor area was filled by the time they arrived, so they went inside and up to the balcony area, which overlooked the rest of the venue.

"How're you feeling?" Jake asked.

"I think the only thing hurt is my pride." Mia replied and Jake smiled. Her back was a little sore, but it was nothing to be concerned about.

"What would you like?" Jake asked, when they found a free table.

"Pint of Amstel, please."

Jake trotted off to the bar and returned with two pints of Amstel. Mia could not help doing the maths in her head:

Jake + Beer = No Driving. No Driving + Mia's flat being closest = Overnight guest? Eek.

"Isn't that your mate down there?" Jake pointed to the lower floor. "Sorry, I can't remember her name."

Sure enough, when Mia turned around and looked over the balcony, she could see Sian and her date eying each other up over their drinks.

"If I was a meaner person, I'd be down there in a flash." Mia laughed, looking back at Jake.

"I don't think you'd have time." Jake said, pointing to them again. They had scraped their chairs back and were heading out the door. "Leaving this early means it's either gone really badly or really well."

Stopping outside the doors to shove their tongues down each other's throats answered the question. On one hand, Mia admired Sian's sheer ability to pull. On the other, she was worried Jake would be expecting the night to go a certain way too.

They had another drink each, meaning Jake was not driving home, unless he was going to take a leaf out of her Dad's book.

"Should I order us an Uber?" Jake asked, looking at her quizzically. When she fumbled over her response, he continued. "I'll order it to mine and drop you off on the way?"

"Yeah, that sounds great." Mia said, shyly. "Thank you."

Less than ten minutes later, they met John the Uber driver outside and he took them to their homes. Jake leaned in to give Mia a quick kiss, which she was sure John watched, before Mia scooted out and up the steps. She waved them away before letting herself in and clambering the stairs up to bed.

Evidently, Sian's date *had* gone well; Mia could hear just quite how well very clearly through the ceiling. Poor Charlie kept thinking someone was knocking at the bedroom door each time the headboard collided with the wall. Burying her need to pee and pushing her headphones in, Mia tried her best to block it out, wondering when she would be inviting Jake back.

[Jake] I had a great time again, hope you did too. x

Chapter Eight

"*Morning,* All." Sian uttered, swanning into the kitchen, dressed in her iconic red spotted dressing gown. Her long, brunette, curly hair hung down her back to her waist. Mia was pouring over her '*Wicked'* script, but she managed to look up in time to receive a wink off Sian.

"God, you're practically strutting." Mia laughed, straightening out her script on her legs.

"How's Amy?" Steph asked, ruffling the newspaper, pretending to be a proper adult at the table.

"Still two dimensional." Sian replied, digging out a frying pan and a mixing bowl to make pancakes. "Since when do you read the newspaper?"

"Then, who's that up there?" Steph mouthed initially, pointing to the ceiling. "And since it started coming free in the post."

"I *really* want to say her name is Ashleigh," Sian looked remotely guilty, but not for long. "But she's very, very Irish so I might have caught it wrong. The places we went to were really loud last night as well."

"You don't even know her na-" Steph began but was interrupted.

"Morning!" A small, blonde, Irish woman bounced into the kitchen, threw herself over the kitchen table and pulled Steph into an unexpected hug. "I'm Aisling." Steph looked desperately uncomfortable. Aisling was wearing Sian's boxers and one of her pyjama tops; she hopped back off Steph like a spritely unicorn and pranced over to Sian, wrapping her arms around her from behind. "I hope it's ok, I found these under your pillow and just threw them on."

Sian looked a little horrified and subtly looked sideways at Steph and Mia for help, as Aisling buried her face between Sian's shoulder blades. Mia tried to keep a straight face and Steph disappeared behind her newspaper. Charlie, who normally followed anyone showing signs of energy, looked slightly bewildered by this stranger in his home. He watched her, cautiously, from his throne.

Meanwhile, completely unfazed by the others in the room, Aisling snaked her way around Sian's body and slipped her hands inside Sian's waistband.

"Let's go back to bed." Aisling whispered loudly, causing Sian to stir faster with embarrassment. It was rare to see Sian squirm. The grins Steph and Mia were desperately trying to conceal were making their faces ache; Steph's newspaper was actually shaking.

"Go up and I'll follow you soon." Sian tried to whisper back, but both Sian and Mia were too close for anything to go unheard.

"But I don't want to go without you." Aisling whined. "I want you to make me feel like you did last night." Both Steph and Mia made silent 'yack' faces to each other.

"I'll be two minutes." Sian hissed, trying to peel her off.

"What if I start without you? What if you walk in and I'm straddling-"

"OK!" Steph and Mia leapt up together.

"I think Charlie needs a walk. Do you want a walk boy?" Mia said, quickly.

Charlie kindly picked up his lead for them, they grabbed their shoes to put on outside and left, not able to sprint down the stairs fast enough. They both shuddered and, this time, made an audible 'yack,' as they stepped out the front door, still in their jogging bottoms and lounge clothes.

"I don't get where Sian finds all these weird and willing lesbians from. I swear, they get stranger every time." Mia said, turning south towards the river.

"I'm still expecting to come in one day and find her handcuffed in her bedroom. All our stuff and the burglar long gone, like in some American film."

"I think you're right." Mia replied. "I might start locking my room."

They walked up the road, along Front Street, passed the priory and down the hill to the small haven on the shore of the river. A small sailing club was the only building by the sand, with a few small pleasure boats scattered at its feet. One was being launched as they approached.

"Ooh, do you fancy an ice cream?" Steph asked, as they happened across the ice cream van at the bottom of the bank.

"Always." Mia replied. "Do you have your purse? I didn't pick mine up."

"Likely story." Steph tutted. "I suppose it's my treat then. What do you want?"

"A 99 please." Mia said, practically licking her lips in anticipation.

"Two 99's please." Steph ordered.

"D'you want monkey's blood, pet?" The ice cream man asked.

"Yes please." Mia replied. Steph wanted it too. "Thank you!"

Ice creams in hand, they set off, walking along the North Tyne pier, discussing how expensive ice cream was now.

"I swear, when we were little 99's were actually 99p." Steph said, lapping up the monkey's blood to stop it running down her hand. "Or am I imagining that?"

"No, I'm sure you're right." Mia replied, crunching her flake. "It's like freddo's though. They used to be 5p. They're probably £5 now."

"I haven't had a freddo for *years.*" Steph replied, nervously watching a seagull that was eying her ice cream.

"We should go to that new sweet shop at some point." Mia said, scooping a little bit of ice cream onto her finger and feeding it to Charlie. "I heard they do all the retro tuck shop sweets – like sour belts and those squidgy toothbrushes."

"Mmm, get me there now." Steph said, drooling over the thought of more deliciously unhealthy food.

Their conversation trailed off as they neared the end of the pier and the end of their ice creams.

"We're so lucky to live where we live." Mia breathed, taking in the fresh sea air. "What are you doing?"

"Seeing if anyone is around." Steph replied, tapping away on her phone screen.

[Steph] Sian's having really loud sex in the flat so we're out and about if anyone fancies meeting up?

[Holly] I just woke up, let me know if you decide anything.

[Carol] I miss you guys.

[Fred] Come to the bakery! Gramps just made some empire biscuits.

[Mia] We're on the way!

They ambled back along the pier and reluctantly climbed the steep hill next to the Priory onto Front Street.

"I am so unfit." Mia wheezed, bending over at the top of the hill while Steph took to one of the benches.

"Me too." Steph breathed. "Maybe we shouldn't head to the bakery?"

Mia waved her down and straightened up. "Nah! Diet can start tomorrow."

As they stepped into the shop, the delicious smell of fresh bread hit them square in the face. Music of The Beatles played over the speakers and the train chugged by on one of its many laps. Some of the empire biscuits had already made it onto the shelves, beside the fresh bread basket. A young mother was at the front of the queue buying some. Taking a seat in the dog friendly section, Charlie drank while they ordered. Two cokes appeared with their biscuits not long after.

"How long have you guys been here?" Fred asked, sliding out of the kitchen.

"Only about 5 minutes." Steph said, pulling up a chair for him. "What have you got going on today?"

He took a seat and scooted closer to the table.

"Freddie, do you want a diet coke?" The waitress asked.

"Yes, please, Becca." he said, and she obliged. "I'm on birthday cake duty today. Trying to perfect a Moana themed one. Maui's tattoos aren't easy, I'll tell you that."

"What are you making for our birthdays this year?" Mia asked, giving him a nudge.

"Ahh." Fred said, tapping his nose. "Wouldn't you like to know."

"Yes," Mia replied. "That's why I asked, genius."

"Well, you'll have to wait 'til Edinburgh." Fred said, crossing his arms.

"Can I know?" Steph asked, and Fred leaned in to whisper it to her.

"Hey!" Mia looked outraged. "How come she gets to know?"

"Because it's not her cake." Fred said and Mia huffed.

When they finally returned home, Sian and Aisling were still occupying each other, as they were for most of the day. They emerged for food early evening but took it back to the bedroom to eat it off each other. Aisling was not shy when it came to discussion and could not have cared that the other two were in ear shot.

With a sympathetic look at Steph, Mia left again once she had grabbed her bag and *Wicked* supplies. Before she even reached the street, Steph was by her side and accompanying her to rehearsals.

"I'm sorry mate, I can't sit and listen to that on my own!" Steph explained. "It sounds like someone is milking a cow in there."

"Ew. Please never, ever say that to me again." Mia winced and shook the images from her brain.

They marched along the seafront together, towards the little theatre, with Steph occasionally pointing out a *Wicked* poster that had been pinned to a lamppost or a bin.

"Are you nervous yet?" Steph asked, tugging at Mia's arm.

"I'm terrified!" Mia squeaked, as they walked by yet another poster.

"You'll be fine." Steph replied, jumping at her shoulders. "You've been on stage loads of times."

"Not as the lead." Mia groaned.

"Oh, come on," Steph said, rolling her eyes. "I hear you in the shower every day and I've heard you do karaoke thousands of times, you're pretty damn good."

Mia blushed and they crossed the road to the theatre.

"Hey, Steph, what are you doing here?" Sam bounded over and embraced Steph in a hug as soon as they walked in. "Finally caved and decided to join?"

Steph laughed. "Er, no. You don't need my dire singing abilities chasing everyone away! No, I'm here because the alternative was listening to Sian have loud sex with a stranger about two metres away from me."

"Fair enough." Sam said, nodding at her choice. "Well, you can come and sit with me if you like? Make sure I don't blind the star of the show?" Sam nudged Mia, causing her to blush.

"Great, thanks, see you soon, Mi." Steph said, following Sam up to the decks.

That evening, Angelika was on a mission. As well as being the show's pianist, she was also the director and she was very good at it. Everyone was either busy or given a job. The set was coming on well; the big clock was almost finished. Even though the show was still two months away, it took so long to get everything right. Two months only meant eight more rehearsals, unless they added in more towards the end, as they usually did. Those eight rehearsals relied on everyone being available and not sick or busy or on holiday which, in the summer, was usually the main difficulty.

"Right, places everybody!" Angelika ordered with a clap; Her strong Czech voice rang through the theatre.

The full set for the 'Popular' scene was now finished, so they practiced the whole scene. Mid way through, they needed a brief pause when Sophie/Glinda's boobs tried to escape from her dress. It was strange adjusting to having real single beds to use as props rather than just small chairs and it took some getting used to, making sure they incorporated the beds into the choreography. Mia spent most of the scene sitting down, while Sophie danced around her. Sophie captured the character of Glinda fantastically well and there was a lot of laughter from the thin audience of cast and crew watching. In the glances Mia managed to grab of them, Steph and Sam looked like they were having a great time, dancing along from the decks.

After a sweaty dance scene, which was the last they practiced for the evening, Mia trapesed off the stage to get changed.

"Ready to go, Steph?" Mia asked, throwing her bag over her shoulder.

"You're not gonna break your promise, are you?" Steph replied; Mia was confused.

"What promise?" Mia asked, with furrowed eyebrows.

"Sam told me you'd promised to go to the pub tonight." Steph said.

Mia groaned and slumped. "Ah, man, I really can't be bothered."

"Don't be like that." Steph said.

"Yeah, Mi, don't be like that." Sam said, appearing behind her. "You're not bailing on me again."

"I'm at work in the morning though and I'm all sweaty and…"

"Mi?" Steph said.

"What?"

"Shut up, you're coming."

"Fine." Mia replied, and allowed herself to be dragged to the Surf café.

"I'm sorry, Sam, but I don't even know what you do?" Steph said, as Sian appeared with a tray of drinks. It was a busy evening, so she had not been able to join them.

Sam stopped drinking mid sip to reply. "I'm actually working in construction at the minute." Sam replied, and Mia listened intently. "My sister has her own bricklaying business so I'm just working with her."

"That's cool." Steph replied, nodding. "You don't hear of many female bricklayers."

"I know, my sister had a hell of a job building a reputation." Sam continued. "She's actually had some people laugh in her face when she's turned up on jobs, others have refused to use her altogether when they found out the builder was a woman. She set up her own business because trying to get equal pay in that environment was practically impossible."

"It's so ridiculous when everyone is doing the same job." Mia chipped in and Sam nodded in agreement.

"She's flying now though; her business just keeps going from strength to strength." Sam smiled, clearly proud of her sister's accomplishments. "I only want to be there temporarily though. I'm trying to get my foot in the door with photography."

"Come on then," Steph challenged, pointing to Sam's phone. "Show us your best! I love looking at other people's photos."

Picking up her phone and clicking to an album, Sam showed them her talent. The photographs were incredible, so clear and well timed.

As Sam showed Steph, Mia looked at her, smiling at how proud and happy Sam looked.

**

As time was ticking on, Jake and Mia were texting each other more. He had even started sending amusing posts to her on Instagram. On Friday night, Sian and Steph were both due to be out. Aisling was, thankfully, taking Sian to her place for the evening and Steph was working late. Mia was tempted to take advantage of an empty flat and avoid another slightly awkward date in a staged setting.

[Mia] So, are you still free Friday?

[Jake] Yeah, what have you got in mind?

[Mia] Nothing, I just wanted to tease you for having no plans or friends.

[Jake] Wow, straight for the jugular. I'll just sit here and cry in the dark. ☐

[Mia] Haha. Anyway, do you fancy dinner at my place?

[Jake] Oh, tempting, what's on offer?

[Mia] I'm thinking, homemade pizza, beer and any other unhealthy things we can muster.

[Jake] It's a date.

**

When Jake turned up, it was with a bottle of wine in his hand. When he buzzed, she ran down to meet him and received a welcome kiss for her troubles, which took her breath away a little. She slid her hand into his and tugged him upstairs to the flat for Charlie to greet him.

"Who is this handsome fella?" Jake cooed, dropping down to greet Charlie properly, ruffling his ears and lavishing attention on him.

"This is Charlie, he's my Dad's dog, but kind of ours, now, too." Mia replied.

"He is just gorgeous." Jake cooed some more, and Charlie brought him a shoe as a present. "Thank you, boy."

After the vital introductions, Mia gave him a tour.

"…and this is my room." She creaked the door but did not lead him in.

"Does the tour end here for a reason?" he asked, with a twinkle in his eye.

"Oh, no, you're not allowed over the threshold."

"Not even to hear you play a song for me?" He pointed to the keyboard.

"Absolutely not." She tried to look defiant, but still with a cheeky grin, and closed the door to him. She knew they were getting closer to sleeping together but not yet.

Before long, their date night was in full swing, and they were in the kitchen, innocently preparing homemade pizza. On the countertop, the surprisingly loud speaker was playing some Jack Johnson, tomato puree was smudged in various places and more cheese had been eaten than used in the cooking. Charlie willingly hoovered up anything that dropped to the floor.

"What are you looking at?" Mia asked, catching Jake checking her out. She had been stretching up to try and reach the extra-large plate from the top shelf.

"Nothing. Nothing." He smiled and gestured for her to go to him as he took a seat. She obliged.

She straddled his lap and he held her steady with strong hands. As they kissed, she ran her hands through his hair; the smell was clear and intoxicating. She pushed her toes against the floor to raise herself a little in the kiss, so she was slightly above him and he held her there. They were at that crossroads where the next move would determine the rest of the night. They pulled apart, both feeling the spark, and looked into each other's eyes, just for a moment, searching for that knowing look.

"Is everyone decent?" Sian sang, as she launched herself into the flat, almost swinging the door off its hinges.

A full marching band parade came with her – Sian, Steph and Holly all trapesed in at once. Unfortunately, Mia was too slow in jumping off Jake and was caught mid leap.

"Oi, oi! Let's keep everything PG people!" Steph hollered, abandoning two full shopping bags on the bench. "I'd shake your hand in hello, but I don't know where it's been."

Jake stood up and held out his hand anyway. "I promise, it's been recently bathed in Carex."

Steph took it and they shook.

"He-ey, gu-uys." Mia drawled, with a 'what-the-hell-are-you-doing-here' look in her eye. The oven started beeping; their food was ready.

"I'll be right back." Jake said, excusing himself to the bathroom; Mia smiled at him and whipped her head to her flatmates as soon as he was out of the room.

"What are you guys doing here?" she hissed and pointed at them in turn. "You're meant to be at work, and you're meant to be doing God knows what with an Irish lass."

"Woah! Calm down, ya horn-dog!" Sian said, with her hands in the air; Mia rolled her eyes. "Plans change."

"Yes, I'm sure they do." Mia replied, contemplating her next move. "And I'm not horny, just a little blind-sided."

"Whatever, I can see your boner through your jeans."

Mia scowled at her and slipped on the oven gloves.

"So!" Steph clapped her hands together as Jake came back into the room. "What's the plan for the evening?"

Mia glared at her.

"We were just about to have dinner." Mia said, sliding the pizzas on to plates.

"Okay," Steph began, beginning her retreat. "We'll be next door if you want us."

Pulling Holly and Sian with her, they moved through to the living room and closed the door.

"Sorry about the friendship brigade." Mia grumbled, cutting up the pizza.

"Don't worry about it." Jake said, curiously observing her choice of kitchen wear. "Why are you using scissors to cut a pizza?"

"Why not?" Mia asked. "What do you use?"

"A pizza cutter." he replied, getting up to huddle behind her. "Or a knife, like a normal person."

"But scissors work." she argued, and he hugged her.

"I think we should spend some time with your friends." he said into her neck.

"Trust me, you don't want to do that." Mia replied.

"I've done it already, what's the worst that could happen?" Jake asked.

Mia spun round to face him and looked thoughtful. "You know, there's so many bad things that could happen I wouldn't even know where to begin the list."

"Okay, what's the alternative?" Jake asked, looking playful. "Our movie night is out the window."

Mia thought for a moment. *They're in the living room, walls are paper thin. If we do have slightly awkward first time anything, they'll hear everything.*

"Okay, we'll join them." Mia replied, reluctantly. "But if I say we're leaving the room; we're leaving the room." Between Steph, Sian and Holly, they knew far too many stories about Mia to make Jake run for the hills.

After the pizzas had disappeared, they opted for Cards Against Humanity as a group of five. It was the even more savage version where names of players could be used.

"Oh my God, who put children on leashes? That is definitely my favourite." Steph laughed.

"Thank you very much." Jake said, whipping the card off Steph.

"Should I be worried about how good you are at this game?" Mia whispered to Jake.

"Yeah, I draw on my own personal kinks to really make this game come alive." he replied with a twisted grin.

"I'm pretty sure I know you're joking, but ew." Sian said, picking another card.

With a captive audience in the flat, Mia walked Jake downstairs to say goodbye.

"I had fun tonight." Jake smiled. "Maybe next time you'll play that keyboard for me."

"Maybe. We'll have to wait and see. I don't want to play it if my friends are in."

"What a shame they were in tonight." Jake replied, slowly. "I was really ready for a song."

Mia smiled at the ground before he lifted her chin. She was tingling from head to toe with want and cursing her friends in her head for coming home.

"Don't let them have your life too much." he laughed and turned to walk home.

"Bye!" Mia shouted after him.

"Bye, Jake! Bye!" Came the chorus from upstairs, all of whom were squashed together and hanging out the window having clearly just watched the exchange.

"And I'm gonna kill them." Mia breathed. She shut the door and trudged upstairs to go and beat up her friends.

Chapter Nine

With the school holidays in full swing, the café was busier every day. The outdoor showers were rarely off, with many people taking refreshing dips in the sea throughout their visit. It was a time of year when surfers were happiest – there was warmer weather but still surf rolling in occasionally. The surf school had plenty of groups out on foam boards; they tended to nip into the café after their session. Mia and Sian had managed to get out for a few early morning surfs themselves. There were at least two surf schools in the area as well as a shop that hired out kayaks and paddleboards. It seemed like a waste to live so close to the water and not use it as much as possible. Seeing the amount of people running had spurred Mia to take up running again herself, that and the strong possibility that someone could be seeing her naked soon enough.

"Why don't you just join my gym?" Sian asked, as Mia dragged herself out of the house for another short run.

"Because then I still have to pay when I give up." Mia replied.

"Exactly, it stops you giving up." Sian said.

"I'm not joining the gym with you, bud." Mia said, tying the laces on her trainers. "I don't have money to piss away on that when I can just as easy run round the block."

"Fine!" Sian gave in. "Talk to me in six months when I've got abs of steel and you're wobbling all over the place."

"When I'm fat and happy and you're raging roid head? will do." Mia flashed a grin and left the flat, starting some arm stretches as she walked down the stairs.

It was embarrassing how little she could manage to run. She kept telling herself she would build up her cardio levels but, in the meantime, she was embarrassed only managing 2km. Detouring past the Co-op on the way home, she killed some time by chatting to Aanya, who was excited about her upcoming trip to Las Vegas with her girlfriends. When she reached the bottom of her street, she ran again, arriving home slightly breathless and making it seem like she had been running for much longer than she had been.

"Good run?" Sian asked from the sofa.

"Yeah." Mia said, pulling off her t-shirt. "Just a short one today."

"How's Aanya?"

"She's go- how did you know I went to the shop?"

"Lucky guess." Sian said with a smug grin.

Mia rolled her eyes and trekked upstairs for a shower.

**

With Jake having six weeks off work, his schedule was much more flexible than Mia's. On Wednesday, Mia was on the early shift, with Steph taking over from her mid-afternoon. With her extra time, she decided to take a trip into the city centre for some impulse buys. She hopped on the Metro and made the twenty-five-minute journey to town.

[Mia] Heading into town last minute if anyone fancies a cuppa?

[Grandma] We're already here, darling! Come to Marks and Spencer's Café.

[Mia] See you soon. I'll be there in the next half an hour.

Jumping off at Haymarket Metro station, Mia jogged down Northumberland street to Marks and Spencer's to meet her family. They waved from the far corner of the café when she walked in.

"Hi, pet." Grandma smiled, greeting her with a kiss on the cheek. "I ordered you a jacket potato with beans and cheese, I hope that's okay?"

"Yeah, thanks, Grandma." Mia said, squeezing in beside her sister. "Hey, Molls."

"Have you dyed your hair?" Molly asked.

"I'm great, thanks, how are you?" Mia replied.

"Yeah, I'm fine, seriously, have you dyed your hair?" Molly asked, again. "It looks really light at the top."

"No, I haven't." Mia said, pulling bits of hair away from her head to look.

"You're just sun kissed, darling." Grandma said, smiling. "You look very healthy."

Mia looked smugly at Molly, who rolled her eyes. Deep down they were still children. With the wedding creeping ever closer, they mainly discussed the wedding. Mia's mind wandered in the conversation and she was grateful for the interruption of food.

"Mi, are you listening?"

"Huh? What?" Mia switched back into the conversation. "No, sorry, I'd wandered off."

Molly groaned. "I *said* we're going to stay at Grandma's the night before the wedding with Lily, is that okay?"

"Yeah, that's fine. I'll make sure I'm on the early shift." Mia replied. "It's not like I'm a brain surgeon, I don't think you need to worry about me switching shifts."

Even when the sisters swiped at each other, Grandma grinned. She was all smiles through the full conversation in her excitement about the wedding. That morning, she had bought a new hat to wear as 'Grandmother of the bride' and had treated her granddaughters to matching silver sterling necklaces with heart pendants. Bar the trips away with their Dad, Molly and Mia had mainly been raised by Grandma from the age when they were old enough to go to school. Though they drove each other crazy sometimes, as families did, they were very close.

"Eat your salad, it's good for you." Grandma said, pointing to Mia's plate.

She ate the tomatoes and prodded the rest around her plate.

After seeing Molly and Grandma, Mia darted off to do her own shopping, before catching the Metro back home. When it started to rain, she jogged with her bags from the station to the steps of the flat.

"What's in the bag, Mi?" Sian asked, not looking up from her phone as she did so, when Mia walked back into the flat. Sian's legs were crossed over one another as she lay back, not really watching the television from the sofa. Her newest *Netflix* binge series was burning away on the screen.

"Nothing that concerns you my vertically challenged friend." Mia sang back, skipping through the living room to the kitchen.

"Don't you have a date tonight?" Sian replied, tilting her head and raising a suspicious eyebrow.

"That would be correct." Mia confirmed, placing her bags on the counter and starting to sort the food items from one, purposefully avoiding eye contact with Sian.

"And this is the *fourth* date, am I right?" Sian pressed.

"You are." Mia said, trying to act blasé. Sian shuffled onto her knees to lean on the back of the sofa, further suspicion creeping across her face.

"Let me guess, you've been to Victoria's Secret?"

"So, what if I have?" Mia said, with a vague play of outrage.

"Interesting." Sian replied, with an eyebrow raise and a twitch in the corner of her mouth. She pretended to add on her fingers. "Fit lad…new underwear…fourth date…interrupted third date…I wonder what that could possibly mean?"

"Oh, shut up. It's not going to happen." Mia said, grabbing her bags off the counter and heading for her room.

"Oh, bullshit," Sian laughed and shouted. "Did you shave your legs?"

Silence.

"Exactly!"

"Oh, bugger off." Mia laughed, with a blush, stepping through to her bedroom. "Damn, *Friends*, for teaching you that."

"Let me ask you this – how can you afford to shop at Victoria's Secret but can't spare money for the gym?"

"Are you on this again?" Mia groaned. "Victoria's Secret has deals on underwear and I only have to pay once."

"Where are you going tonight anyway?" Sian shouted through, not moving from the sofa.

"We're going to the JamJar." Mia shouted back. Charlie jumped onto her bed to nosey in the bags.

"Is that the cinema in Whitley?" Sian asked.

"Yeah." Mia replied, stepping back into the living room. She had lifted her t-shirt and was hopelessly prodding at her stomach. "Eurgh. Why is food so delicious?"

"Put your belly away." Sian said, wafting a hand at her. "And retro cinema – I like it! Do you think you'll let his hands wander in the darkness?"

"Is your mind ever out of that dark place some call a gutter?" Mia asked, dropping her t-shirt.

"It's warm down here, come join me." Sian said, patting the sofa beside her. Mia smiled and flopped down beside her.

"Will you help me choose something to wear?" Mia asked.

"If I have to." Sian replied. "Can we wait 'till the end of this episode?"

"I'm in no hurry." Mia said, snuggling in closer to watch the series.

Two hours and four outfit changes later, Mia was finishing her make up in the bathroom. When the *Uber* driver sent his 'arriving soon' text, she shouted her goodbyes to Sian and Steph and ran down the three flights of stairs. Jakob the driver picked her up and drove her the seven minutes to the JamJar. She bounded out of the taxi, wrapped Jake in a hug and smacked him with a kiss.

"Woah, you're in a good mood." Jake said, blind sighted by her forwardness.

"Sorry, I didn't mean to pounce on you." Mia replied with a blush.

"Hey, I'm not complaining." he said, taking her hand and allowing himself to be led inside.

Nestled between an Italian restaurant and a charity shop, the Jam Jar cinema was a small, independent cinema in Whitley Bay. It only had one screen and a small bar area, that served drinks in jam jars with paper straws. All the listings were written on a noticeboard outside and updated every month. Half of the shows were brand new releases, the other half were classics shown for adoring fans. Jake had done well and surprised her with two tickets to watch *Grease.*

"I thought you might be a fan if you're into musicals." he said. "And there's less chance of falls or winding at the cinema."

Mia practically squeaked with excitement as they made their way up the stairs. She reminded herself it would not be cool to sing all the way through.

"Hey, look." Jake said, pointing to a piano as they walked down the corridor towards the bar. "You could give everyone a rendition as they wait."

"Oh, shut up." Mia said, giving him a gentle shove closer to the bar. "Anyway, I've got a really important question to ask you."

Jake looked grave for a second, mimicking Mia's expression.

"Are you a sweet or salted kind of guy?" Mia asked.

"Hmm." Jake rubbed his forehead, keeping the serious look on his face. "I mean, that is one difficult question. I suppose, I would have to go with sweet."

Mia let out an overexaggerated sigh of relief. "Oh, thank the lord for that. We could have had a problem there."

They ordered two cokes, which were also served in jam jars and a large, sweet popcorn to share before finding seats in the bar by a large painting of a giraffe.

"You've seen Grease before, right?" Mia asked.

"I haven't lived under a rock, of course, I've seen Grease before." Jake laughed.

"Okay, tell me honestly then, which of the girls would you date if you had to pick one?"

"Well, considering there'll all about forty, I feel like describing them as girls is a bit of a stretch, but anyway …." Jake started. "Is it too obvious to say Sandy? But only when she's bad Sandy, of course."

"Of course."

"What about you?" Jake asked.

"What girl would I date?" Mia laughed.

"I did mean guy, but we'll go with girl." He replied with a shrug.

"I'd have to go with bad Sandy too. I'd have probably said Rizzo if she was about fifteen years younger." Mia said. "What guy would you pick?"

"Oh, that's hard, none of them are really attractive." Jake replied. "If I was gonna pick a guy from a musical, it would be Zac Efron's character in Hairspray."

"Nah, Donny Osmond in Joseph, he wins that contest."

"Never seen it." Jake said, taking a handful of popcorn.

"You've never seen it?" Mia said. "I thought you said you hadn't lived under a rock?"

"We'll have to watch it sometime then." Jake smiled.

When the cinema doors opened, they moved through to their seats. In the front row, where they sat, the seats were all small sofas for two people. Jake and Mia snuggled into one together. Ignoring her own rule, Mia was already dancing and quietly singing when the BeeGee's started up. Jake laughed at her and placed a hand on her thigh. She ran her own hand over his and tangled their fingers together.

**

"Do you want to come in?" Mia asked, slowly pulling away from his kiss, but not removing her hands from around his waist. They were standing on the steps leading to the main door of the flats. Her butterflies were wide awake and making themselves known but, she still wanted him to come in.

"Yeah, I'd love to." he replied, smiling his perfect smile at her. *That* feeling was back.

Before she knew it, they were tumbling their way up the stairs to the flat. It was not romantic, like in the films. They were very drunk and keen to get straight to the bedroom. There was none of this 'kissing against every wall' malarkey, it was too hard to kiss and climb at the same time.

135

"Shh, don't wake the girls." Mia pressed a finger to her lips as she turned the key in the door. His size thirteen feet seemed to cause echoing footsteps. She let them into the flat and moved straight to her bedroom, swiftly closing the door behind them, holding her finger to her lips when they were inside to check the girls and Charlie were still quiet. She was thankful her room was so close to the front door.

"Sorry, I'm such a bull in a china shop." Jake whispered, wrapping his arms around her from behind; she tingled and smiled. She could not help but love how warm and muscly he was and how good he smelled. The alcohol was not helping. She wanted to play it cool but knew that hope was long gone.

His warm breath breezed her neck and she spun around, so their noses were less than a centimetre away from each other. Her teeth bit into her bottom lip; she was so nervous and was sure her pulse was glaringly obvious at her neck. They kissed again with more force and passion, his tongue entwining with hers as their hands explored. His hands finally moved below her waist as hers brushed through his tousled hair.

She pushed him back onto her bed and he lightly chuckled with surprise, looking up at her, slightly dishevelled. Ripping her t-shirt over her head, she climbed on top of him, kissing him and unbuttoning his shirt at the same time, before, reluctantly, tearing herself away from him.

"I'll be right back." she said, slipping out and upstairs to the bathroom.

Once inside, she stuck a toothbrush quickly in her mouth, ran a brush through her hair and poured moisturiser over anywhere that needed it. It had been a while since a man had been in her bed and she did not feel prepared for it. Holly would have labelled it 'cock fright.' She did a final stubble check on her legs, plucked a stray eyebrow hair and took a very deep breath.

When she re-entered her bedroom, Jake was sat on the corner of the bed and stood up to meet her. His shirt was not fully unbuttoned, revealing some of the muscles that had been at work during climbing.

"You look beautiful." he whispered, making her cheeks flash a prominent shade of scarlet, as she skirted past him onto the bed.

She gazed up into his eyes as she knelt on the duvet; they lit up when he smiled. At that point, she grabbed his half open shirt and pulled him down to her level on the mattress.

**

The next morning, Mia woke up face down in her bed alone. It was not that he had scarpered in the night; she had shown him out before going to sleep. A few years earlier, she had watched a really cheesy romantic comedy, which starred a pretty sleazy guy. Pretty much everything he stood for, Mia disliked, except his 'nobody stays overnight' rule, that seemed to make sense. No awkward half cuddling in the morning, no small talk and no last-minute master plans to get rid of people if they just would not leave.

Sian was the worse sometimes with overnight guests. Often, she had to enlist the help of either Mia or Steph to 'get rid' of her lady-friends. None of them seemed to want to leave. If Sian was a character on *Friends,* she would be Joey, minus the obsession with pizza – that trait belonged to Mia.

"Morning, Sunshine." Steph chimed from the armchair, grinning like the Cheshire cat as Mia emerged from her room.

"You're going to say something, aren't you?" Mia said, she had hoped to sneak to the kitchen unnoticed, but that was wishful thinking. She knew they had not been quiet enough the night before.

When Mia turned to face her, Steph was resting her chin on her arm and looking very smug. "I just love payback, don't you?" She snapped her fingers for Mia to sit and got up to do tea duty. "SIAN!"

Mia rolled her eyes and did as she was told.

"I'm coming! I'm coming!" Sian yelled back, running downstairs in her slippers and trademark dressing gown.

"Tell me everyth-"

"While you're both in earshot," Mia interrupted, stopping Sian in her tracks. "You both owe me £12.79 each for the gas bill."

"Ok, ok." Steph tutted, leaning in the doorway as the kettle purred in the background. "Stop trying to change the subject, we're not here to talk about gas."

"I don't know, I thought some sparks might have been flying last night." Sian sang.

"Transfer me and I might consider thinking about telling you guys something." Mia said.

"You know I don't respond well to blackmail." Steph replied, raising her eyebrows, before dipping back out to make their drinks.

When they were settled with teas and coffee, the real grilling began.

Mouth of the Tyne, Anna Heslop

Chapter Ten

By the end of July, they had been in the flat over month and it was starting to feel much more homely. Carol had kindly made them some new curtains that fit the windows; the old ones had hung four inches too short. Steph's Dad had bought her an Amazon Firestick, so they could stream on the TV without attaching a laptop and they were starting to buy non-essential items for the flat, such as a toothbrush holder, a bread bin, new glasses and even a cheap wine rack.

Both Jake and Dimitri were at the flat most days, though Jake had still not stayed the night. Dimitri was in the kitchen most mornings when Mia dragged herself out of bed, along with whomever Sian had claimed as a victim the night before. All in all, the flat was a hive of life, with Charlie lapping up the additional attention he was receiving.

Movie nights were more crowded than they had ever been. When they were all together, there were ten of them including Dimitri and Jake. They all squeezed into the living room and fought over space.

"You guys really need a bigger place." Carol laughed, surveying the sardines packed into the living room. Carol was home more frequently, enjoying the sun at the coast and putting them all to shame with her morning sea swims in just a bathing suit.

"We could go around to one of your houses if you'd prefer, Carol."
Mia said, with a wink.

"You know, you're always welcome at my house." Carol said. "But
your place has more beds."

It was rare the whole gang managed to get together, with there being
so many of them and with everyone leading such busy lives. Mia
loved it. It was always so warm and comforting having such a full
living room. Blankets were scattered around; Charlie kept trying to
sneak scraps where he could. Jake cuddled Mia in, and she smiled
into his chest. Fred was completely unfazed being the fifth wheel on
the sofa.

"Beer anyone?" Holly asked, peeling herself off the floor.

"Yes!" A chorus sang.

"Please."

"Okay, how many was that?" Holly asked, stepping carefully over
the tangled legs and plates of food. "Five? Okay, let me through."
Charlie nipped at her heels. She clattered around the kitchen and
popped the lids off the bottles.

"Does anyone fancy going kayaking tomorrow?" Holly asked,
curling back into the room again with six cold beers.

"I can't." Zoe grumped; she was sick of her cast. It was beautifully
decorated by them all, but it was still an unwelcome guest.

"We could tow you behind?" Holly suggested and was met with a stony glare from Zoe. "Okay, anyone else?"

Everyone else was keen, bar Carol, who offered to make the picnic and Dimitri, who already had plans.

"Okay, now that's sorted, enough with the faff, what are we watching?" Sian asked, taking control over the remote and the evening.

They opted that evening to watch Easy A, a 2010 romantic comedy starring Emma Stone. While the boys and Sian debated over Emma Stone and other female actresses, Holly and Maria discussed the hate they now held for their workplaces. Carol was telling Mia about her recent trip to scout camp with her troop.

"Will you guys shut up?" Zoe grumbled. "I can't hear the movie."

"Aw, we're sorry, Zo." Holly said, wrapping Zoe in a suffocating hug.

"Oh, get off." Zoe gave her a shove and she landed on her floor with a bump.

"Ow, you sat on my hand." Maria squeaked.

"Ladies! Ladies! Watch the beer." Sian said, rescuing the bottles.

Mia laughed at her friends. It was like living in Cheaper by the Dozen, except they were grown up and not related. Every window in the flat was open and it was still boiling hot. The blankets were simply used as extra padding. After stealing as many scraps as he could, Charlie retreated to the kitchen, to sprawl out on the cold floor. Mia cringed when she had to physically peel herself off Jake to go and lie on the floor – her skin stuck to his with sweat.

"I brought some ice lollies, if anyone wants one?" Carol said, shuffling into the kitchen.

"Carol, you literally think of everything, I love you." Sian said, graciously accepting her fab.

They munched away, scattering bits of fab around the room, occasionally dancing on the spot to the soundtrack.

"God, what a throwback, Avril Lavigne, I haven't heard this song for years." Mia said, wiggling with the music and wiping some liquefied lolly off her chin.

"The original was better." Carol replied.

"Original?" Holly asked.

"Yeah, the original was by Joan Jett and the Blackhearts." Carol replied. "I loved her back in the day."

"I never knew that, I always thought Avril Lavinge's was the original." Holly shrugged.

"Every day's a school day." Carol said with a smile.

At the end of the film, the party stirred and stretched.

"Anyone need a lift?" Carol asked, rubbing her tired eyes. Fred and Zoe jumped on the offer, and Jake looked at Mia to answer. Her sheepish look gave him an answer.

"Can I have a lift please too Carol?" Jake asked, trying to hide his disappointment.

"Of course, do you want a lift in the morning, too?"

"If it's not too much trouble?" Jake replied, getting up from the sofa.

"Not at all!" Carol smiled. "I'll pick you up at 10:30?"

"I'll be at the door." he said with a salute.

"I'm gonna jump in the shower." Dimitri said, kissing Steph and starting up the stairs. "See you all later."

As Jake left with the others, Mia could tell he held a pang of jealousy towards Dimitri, who was able to make himself at home.

"See you in the morning." he said, quietly. They kissed and she waved him off with Carol.

Ten minutes after he left, Mia was lying on her bed, debating with herself.

[Mia] What are you doing Monday day and night?

[Jake] Something really cool and exciting, unless a better offer comes along, why?

[Mia] Steph and Sian are both away. Do you fancy a sleepover?

[Jake] Can we have a pillow fight in our underwear?

[Mia] Only if you let me win.

[Jake] Deal.

Mia grinned to herself, nervous and excited at the same time.

"What are you smiling about?" Maria asked, with a half-smile. She was sharing with Mia while Holly piled in with Sian.

"Nothing. Nothing." Mia said, blushing a little.

"You can't lie to save your life." Maria said, digging through her overnight bag. "Were you texting Jake?"

Mia nodded.

"How are things with you two?" Maria asked, changing into her pyjamas.

"Good, yeah, thanks. I think I really like him." Mia replied, getting changed herself.

"You think?" Maria furrowed her eyebrows.

"Yeah, I think so. It's nothing bad, I think I just always doubt my own judgement. Like, I'm always a bit hesitant in case I picked wrong, you know?"

"I don't know how you don't need more sleep. I'd be exhausted if I thought and worried as much as you do." Maria laughed.

"I do need a lot of sleep mind." Mia replied.

Maria was one of those friends that Mia could go seven years without seeing, then they would meet up and nothing would be different; they would get on as though they had seen each other the day before. She lived on the south side of the River Tyne, in Jarrow, and had a soft Geordie accent, a kind face and an even kinder heart. Her stunning looks came from her Italian mother's side and her natural humour came from her father, who was one of the funniest men Mia had ever met.

They climbed into bed and lay, chatting away while the bed springs creaked above them.

"That didn't last very long." Maria laughed.

"Don't worry, I've already teased Steph about it." Mia smiled.

They chatted until they were too tired to continue. Mia set the alarm and apologised in advance in case she accidentally crept in for a spoon in her sleep.

**

Dressed in her wetsuit and borrowed buoyancy aid, Mia pulled her rented kayak down to the beach on its wheels. When Jake had walked out in his wetsuit, she could not help but whistle or take a sneaky look.

"Holy crap." Holly hissed when Jake walked inside to store his clothes in a locker. "Mate, how did you not break?"

Leaving the wheels on the sand, they dragged the kayaks down to the shore and climbed in. Jake and Fred raced each other off the beach, making a mad dash for one of the mooring buoys just beyond the piers. Maria climbed in her kayak prematurely then struggled to get off the beach – Holly ended up dragging her in.

"You know, I think you've finally found a boyfriend that I approve of." Fred said when Mia caught up with him. Jake had paddled back to keep Maria company at the back of the group.

"He's a good one, isn't he?" Mia replied, looking back over her shoulder.

From all around them, the sea glistened as they paddled. It was flat like a mill pond, not a ripple in sight, and not a breeze of wind. Plenty of people were packed onto the sand but they were segregated, absorbed by the peaceful bliss of the sea. The café was swarmed with customers; Bill would be happy. Cars snaked along the seafront, battling for spaces so they, too, could join the parties on the beach. Smoke plumed from select areas as BBQ's were lit. Volleyball nets were up, footballs bounced back and forth, and children squealed with delight as they ran into the freezing North Sea.

"So, what are you planning for Monday?" Jake asked, skidding into the space beside her.

"Well, Steph and Sian are both away, so we have the flat to ourselves."

"Interesting." Jake nodded, hiding his smile.

"So, I thought we could make best use of the space." Mia was trying very hard to be flirtatious but managed to flick a paddle full of sea water onto herself with her next stroke. Jake burst out laughing.

"Oh, shut up, you." she said, splashing him too.

They paddled south from Cullercoats towards Tynemouth Longsands, weaving through and playing in the caves between the two beaches. Holly very narrowly missed being pooed on by one of the pigeons nesting in the caves as it swooped around.

"A five-mil wetsuit was a mistake." Mia said, starting to unzip her buoyancy aid.

"What would Carol say if she could see you taking that off?" Maria scolded.

"It's only for a minute." Mia replied, wiggling the top half of her wetsuit down to her belly then putting her buoyancy aid back on. "I was just getting far too hot."

When they reached the far end of Longsands, by the headland known as Sharpness Point, Mia shuffled back into her full wetsuit and slid in for a swim.

"Oooh!" she shuddered. "It's not as warm as it looks."

The sea water slowly trickled down her spine and she whined; the cold spread across her skin.

"God, you're not getting me in there." Steph twisted her face at them as they splashed around.

"Oh, you shouldn't have said that." Mia said, looking at Sian.

"You really shouldn't have said that." Sian grinned back.

"Don't you dare!" Steph warned, pointing her paddle towards them like a weapon.

But they dared, leaving their kayaks behind and swimming as fast as they could in her direction.

"No, no, NOOO!" Steph half protested, half laughed as they tipped her over into the sea, causing an almighty splash.

"God, I hate you both so much sometimes." Steph said, but her laughter betrayed her.

They swam back to their kayaks, which had been rounded up by Fred, and hung onto them as they floated.

As she bobbed in the water, Jake swam over to give her a kiss, a snotty, salty, pretty slobbery kiss, but a kiss all the same.

When they climbed back in, Maria needed a helping hand, before they started back North. Every so often, Mia would splash sea water on her arms and face to help keep her cool, it was still so warm.

"Did you guys see that?" Fred called back to them.

"What? Is it a jelly fish?" Mia shouted back. She hated jellyfish.

Suddenly, a ripple appeared by her kayak, followed by another seconds later.

Then, as though the day was not beautiful enough, they found themselves in the heart of a dolphin pod as it passed by. The magnificent creatures rose out of the water beside them, weaving between their kayaks, occasionally nudging them slightly. There was no warning before they appeared, they simply emerged, shockingly elegant and playful in the water.

"I can't believe I don't have my camera!" Sian said, her mouth opened in awe at what they were beholding.

Mia's mouth dropped too as a dolphin bumped the front of her kayak, rising out of the water beside her. The sea was dark so there was little to no warning before they would appear, breaking their dorsal fins on the surface, slicing through the water so cleanly.

"Oh my god!" Maria squealed. "This is both beautiful and terrifying."

"Terrifying?" Sian asked with confusion.

"Well, I don't want to be killed by a dolphin, Sian!" Maria replied.

"Why would you be killed by a dolphin?" Holly asked.

"What if I fell in and got between a mother and it's baby? Maybe they're like cows and they kill if you get in the middle. Imagine. It would be so embarrassing if I was killed by a dolphin and definitely something that would happen to me." Maria said.

"Don't fall in then, you muppet." Holly said, then quickly pointed. "Oh, look a baby one."

It was one of the most amazing moments for Mia, surrounded by her friends, in glorious weather, appreciating nature at its best. It made her all tingly and smiley. The dolphins past by within ten minutes, and the gang turned to head back to the beach, delighted with the scene they had witnessed.

"Oh, guys," Fred began, stopping in the water ahead of them. "Maybe we should be careful about how buzzing we are in front of Zoe. She might actually cry if she knows she missed this."

They all agreed to keep it quiet for Zoe's sake.

When they were dried and changed, they tumbled back down to the beach to meet Carol and Zoe, who had set up camp on Cullercoats. The BBQ's were already lit. Carol had outdone herself. She arrived at the beach lugging a cooler bag so big she should have used a trolley to assist her. There were two party sized disposable BBQ's, Quorn burgers, sausages, halloumi, peppers, cheese, buns, beers, ketchup and even two picnic rugs. Sian lit the BBQ's and Steph shuffled away when the smoke began wafting in her direction. Together, they lay in a cluster, surrounding their food, watching the world go by. Mia was so relaxed and tired from kayaking she felt she could have fallen asleep. Poor Zoe had wrapped her leg in a bin bag again to prevent sand from creeping in the crevices.

"Carol, I swear, you need to become a chef or something." Sian said, scooping delicious fillers into a sandwich for herself.

"Don't be silly, I bought a lot of it." Carol replied, looking coy.

"Did you make the pavlova?"

"Yes."

"And did you make the skewers?"

"Yes."

"Well, they are my favourite, so take the compliment."

When the chill crept into the air, they retreated to the Surf café. Sian lost the 'Rock, paper, scissors' and ran back to the flat to get Charlie, who was delighted to see all his favourite people in the Surf café. He was spoiled rotten with treats from the dog bowl as soon as he walked in.

"Is it bad that I don't want your Dad to take him back?" Sian said, ruffling his ears.

"I don't want him to either." Mia replied, smiling down at the dog, who was happily wagging his tail.

Steph wrote their names on the performer list and Holly did the ordering for them all, opening a tab. When it was their turn, Steph and Mia got up to perform 'Rotterdam' by The Beautiful South. Each performer was thanked with a free drink, so it was always worth it.

"I'm tempted to go up there just to get a free drink." Sian said, eyeing up the stage. The table they were at was homemade and had bottle tops from hundreds of different beers sealed in glass to make the top surface.

"Mate, I'll get you a free drink for you *not* to go up there." Steph replied. "I like having working eardrums."

"I wish I could argue with you, but it's too true." Sian signed. "Although, I might argue I'm a better singer than Holly."

"Mate, I think we're as bad as each other." Holly replied.

"Oh, well, at least we can drink." Sian said, and they clinked their glasses.

Chapter Eleven

When Jake pressed the buzzer, Mia found herself taking a deep breath before opening the door.

"For a giant man, you sure do pack light." Mia laughed when Jake arrived, eyeing his tiny rucksack.

"I don't need very much, though do I?" Jake replied, bundling into her bedroom and unpacking as he listed his items. "Toothbrush, underwear, deodorant, razor, towel and, the most essential item…"

He waved a small red box at her.

Mia faked disgust by allowing her jaw to drop. "How dare you be so presumptuous."

"I'm sorry, Ma'am, a good scout is always prepared."

Steph had been away with the sunrise at a ridiculous time in the morning. As soon as Sian left too, Mia had texted Jake, changed her sheets and done a final shower and shave before he arrived. Although it made no sense, Mia had found herself shaking with nerves and anticipation. Perhaps because the sex was guaranteed and therefore not spontaneous, so she had time to overthink and get nervous. Having always lived with other people, either family members or flatmates, Mia could not remember a time where she had ever spent forty-eight hours alone with a man.

There were no obligations to go outside, bar to let Charlie out for the occasional wee, until her Wicked rehearsal in the evening, no visitors due and no pending shifts at work for at least twenty-four hours. What else was there to do?

Jake moved in and brushed his lips over her ear, breathing on her neck as he did so; she recoiled slightly with a shudder.

"What's wrong?" he asked, moving to catch eye contact.

"I don't know." Mia said, stepping back and rubbing her arm. "I think I'm nervous."

"Nervous?" Jake replied. "You know, we've done this before?"

"I know," Mia said. "It just feels like a lot of pressure this time."

"There's no pressure, you know. None." Jake gestured as he spoke.

"I know that really, I'm just - tingly." she said.

"Tingly?" he looked perplexed.

"Yeah, tingly." she scrunched her hands.

He stepped back towards her and placed a hand on each arm, looking up at the ceiling as he thought.

"How about we go for a swim?" he asked.

"A swim?" she replied.

"Yep." Jake replied, looking to console her. "A nice sea swim, then see where the day takes us?"

"Okay, yeah, that sounds good." Mia said with a nod. "Sorry, I'm being weird."

"Nothing weird about wanting a swim." he said, kissing her on the forehead. "You'll need a wetsuit though."

Giving him a sheepish smile, she removed herself from the room and ran upstairs to recover her wetsuit, running back up one more time when she realised, she had forgotten her bikini. Jake called her a 'numpty' and she accepted it. As she dressed, she questioned her hesitation, hoping the sea would help flush it away. She also noticed a small patch of eczema was becoming an irritation on her inner thigh and she worried it would sting in the salt water.

"Do you ever feel like a superhero in one of these?" Jake asked, as she reached the bottom of the stairs. He was standing in the living room doing the best superhero poses he could muster.

"Wow, don't wear that in Florida, they'll think you've escaped from the Marvel Universe." Mia replied with a laugh.

"You won't be laughing when it turns out I'm not a hero after all, I'm a villain!" He ran at her making scary noises and lifted her off her feet when he caught her, swinging her onto his back. "To the beach?"

"To the beach!" she repeated, and off they shot, with Mia making him drop her before they attempted the stairs.

No matter what time of year it was, it was always a cold entry into the North Sea. They wandered down to King Edward's Bay, past the watching lifeguards and into the sea. It was nineteen degrees. One lifeguard paddled around on his rescue board, supervising those enjoying the water. Jake was like a fish, dolphin diving under non-existent waves and collecting objects off the seabed. Mia rolled onto her back and allowed herself to float, admiring the treasures he brought to the surface to show her. Seeing the children run in to the water in nothing but their underwear made her feel slightly embarrassed that she was in a wetsuit. Planes flew overhead, coming into land at Newcastle Airport and she wondered what adventure she would be jetting off on next. Sometimes she missed the warmth of places like Barbados.

"What's the best thing you've ever found in the sea?" Mia asked, as he treaded water beside her.

"Living or not?" he asked.

"Not."

"I found a full-on Rambo knife a few years back, like a super sharp, really expensive one."

"Do you still have it?" she asked, allowing her legs to fall and starting to tread water too.

"Yeah, I don't know what I'd need it for really but it's too cool to give away." he replied.

In some of the shallow sections, Mia tried her hand at diving alongside him. She called him crazy for opening his eyes in the salt water and refused to do it herself.

"But then how are you going to find things if you can't see?" he asked, wiping his face with his palm; a huge grin was plastered on his sodden face.

"I'll bring goggles next time." she replied.

"Hot." he said with a wink, before diving beneath the surface again.

They were in the water for over an hour, swimming and floating around. At one point, the lifeguard on the board told them off for drifting outside the red and yellow flags so they sheepishly apologised and swam back to the middle of the swim zone. When they waded out, Mia rolled the top half of her wetsuit down, before climbing the torturous stairs out of the bay. It was a slightly uncomfortable walk with the wetsuit rubbing against the eczema patch on her inner thigh, though luckily not far.

"Is it hurting?" Jake asked, as she pulled at the neoprene.

"Yeah, it's stinging a bit." She winced. "You know if you have a cut on your finger then eat salt and vinegar crisps?"

"Ouch, yeah?"

"That's what it feels like."

"Do you want another piggyback?" he asked, trying to help.

"No, thanks." she smiled. "I'll just jump in the shower as soon as we get home."

Getting home always felt like lining up at the start of a race. From the front door to the bathroom, it was a mad dash up the stairs to try and leave as small a trail as possible of sand and water. On the stone steps outside, they rung out finishing stripping off their wetsuits and rung them out as much as possible before darting straight up to the bathroom.

"God, I hate that run." Mia panted, trying to catch her breath. Jake had slipped by her to start the shower.

"How's your leg?" Jake asked, stepping closer to her.

"Sore, but I don't think we'll have to amputate." Mia said, inspecting her skin.

"Where's your sudocrem?" he asked.

"On my bedside table – I think."

"Jump in the shower, I'll bring it up." he patted her bikini bottoms and walked out.

By the time she had showered and towelled off, Jake still had not returned.

"What happened to you? I was about to send out a search party." Mia said, as she waltzed into her bedroom in a towel to find Jake sitting on her bed.

"Your window cleaner came but I couldn't find change. Poor guy had to wait while I dug some out." he replied, popping the lid off the cream and patting for her to sit beside him. "Where does it hurt?"

She inched the towel up to the patch of eczema that ran at least seven inches down her thigh.

"O-oh, that looks really bad." he winced, recoiling away from her inflamed leg; she quickly pulled the towel back over it and snatched the sudocrem off him.

"If you think it's so horrible to look at, don't look at it." Mia snapped, clearly hurt.

"I didn't mean that." Jake said, taking the sudocrem back off her. "I just meant it looks painful. Now, lift your towel back up or I can't reach it."

She obliged, letting him find her sore skin and rub the healing cream into it. She watched as he took such care, trying hard not to hurt her or cause further irritation, covering every speck that had turned red. It only offered a moment of thinking time, but she used it wisely, to think about how kind, thoughtful, funny and sweet Jake was. As he finished massaging her skin, she leaned in a kissed him, softly, telling him wordlessly what he meant to her.

**

By the time she was due to leave for rehearsal, Mia considered phoning Angelika to say something had happened and that she would not make it. But, as a believer in karma, she decided against it and dragged her reluctant body out of bed.

"Do you feel secure?" Angelika shouted up at Mia, who was hanging from her harness fifteen metres above the stage. She had left it until the very last minute before running along to rehearsal and felt that Angelika was punishing her for her almost lateness.

"Secure, yes, comfortable, no." Mia yelled, while receiving the wedgie of her life. She was sure everyone was currently getting a nice flash of camel toe as she danced like a puppet on a string.

"I don't care about comfort, as long as you can sing." Angelika said, with a wave of her hand, stepping towards the piano. "Let's try and see. From the top."

On the first attempt, Mia felt like a cat being strangled; she even saw Sam wince from the decks. The harness seemed to push against her body in all the ways that were counterproductive to singing well. Angelika need not have told her it was bad; she already knew it was.

"Okay, that wasn't up to the standard I'd be expecting." Angelika said, bluntly, straightening her sheet music. "Let's try again, shall we?"

Mia could not help but roll her eyes. As much as she loved performing, she hated it sometimes too. The whole rehearsal felt tedious. Mia was so uncomfortable and hung in her harness for over an hour, singing on and off. She was lowered only once in this time for a drink of water then proceeded to need a wee for the remainder.

"Are you coming to the pub tonight?" Sam asked, nudging Mia, when she was finally released.

"Nah, sorry, not tonight." Mia said, throwing her bag over her shoulder. "I've got plans."

"Boy related?" Sam asked.

"Yeah."

"Say no more." Sam said with a wave of her hand. "I'll maybe catch you next week."

She walked backstage and Mia watched her go.

Though it would have gotten her home quicker, she politely declined Angelika's offer of a lift home. Although she understood why the practice was necessary, she was still a little angry about being dangled for so long. She half jogged, half walked home, snuggling up with Jake on the sofa as soon as she was able.

"Are you sure you want me to stay tonight?" he asked. They had decided to watch, or in Mia's case re-watch, Sex Education, the original Netflix series.

"You're not allowed to leave." Mia said, taking comfort in his boyish smell, as something embarrassing unfolded on TV.

**

"Who is texting you so much?" Jake asked, as her phone pinged for the seventeenth time. It was nearing lunchtime, but they still had not rolled out of bed.

"It's the wedding chat." Mia replied, rolling over to silence her phone. "It never stops now."

"I've noticed." Jake said.

"It's such a pain, but it's her wedding, I can't exactly ask her to calm down."

"You could," he replied. "But you might not be maid of honour for much longer."

Molly's wedding was fast approaching, and her nerves were becoming more and more apparent. The Wedding Whatsapp had shifted from buzzing once a week to multiple times per day and Mia was running out of comments that made her sound enthusiastic. Luckily, Molly's friends had it covered and they genuinely seemed interested in designs for place cards.

Mia had told Jake snippets about the family drama, but there was too much to explain it all.

"Can I ask you a question?" Jake said, half propped against the headboard.

"Of course." She shuffled up the bed so she could lie across his chest.

"Why doesn't Molly speak to your Dad?" Jake asked. "Surely if he was such a bad guy you wouldn't talk to him either."

Mia sighed and looked to the side; it was not something she discussed very often. Mainly, because it should not have mattered, but, somehow, it still did when it came to Molly.

"It all happened a long time ago really." Mia began. "And I suppose we both see it differently because of the age gap between us. I was nine and Molly was sixteen when it all really peaked, so she suffered the brunt of the bullying; everything was over and done with by the time I reached high school."

"What happened?" Jake stroked her hair.

"Have you ever noticed I don't speak about my Mam?"

"Yeah, I just didn't ever want to ask in case it was a sensitive subject."

"Well, Dad used to be my Mam."

Mia appreciated that Jake's reaction was not a big one. Some people still struggled with the unfamiliar. Mia continued, pausing briefly at the end of each sentence.

"Mam had us both through IVF on her own. She always knew she wanted to be a parent, but it took her a while to realise what body she was meant to be in. Finally, she decided to go through with the operation and become 'Dad.' Ever since, he has been so much happier, he's himself and he suits being in his own skin. We had a great childhood, but he always had this underlying depression. Now that's gone, it's so lovely to see. But Molly still feels 'betrayed' in some way. She moved in with William when she was 17 and never came home again. I don't know if that relationship will ever be repaired."

"Man, that's so sad."

"It's hard, because if anyone else had a problem with it now, they wouldn't be in my life for very much longer. But, because, it's my sister, it's a difficult one." Mia said, scrunching her face. "I love Molly to bits, but you'd think she was born in the 1800's sometimes."

"My brother's a bit like that." Jake replied. "He's married, 2.2 kids, house, car, all that. My niece is older, absolutely loves gymnastics, goes to lessons twice a week. When my nephew decides he wants to try, is he allowed? No. Might turn him gay. He's five. I even offered to pay but my brother won't have it. Football, rugby or nothing."

"No offence, but what is wrong with people?" Mia asked.

"I guess some people fear the unknown." Jake replied. "It's not an excuse, but it offers an explanation, I suppose."

They had a brief break in conversation to smuggle food in from the kitchen then dropped back off to sleep next to their empty plates.

"Crap! What time is it?" Mia looked at her clock and realised she had spent the first hour she was meant to be at work drooling on to her boyfriend's chest.

Luckily, Jay was the only person in besides the chef when she turned up over an hour late.

"I'm sooo sorry." Mia apologised, as she rushed through the door.

"You can apologise by telling me everything." Jay replied. "There's been like three customers anyway this afternoon so don't worry. The rain kept most of them away."

"Phew." Mia breathed.

"I would hide that massive hickey on your neck though before someone notices it that's not me."

Mia cursed under her breath and repositioned her ponytail to fall on the opposite side. Last time she had an obvious hickey, she was about fifteen and Molly spotted it. She had managed to get away from her sister just in time before she took a picture to send to all her friends.

With very little to do after cleaning, Jay and Mia poured drinks for themselves and took seats next to the window to watch excited surfers jog down through the rain to the building swell.

Chapter Twelve

When she got home, a postcard from her Dad greeted her before Jake did. It was on the bottom step and slightly chewed by Charlie:

Hey Darling,

I hope you're good, and Charlie too. Do you still have a matching pair of shoes or has the boy hidden them all? Say hi to the girls for me. All good here in South Africa. It's absolutely gorgeous as usual. Made friends with some locals and we've been free diving with tiger sharks. You'll need to come out here one day with me. It'll be like when you were little again. Say hi to your Grandma for me too. Keep safe and don't do anything I wouldn't do.

Love, Dad x

'Don't You Want Me' By The Human League was blasting from the kitchen speaker when Mia moved through to pin the postcard on the fridge; a beautiful picture of an elephant stared back at her.

When she pushed open her bedroom door, she was surprised to see it vacant, until Jake started plodding down the stairs from the bathroom in his black, cotton robey.

"Hey, Mi." He said with a grin, scrubbing his wet hair with a towel. When he reached her, he leaned in to kiss her on the head. "Good day?"

"Yeah, it's been alright." she replied, holding up a paper bag. "I brought you a muffin."

"O-oh, chocolate chip?" Jake asked, following her back into the kitchen.

"Double." she replied, and he practically drooled on the floor.

It had just turned 9pm; with no customers in they had closed early. Jake had surfed most of the afternoon and evening and she was very jealous, she had watched him from her perch with Jay. She had been jealous of all the people in the sea that day, to be fair. He had also napped with Charlie, something she was even more keen for than a dip in the sea. His surfboard was propped up against hers in the corner of the bedroom looking smug.

"I think I've got a fan." Jake said, pointing to Charlie, who had followed him downstairs. "He loves me so much he was drinking my shower water."

"That is gross." Mia said with a grimace.

"So, he can lick himself, but drinking my shower water is the line?" Jake asked, tilting his head.

"Ew, it's just its hairy, sandy, dirty water?" Mia replied with a shudder.

"Hey, I'm not that dirty." Jake argued.

"You are when you've been to the beach." Mia said.

"Says you!" He said, lightly grabbing her chin and turning her head to the side. "You've still got green paint in your ear from last night!"

"Yeah, well, that's really hard to get off." she said, wriggling out of his grasp.

"Minger." he said, quietly.

When they curled up on top of the covers, Mia snuggled into his neck, tasting salt when she kissed it. Mia had stripped her work clothes off and littered them on the floor; Jake was still in his robey.

"I knew you were manky. You're still salty." she said, wiping her tongue to prove a point.

"I must have just missed a bit." he replied, rubbing at his neck.

They lay, cuddled up together; Jake stroked her hair with one hand and Charlie with the other.

"I was having a proper nosey at your map today." Jake said, angling his head towards the new addition on her bedroom wall. He had been too occupied previously to properly study it. The previous Thursday, after their Lego building session, she and Fred had installed a world map poster with a home-made frame on her bedroom wall. Mia had since covered it in polaroid photos of her different adventures around the world.

"You've had quite a life already." Jake said, running his eyes over the collection.

It was true; she had been fortunate. Before he retired, her Dad was a Professional Diver, working mainly for the National Geographic. Although it had meant long periods of time away from the girls at times, it had also meant they had travelled to some of the most remote corners of the globe.

On top of the adventures with her family, Mia and Holly had travelled as much as possible in the summers between university, collecting memories and enjoying experiences. Her Dad had always encouraged her to save all she could in a travelling fund then jet off whenever she could. Saving up for post-university had taken priority at the start of the year but she really needed to book the next trip; she was getting itchy feet.

"Why do you and Holly look like a married couple in most of these photos?" Jake asked, and he was not the first to.

"Because we practically are an old married couple, minus the sex part." Mia replied. She rolled over and lay a hand on his bare, muscled chest. "I swear, if we aren't married by the time we are fifty, we'll marry each other."

"To be fair, I bet some old married couples never have sex." Jake replied.

"I bet they have done in the past though." Mia replied. "And we - definitely - have not. It would be like shagging my sister."

"Is it bad that I'm a little disappointed?" Jake asked.

"Ew." Mia replied, shaking her head. "No, just, no."

"Damn." Jake said, with an exaggerated sad face. "No threesomes in the near future then??"

"Absolutely not." she replied.

They lay in silence while Mia let her thoughts flutter in her mind, staring out the window as she did so.

"What are you thinking?" Jake asked.

"Do you want to come to my sister's wedding with me?" she asked, drumming her fingers on him. "I get to bring a plus one and I'd rather not be the sad, lonely, sibling, you know?"

He swept her hair from her face. "I'd love to."

She smiled and kissed him on the nose.

"But only if I'm allowed to gawp at the Maid of Honour." he said.

"I think I can allow that." Mia replied.

"Actually," He began. "I have a second request."

"Oh?"

"I want you to meet my friends." Jake said. "And not just Dimitri, he's not really a friend, just a flat mate."

"Don't tell Steph that, she's planning on us being a fab four." Mia warned.

"So, threesomes are a no, but foursomes are in?" Jake laughed.

"Can you stop making me sick in my mouth please?" Mia replied, making a face.

Jake shrugged with an innocent grin.

After a little while, they heard a disgruntled Charlie bat his empty food bowl across the kitchen floor.

"Oops, I better go and feed the boy before he learns to open the cupboards." Mia said, sliding out of bed and reaching for her pyjamas.

"What are you doing?" Jake asked, pulling the clothing out of her hands.

"I'm getting dressed to go to the kitchen." she said, looking confused.

"Er, is there anyone in?" he asked.

"No-o." she replied.

"Then why do you need to get dressed?" he smiled.

"Force of habit?"

She rolled her eyes and turned out of the room, in underwear only, smacking her backside as she did so.

When Charlie was taken care of, she crawled back to bed and turned the conversation to suit her own hunger needs.

"Where do you fancy for food tonight?" Mia asked, noticing her hunger; it was getting quite late.

"Well, I was thinking about this before." Jake said, slipping an arm from behind his head to put around Mia. "There's that little place down by the Quay, it does fancy fish and chips and stuff, or we could go to the Thai place round the corner that you like, or we could go completely out of the way and head into Newcastle, your choice?"

"Ooh, so many choices." Mia said, tapping her chin. "I do quite fancy Thai. Then again, I'd love a night in Newcastle, but I've got work tomorrow. Can we go into Town when I've got a day off the next day? I'm not eighteen anymore."

"Okay, so Town maybe next week? Thai tonight then?" Jake said, running his hand over his beard stubble.

"Sounds wonderful." Mia smiled. "Can I take an annoying amount of time to get ready?"

"Only if I can wear you out a little bit first." He said with a grin, pulling her up to sit on top of him.

"Wow, you're really king of the cheesy lines." Mia said, kissing him.

**

It was a luxury to have a bath with no one else in the room though that did not last. Before long, Jake had knocked on the door and was sitting on the floor to chat while she bathed, bringing Charlie with him.

"When you said you were going to take a while to get ready, I didn't realise you meant 'take a bath' long, I'm hungry." Jake said, as his stomach growled in agreement.

"Sorry, I just couldn't resist a bath in peace." Mia said, slipping further into the bubbles. "I'll be done soon."

Leaning over the side, while cross legged on the floor, he began playing with the bath water.

"Do you not get bored in the bath?"

"I don't have the chance when I've got an audience." Mia said, with her eyes closed.

Eventually, with lack of attention, Jake retreated downstairs with Charlie to watch Netflix and Mia enjoyed pottering to get ready.

Not having to share the bathroom and dressing room with two other women when dressing for a night out really did make a difference. She did not have to lean over anyone to use the mirror or wiggle around other bodies to find her outfit in the wardrobe. Though, she did miss the girls' opinion on outfit choice. She decided on high waisted, skinny black jeans and a crop top, letting her hair, that was growing ever lighter in the sun, hang naturally down to one side.

Jake physically stood and applauded when she came downstairs. Though she blushed, she secretly liked it.

"Ready?" She asked.

"If you are." he replied, and she led the way downstairs.

Koh Noi, the local Thai restaurant, was a stunningly decorated business. Set up in an old church, like the climbing centre, it occupied the corner of Tynemouth Front street. Tall and proud before the line of bars and cafes ran down towards the priory. Golden fairy lights illuminated the heart of the building and a large statue of Buddha towered over the dining guests. The waiter seated them upstairs, on the balcony overlooking the rest of the venue. It was busy for a Tuesday night, but they were immersed in their own little world anyway.

When she was getting ready, Mia had taken a sneaky look at the menu. She was notoriously slow at choosing what to eat, so gave herself a head start. They ordered tapas to share and martinis on special, eating until their clothes pinched at their stomachs.

"Whose turn is it?" Mia asked.

"I think it's yours." Jake replied, taking a mint off the bill plate. "Cheers me dears."

Mia paid the bill and Jake dug out change for the tip before they left.

"I'm just gonna grab some milk." Mia said, as they passed the Co-op on Front street.

"Oh, actually, I need some bread." Jake said, patting down his jacket to find his wallet.

As Mia made a beeline for the fridges, Jake wandered to the bakery section at the back of the shop.

"WHAT DO YOU MEAN YOU WON'T SERVE ME?" Mia heard a shout coming from the tills and began to follow it to investigate. A highly intoxicated man, whom Mia did not recognise, was screaming in Aanya's face. "YOU CAN'T COME TO THIS COUNTRY AND

176

TELL ME WHAT I CAN AND CAN'T BUY. YOU DON'T EVEN BELONG HERE. YOU STUPID-"

And then he called Aanya a name no one should ever be called. Aanya looked close to tears, trying so hard to stay calm, while not letting the pain drip down her face.

"Excuse me." Mia said, puffing her chest out to feel confident. "What did you just call her?"

The man turned around to see what ignorant person was interrupting his rant.

"Stay out of this, sweetheart." He said, waving her down, before turning back to Aanya. "It's got nothing to do with you."

"I *said* what did you call her?" Mia said, finding herself unexpectantly advancing on the man. "I think you need to leave, *now.*"

"Or what?" he smirked, meeting her advance.

"Mia, leave it." Aanya whispered, as Jake appeared around the corner with his bread, looking utterly bewildered.

"What's a pretty blonde thing like you going to do about it?" The man hissed and Mia used a warning hand to keep Jake from jumping in.

"Well you've got two options. Either you can leave now, nice and quietly to avoid being arrested. Or, do you see that camera over there?" Mia waved at it in the corner. "You can keep ranting and raving like the racist, sexist, idiot that you are and build up some more evidence for when the police do arrive."

Though he considered his options for a moment, the man pulled his jacket up around his face, shot Mia the stoniest glare he could muster and stormed out of the shop.

Mia took a breath of relief. "You ok?" she asked Aanya, who nodded with a 'thank you.'

She paid for her milk and Jake's bread then they wandered back out to head home.

"Question." Jake said, still looking confused at what had happened.

"Mm?"

"Since when am I going out with a bulldog?" He laughed. "I never thought I'd find you fighting in public."

Mia shrugged. "No one should be spoken to like that."

"You tell 'em." Jake said, wrapping her in a one-armed hug.

When they reached the flat, Jake jumped in his car and headed for home. Sian and Steph were back and settled in the living room.

"Hey, Mimi." Steph shouted through as she kicked off her shoes; Charlie greeted her at the door.

"Hey, boy." Mia said, ruffling his ears and stepping into the living room. "Hey, guys. Good few days?"

"Yeah." They both replied.

"Nice and chilled." Sian said.

"Same." Steph said. They both looked worn out; Charlie was still wiggling round Mia looking for a gift to bring her. He resorted to digging under the sofa.

"Hey, boy, what you got there? EWWWW! Dude!" Steph squealed, as Charlie dropped a present in her palm.

"What? What is it?" Mia asked, jumping up to her aid. In Steph's hand, clutched between the furthest tips of her fingers, was an empty condom wrapper.

Sian threw both her hands in the air in innocence. "Not mine."

"Thanks, Sian, I figured that much out, funnily enough." Steph said, sarcastically and Mia smiled apologetically, taking it from her to put in the bin.

**

Arriving at work the next day was unusual. She was working the long and late shift that day – twelve hours, 9am-9pm, with Jay, who was acting distinctly different from her normal cheery self.

"What do you think marriage is like?" Jay asked, dreamily looking into the distance.

"I have no idea." Mia replied. "I feel like it's too far away to worry about. Why do you ask?"

Jay sighed and placed the glass she had cleaned in its holder.

"It's just on my mind a lot at the moment, that's all."

"Do you want to talk about it?"

"I just don't know what to do. I always thought, when the time came, my parents would find me someone who I was suited to and it would all just kind of happen. Of course, I always hoped for a middle child so it would just be him and me but now.."

Mia let her pause.

"But now, I've got this boy, this *haram*. And he's the only son! So not only do his parents not like me, I'd have to live with them for the rest of their lives, unless they killed me off first. It's all just a massive mess."

It had felt like a long shift. Without Jay's usual bubble and lack of infectious energy, Mia had drained herself trying to support her friend. By 9pm, she was exhausted. Walking out of work, she paused at the bottom of the hill and could not bother herself to climb it. Instead of wandering the ten minutes back to the flat, she put her headphones in and strode along Tynemouth Longsands. It was a low spring tide, meaning the tide was extremely low. Rocks that were not often uncovered were high and dry out of the sand. She skipped between them, listening to '*Cough Syrup*' *by Young the Giant* and feeling all kinds of dramatic. The sea air seemed to revitalise her. Small waves were starting to push onto the beach and a little swell was due.

Arriving home forty-five minutes later, she entered the flat quietly, hoping not to be heard. She loved her friends but did not feel like socialising that night. Keeping her headphones in, she kicked her shoes off and pushed the door to the kitchen.

Just as Mia walked in, Aisling looked up at her then orgasmed on the kitchen bench, unfortunately, making eye contact with Mia as she did so.

"Dude!" Mia yelled. "What the hell?"

Scrambling into his boxers as he did so, Jake stumbled out of Mia's bedroom to see what was wrong. Mia was surprised to see him.

"I'm so sorry!" Sian and Aisling were saying together. To add insult to injury, Aisling had lifted the tea towel she had been sitting on off the bench and was using it to shield herself; it was the tea towel Mia's Dad had brought her back from Cuba.

"Just, just clean up after yourselves!" Mia stuttered and turned, pushing Jake back towards her bedroom, as Steph appeared on the stairs.

"What the hell is going on?"

"Just don't go in there." Mia said, pointing to the kitchen door.

"Why not?" Steph asked.

"Trust me." Mia said.

Not saying much at all, Mia changed out of her work uniform and into a baggy old t-shirt and climbed into bed.

**

When they woke, Charlie and Mia were both laid in the same position on the bed, on their backs with hands and paws stretched above their heads. When he noticed she had woken too, he lazily wagged his tail and began to stretch.

"Hey, boy." She ruffled his ears and pulled him into a morning cuddle.

When Jake stepped into the bedroom, he brought with him a glorious smell of cooked breakfast.

"Tell you what, you need to walk in on Sian more often." he said, climbing back into bed. "She's cooked one hell of an 'I'm sorry' breakfast."

"I hope she cleaned the benches." Mia groaned, burying her face in the warm duvet. She was due at work at 3pm, a good five hours away, but she felt tired just thinking about it. She really needed to stop being so lazy.

"Oh, come here." he said, ripping the duvet from her and pulling her close. "Stop being so grumpy."

She huffed again.

"So, your friend had sex on the kitchen counter? We did the other day! Just no one walked in on us. Ey?"

Reluctantly, she nodded and blamed her upcoming period for her excess grump.

"The surf looks great today." he said, with an expectant face. "How about we go for a surf, you can show off your *mad* skills to some of my friends then we can have beers on the beach with them later when you finish work?"

Mia smiled, nodded and snuggled in to find his smell.

"Snuggle then sea?" Jake asked.

"Will you go to work for me too?"

"Oh yeah, I really suit the apron look."

"You know, waiters are a thing."

"I think I'd suit the apron." Jake smiled.

"I've got one in the kitchen if you'd like to try it out."

He rolled out of bed and, with a wink, darted out the door to the kitchen.

"Where did you keep your aprons?" Mia heard Jake ask Sian.

"Bottom cupboard on the left." Sian said. "I'm not even going to ask what you're using that for."

"Do me a favour, play this on the speakers and don't turn around when I get going." Jake whispered; Mia heard certain words.

The speaker started up in the kitchen and Sian slowly inched up the volume. As the bedroom door burst open, revealing Jake in nothing but her apron, Dr Dre's *The Next Episode* crept into the room too,

"God, my eyes are burning." Mia said, covering her face, embarrassed on his behalf. He twirled the tie in his hand and started a semi dance.

"Oh, well." Mia heard Steph exclaim as she came down the stairs. The view she got was a full monty angle of Jake. While Mia saw him in the apron from the front, Steph got the open unexpected back view.

"Sorry, Steph!" Jake laughed, and nipped back into Mia's bedroom.

"Nothing wrong with seeing a fine backside to start the morning!" Steph shouted back.

"Oh, stop it, you're making me blush!" Jake yelled, as he paraded around in the bedroom for Mia's benefit.

Mia could not help but laugh. "Get that fine backside over here."

Mouth of the Tyne, Anna Heslop

Chapter Thirteen

Mia yawned through the first half of her shift. Fred had been at hers until 2am finishing off the Lego version of Hagrid's house. It was a grey and grizzly start to the day. Very few people had ventured out of their houses; only dog walkers were braving the beach and the occasional person dropped in for a takeaway coffee. By midday, the clouds had cleared, and the sun was shining. Jake and his friends had made a beeline for the beach, setting up camp on the beach not far from the café. On her lunch break, Mia skipped the few metres over the sand, kissed Jake on the cheek and crashed their BBQ without the beer. Steph had already joined and was tangled in Dimitri's arms, occasionally moving herself to turn the food on the BBQ. Mia was pleased to see Steph's famous halloumi and pepper burgers taking pride of place on the grill. Though she could not stay more than half an hour, it was long enough to say hello, grab a burger and promise to still join for a surf when she finished at 3pm.

[Carol] Does anyone fancy heading to the beer garden later?

[Mia] What time?

[Carol] 6:30?

[Mia] I'm there, surfing first so might be a little late.

[Carol] Stay safe. Text me when you're getting in and out!

[Mia] Will do.

She closed her phone before waiting for responses from the others.

At 3pm on the dot, Mia jumped into the bathroom and changed as fast as her wetsuit would let her. Grabbing her surfboard from between the bins behind the café, she waved goodbye to Jay and jogged down to the water's edge, stopping only briefly to attach her leash. There were easily forty surfers in the water, and she struggled to see Jake until he waved.

Even in the summer months, the North Sea temperature rarely crept above fifteen degrees. In the winter, she would wear a hood which made a little difference. As a child, her Dad had taken her surfing in Australia plenty of times. It was much warmer and more pleasant, but there was the added risk of sharks. Every now and then a tannoy would call across the beach telling everyone to get out of the water because a shark had been spotted. It was riskier but she did miss it.

As a child, her favourite film had been Lilo and Stitch and she had made her Dad and Molly watch it on repeat. Each time she surfed, the songs from the film rang blissfully in her ears. *I need to get back to the warmth,* she thought, as she ducked under a wave to get to Jake. Three of his friends were in the water with them, including Dimitri.

Her first wave was a flop, but the second she dominated, smugly leaping into the white water when the wave ran its course. The cool water washed over her as she resurfaced and reunited with her shackled board.

Considering his large stature, Jake was an agile surfer. With powerful arms propelling him forward, he rarely missed a wave and whizzed around like a semi-professional. She loved to watch him playing around with the waves as though teasing them.

"Do you want to stop checking me out and catch another one?" Jake called and they paddled out back together.

***

As though it had been a special addition just for Charlie, the Sand Piper pub now had a Dog Friendly menu, consisting of Dog Beer and meals, such as Bangers and Mash. Fred and Maria came together, as did Holly and Zoe. Holly drove, with Zoe's leg still being in a cast. Carol collected all three girls from the flat.

"I cannot wait until this stupid thing comes off!" Zoe spat, swinging her cast under the picnic table.

"I wonder how hairy you'll be underneath." Holly said, taking a sip of her freshly poured pint.

"What do you mean?" Zoe looked alarmed. "Do you think I will be?"

"Well, you haven't been able to shave for six weeks by the time it comes off, so I imagine so."

"How long do you have left?"

"Two days!" she picked a knife off the table. "I'm at the point where I just want to slice it off myself."

Carol placed a hand on Zoe's to lower her weapon.

"Seriously though, is it Monday yet?" Zoe huffed in the corner. She had started listing all the things she was going to do when she was 'free.' She initially claimed to have become queen of partial isolation, taking up cross stitch, reading more and binge watching all the most important series. But the novelty had worn off and she was ready to return to reality.

The conversation rounded onto the Netflix original series, Sex Education, after Mia, Steph and Sian had all started watching it again.

"You know, I had never even really thought about gay sex education." Carol said, swirling the wine in her glass. "That episode really made me think. I don't know if Don or I would have known how to approach a safe sex talk if my son had been gay. Did your parents have 'the talk' with you?"

"My parents still think I'm going through a phase and that I'll get over it eventually." Sian replied, with a disbelieving half smile. "Any girlfriend I've had has never progressed to be any more than a 'friend' in Mum's eyes or vocabulary."

"I can't believe people are *still* that closed minded." Carol looked irritated. "If you don't mind me asking, where did you actually learn about having sex with a girl?"

"Erm, trial and error, I suppose?" Sian replied, thinking back.

"Oh, is that what sleeping around is called these days?" Mia laughed and Sian punched her in the arm.

Sian gave her a disapproving look and she cast a cheeky one back.

"I tell you what episode really got me," Steph began. "Where all the girls bonded over sexual harassment and assault. I didn't even think she'd been assaulted until the story unfolded a little bit more."

"You know, I thought exactly the same." Holly replied. "It made me wonder how many times things like that have happened to me and I've just brushed them off thinking they were nothing."

"I didn't realise so many women had been sexually assaulted." Sian said. "It's so sick."

"So many cases go unreported though." Carol said, sadly. "I remember back in the hospital we used to get severe cases and some women were too scared to report it. It was horrible to see them so broken and know no one was going to answer for what they had done."

"God, we took a dark turn, didn't we?" Holly said, realising the mood. "Anyone for another?"

"Excuse me, I'll be right back." Maria drew back from the table and disappeared through the nearest door.

When Maria failed to return after ten minutes, Mia excused herself to go and find her.

After weaving between the different rooms of the pub and having no success, she finally found Maria, perching on a bus shelter bench outside the pub. Her back was turned, and her shoulders slumped.

"Hey? You okay?" Mia asked, gently touching her shoulder and sliding onto the slanted seat beside her. "What's going on?"

When Maria turned to look at Mia, it was clear the tears had just stopped falling down her cheeks. Mia pulled her into a hug and waited there, in a consoling embrace until she was ready to talk.

"I'm sorry." Maria sniffed after a few moments and rubbed her cheek on her sleeve.

"What have you got to be sorry for?"

"I didn't mean to get upset."

"Hey," Mia replied, lifting Maria's chin, lightly. "Never apologise for that. I'm your friend, that's what I'm here for."

Sinking her head back onto Mia's shoulder, Maria sobbed for a few moments longer.

"You know that episode where all the girls bond over sexual assault?"

"Yeah?"

"It just really rocked me; you know?"

"Has something happened?"

"Kind of." Maria replied with a sniff. "Nothing really, really bad. Nothing that I really even thought was illegal, I just knew it was stuff I wish wouldn't happen."

"What's been happening?"

Maria took a deep breath and Mia waited, watching her anxiously rub her palm against her knuckles.

"Do you want to go for a little walk?" Mia asked, offering out her hand; Maria nodded and took it, willingly. "I'll just message so they don't send out a search party."

[Mia] We'll be back soon. Don't send out the search dogs. x

They started towards the sea front, still hand in hand, and shivered only slightly at the coolness of the evening.

"I don't even know where to start." Maria said, looking at the floor. "I might be overthinking something that's nothing."

"Does it keep going around in your head?"

"It does now."

"Then, I don't think it's nothing." Mia reassured and squeezed her hand at the same time. "And I'm always here to listen."

Maria took a deep breath and let the previously trapped words fall out of her mouth. "It's not every day, but it's most days. Sometimes it's a thigh graze, sometimes it's a slap on the bum, sometimes it's a comment or a proposition. Like I say, it's not terrible but it's enough to make me not want to go in. Ever since I've started letting myself properly think about it, I just feel dirty and ashamed. But it shouldn't be me who is embarrassed, should it, really? But, I am. Like, if people found out it would be me who has let him do it, you know? I've ignored it for so long."

Taking a pause, Mia let Maria breathe and allowed herself time to absorb the information.

"I don't want to tell anyone though. What good would it do? It would only make it worse, I'm sure."

"Who are you talking about? Who has been doing and saying these things?"

"My boss."

"Your boss?"

"Yeah, I quit this morning."

"You what?" Mia replied. "Did you tell anyone before you left?"

"I tried." Maria said. "His wife is the HR manager. She couldn't have given less of a shit."

As they sat on a bench looking out to sea, Mia hugged her friend.

"It's okay." Maria said, taking a deep breath. "I'm going to work in the restaurant with my Mam in the meantime. I just hope some really bad karma comes his way."

"Me too, buddy."

**

First thing in the morning, Carol took Zoe to the hospital to get her cast taken off.

[Zoe] It's off! I'm free! Whose around tonight? If you're not free, cancel your plans. Mimi, I know you've got rehearsals but you're mine from 8. Pick up your tits, girls, we're going to Tynemouth."

Everyone replied with a yes, even Carol. Mia messaged Jake and told him to bring his pyjamas, they were staying at hers. Not that it made much of a difference; her flat was much nicer than his and he was happy to be away from it.

"I am *so* ready for a night out." Sian said, stretching on her perch and encroaching on Charlie's space. He looked at her, indignantly, and kicked her back. "I feel like we're old and boring now. We need to go away somewhere."

"Speak for yourself." Mia replied. "You're practically over the hill."

"Oh, come on, I'm like a couple of months older than you." Sian argued.

"Still counts." Mia said.

"Shut up, dick head." Sian said. "Are we still going away for your birthday?"

"What do you mean are we still going away?" Mia asked. "You've transferred your money to Steph. It's only, like, three and a bit weeks 'til we go."

"Is that all?" Sian said. "God, before we know it, summer will be over."

They vowed to have more meals on the beach or in the park over the coming weeks.

With her birthday being at the end of August, Mia had always been one of the youngest in her school year; Fred was one day older. For their birthdays, the gang had planned a weekend trip up to Edinburgh. The hostel was booked, the plans were made, and their livers were gearing up.

"Don't leave rehearsals without Sam." Steph said.

"Sam?" Mia asked, unnecessarily quickly.

"Yeah, I said I'd invite her along for drinks one night. She's a nice girl."

"Yeah." Mia said, slowly. Steph left the flat to take the recycling out, so Mia spoke to herself. "Yeah, she is." She sat, thinking to herself.

"Come here, I'm cold." Sian demanded, beckoning Mia, who scooted over to join her. One of the many episodes of *Law and Order: Special Victims Unit* was playing on the television while they ate their breakfast. It was definitely a pre-2000 episode. Mia's Dad was a big fan of the show; it was the only show they agreed on watching together.

"What do you want to do today?" Mia asked, as she stole some of the blanket from Sian.

"Any surf? I haven't checked." Sian asked.

"Flat as a pancake." Mia replied and Sian sighed. "We could go for a swim. It's high tide in two hours, we could have a dig around the caves."

"Ooh, that's a good idea." Sian said, as Steph re-entered the flat. "I still haven't swum through those caves yet. Every time I've been, the tide has been out, except when we kayaked, I suppose. They're still lush to walk through but it would be nice to swim."

The notorious *Law and Order* 'Clunk, Clunk' sounded.

"I swear, every time I walk in the front door there is an Amazon delivery girl waiting for me." Steph huffed, dropping a parcel onto Sian, who was stealing some of the blanket back off Mia.

"Is she cute?" Sian asked, rattling her package before tearing into it.

"Have you not seen her? She practically lives here now." Steph responded, clunking her backpack onto the counter and undoing the toggle. "I'm starting to think she might be our own personal Amazon person, considering you order so bloody much offline. What have you even bought now?"

"You know what, I don't even remember." Sian replied, before she reached the centre.

"Where do you even get the money to buy all this crap offline?" Steph asked.

"It's not crap." Sian said.

"Oh, yeah, Charlie really needed that doggy life jacket." Steph replied.

"*Actually,* he can wear it today." Sian said, looking smug. "You fancy coming swimming with us?"

"What's happening today?" Steph asked.

"We're going for a sea swim, you coming?"

"Ah." Steph sighed. "That sounds like exactly what I need right now. Yes, I'm in."

Mia leaned over Sian to peer inside the box she had opened. "What did you get?"

"Never you mind." Sian said, shoving her off.

"Is that a bullet?" Steph asked, she had leaned over Sian's shoulder while she was focused on Mia.

"It looked like a bullet." Mia said.

"What do you need a bullet for?" Steph asked.

"Maybe she's not good enough for the ladies anymore." Mia grinned.

"Maybe she never has been." Steph replied.

"Oh, get lost the both of you." Sian hissed, stomping out of the room with exaggerated frustration.

"There are batteries in the kitchen drawer if you need a test run." Steph called as Sian trudged up the stairs.

**

"I don't care where we go or what we do but one way or another, I am wearing heels, dressing up and we are having some celebration drinks!" Zoe squeaked excitedly.

"That sounds like a good plan. Put yourself straight back in heels and break your ankle next." Steph laughed.

"God, don't even joke." Zoe said. "I could not deal with another six weeks."

"Well, just don't stack it tonight and you'll be grand." Mia said. "What's the plan anyway?"

"Well," Steph propped up her hypothetical drawing board. "I thought we could go along to that Tapas place; you know the one we can never pronounce the name of?"

"Oh yeah?" Zoe replied.

"They have such a good drinks menu. And the food is amazing." Steph said, licking her lips. "I've put it in the chat already. We'll come home after for some proper pre-drinks. Then, when Mia gets back, I was thinking we start at the far end of Front street and just ping pong our way back towards home."

"What's the food option for home time?" Zoe asked, looking serious.

"Subway is open late, or I've got nachos, cheese and frozen pizzas waiting on standby." Steph replied.

"Perfect!" Zoe squeaked, clapping her hands.

Mia was in the bath; Zoe and Steph were sitting cross legged on the floor. They had been for the most therapeutic sea swim in the glassy, cool water. Zoe had floundered around like a newly christened mermaid, making the most of her freed limb. Much to Sian's delight, Charlie loved his new doggy lifejacket and swam circles around them all, like a sheepdog herding its flock. When they got back to the flat, Sian's latest date was waiting on the doorstep and was whisked upstairs away from prying eyes immediately. With the bathroom window open, they, unfortunately, could hear everything clear as day coming from Sian's room as the noise got louder and louder. They all looked at each other; uncomfortably certain about what was happening.

"Why have I heard Sian have sex more times than I've had sex myself?" Steph said, trying to talk over the high-pitched noise.

"Who do you think that was?" Zoe asked, innocently, as an individual cried out.

"To be honest, Zo, I don't really need to know!" Steph said, looking mildly traumatised.

Mia chuckled from the tub as Steph shut the window and turned the music louder. Her baths were becoming increasingly less peaceful. Banishing Zoe and Steph from the room, she climbed out, dried herself and moved through to the wardrobe to pick some clothes for rehearsal. Just in case Angelika planned to dangle her from the ceiling again, she went with the shorts that were least likely to give her another camel toe and a baggy t-shirt that was comfortable to practice dancing in. Thinking ahead to how late she would finish rehearsal, she packed an outfit and her make up bag to get ready for Tynemouth at the theatre.

Evidently, Sam had the same idea and they both dressed ready for a night out after rehearsal. To get herself in the drinking mood, Mia put on the playlist that always got her geared up for a night out. It was mainly painfully tragic music, but always made her want to drink. The first song: 'Is this love – Remix by Bob Marley and The Wailers. They were soon dancing around in front of the bathroom mirrors.

"Is this love? Is this love? Is this love that I'm feeling?" They sang out. Mia shifted her gaze and turned back to the mirror to finish her eyes.

"You really can't dance, can you?" Sam laughed, as the song died out to the next.

"I'll never get paid for it, if that's what you mean." Mia laughed back.

When they were completely ready, they jumped in an Uber to head for home. It was too far to teeter in heels.

"I've never seen you look so clean." Sam said, eying Mia in her finery.

"Wow, you're full of the compliments tonight." Mia smiled, linking her arm to conquer the steps to the flat.

"You know what I mean!" Sam replied. "You're normally in comfy rehearsal clothes. Who knew you had a waist?"

Mia blushed and let them into the lower door.

When they walked into the flat, they were greeted with the instant party atmosphere. As predicted, Zoe was halfway to being legless and struggled to make her way towards them.

"Mimi!" she squealed, falling into Mia's arms. "And you must be Sam! I've heard basically nothing about you."

"Sam, this is Zoe." Mia said, leading her into the kitchen. "And this is everyone else. You already know Steph, Sian and Jake."

"Ah! We meet again!" Sam said, shaking his hand.

"Right, we said we'd go when they got here!" Zoe yelled, falling on the door frame. "They're here, let's go!" She flung the front door open and performed a high kick to exit the flat.

"Someone put a lead on her." Sian mumbled.

"I heard that!" Zoe shouted back.

Leaving Charlie with a long-lasting chew, they made their way to Tynemouth immediately, with Zoe and Maria leading from the front with a rendition of 'Blaydon Races.'

"See, I could be a Geordie, I know the songs and everything." Zoe squeaked.

"Yeah, it's just a shame your accent gives you away." Mia winked at her. She was arm in arm with Steph and Sam. Holly and Sian followed, with Jake and Fred bringing up the rear. Carol was enjoying a rare night with her husband and children but sent her love. They passed the tapas place to get to The Boardwalk; Mia was gutted she had missed the earlier meal and her stomach rumbled. She had made a rookie mistake by not eating quickly at home but managed to snaffle some crisps once inside.

"I love this song!" Zoe squealed with delight and started dancing enthusiastically in the middle of everyone.

"I feel like I've got some catching up to do." Mia said, leaning on the bar next to Sian.

"I don't know if we'll catch up with her tonight." Sian laughed, watching as Steph stopped Zoe from attempting the splits.

"We can try." Mia challenged.

"We certainly can." Sian nodded and gestured with her card. "Shots?"

"You read my mind." Mia smiled.

Two hours later, Mia had a straw loosely hanging out of her mouth as she found herself dancing to The Bad Touch by Bloodhound Gang. Lights were flashing around her, all different colours, and her friends had interchanging faces. Zoe had been sick twice but was still going, emerging from the bathroom both times victorious.

Why does this bother me? Mia thought, watching Sam and Jake from the bar. They were getting on well, *really* well, laughing and joking.

"What's up?" Maria asked, appearing at her side.

Mia nodded her head in the direction of Jake and Sam, still sipping from her straw. "It shouldn't bother me, but it does."

"Hot girl flirting with your boyfriend?" Maria asked, rhetorically.

"You think she's hot?" Mia replied.

"You don't?" Maria asked.

"I've never really thought about it." Mia mumbled catching her escaping straw with her tongue.

"Well, I get why you're worried, but I wouldn't worry." Maria said. "Does that make sense? Jake's a good guy."

Mia shrugged.

"Come on, you need a dance." Maria said, twirling her away from her post.

**

As Mia opened her bedroom door in the morning, Sian was scooping a letter off the doormat.

"Morning." Sian croaked and Mia grunted in reply, stepping into the kitchen to the same exchange with Steph.

Holding the open letter in her hands, Sian read it and walked at the same time. "How many times have you shagged, lover boy?"

"Who you talking to there, bud?" Mia asked.

"Either of you, really."

"Do you want specifics or?" Steph asked.

"No, I mean, have you been sneaking him round or something? Or have you been doing the guy from upstairs again as well as Dimitri?" She pointed at Steph.

"No, why?" They both replied.

"The landlord has had a complaint from the neighbours. They think we're running an Airbnb."

"You what?" Steph said.

"Let me see." Mia took the letter from her and scanned it.

They surveyed the situation in their flat – Sian, Steph, Mia, Jake, Zoe, Holly and Maria, all currently under the same roof. Sam had taxi-shared home and Fred had merely stumbled across the street to the bakery when the night had ended.

"I suppose I can see why." Sian laughed. "I'll talk to the landlord. There's nothing wrong with us having guests."

"You'll just have to explain that you've been sleeping around and that you're sorry the neighbours mistook your multiple lovers for Airbnb users."

Sian glared at her and Mia snuck back to bed.

Mouth of the Tyne, Anna Heslop

Chapter Fourteen

For the week running up to the wedding, most of Mia's time was reserved for Molly, bar the occasional night she had with Jake. All the dresses were hung up in plastic, ready to be released on the big day. Molly's fiancé, William, had been told to stay well out of the way. They had checked and rechecked the seating plan, reconfirmed with the florist and the caterers and even practiced walking down the aisle in time to the music. Molly wanted no stone left unturned.

The night before the wedding, Mia, Grandma, Molly, and Molly's best friend, Lily, were all together, in the fire warmed living room at Grandma's house. It had the classic Grandma feel to the house, with pictures of the girls taking pride of place in every room. The kitchen, with its 1960's design, always smelled of something delicious that Grandma had baked. All the cupboards, the fridge and the freezer were stocked with food, there were enough snuggly blankets to cover a football field and at least one novelty item with 'World's Best Grandma' on in every room.

"I miss having you girls here." Grandma said, as they all snuggled together. "This is just like when you were little. How many times did you sneak down in your dressing gowns to stay up late and watch the telly with me?"

Mia did enjoy being back at Grandma's and vowed to spend more evenings with her. She always felt so safe and happy in her presence.

She was, however, so full of food that she was worried about fitting into her dress the following day.

"I remember thinking it was so naughty if we got to stay up until 9pm to watch Coronation street." Molly laughed; she was cuddled, in slippers and her dressing gown, into Grandma's right-hand side.

"Wow, you really were little girls then." Grandma smiled. "Mia could never quite stay up long enough. You'd be a bit too heavy to carry up the stairs now!"

"I don't think anyone could carry me after that dinner, Grandma." Mia breathed.

"Maybe if I hadn't fed you so much you wouldn't be seven foot two." Grandma chuckled. "And you wouldn't have to duck under the light in the kitchen."

They reminisced and chatted late into the evening, until Grandma was struggling to keep her eyes open.

"Love you, darlings." she said, kissing them both in turn. "Don't stay up too late."

"Night, Grandma." They wished and she shuffled upstairs in her slippers.

When they heard her bedroom door close, Lily dug more wine out and things went south from there.

"I'm excited to meet your new man." Molly said, swirling the wine in her glass.

"Ooh," Lily said, lifting her eyebrows at the impending gossip. "What's he like?"

"Literally, we are sitting here the night before your wedding and the thing you are excited about is meeting the stranger I'm bringing along with me?" Mia said, ignoring Lily. She liked Lily, but she had known Mia her whole life and still treated her like a child. It was a little annoying.

"I remember when you were little." Lily said, sitting like an old woman in her chair, with a glass of wine by the fire. "You'd stomp around in your walking boots, always covered in mud and playing football, hating anything girly. You remember, Moll? To be honest, for a while, we were convinced you were going to be gay, Mi."

The word struck a chord with Mia for reasons unknown. One way or another, she felt offended and defensive, but held back.

"And then you rocked up with that swimmer, what was his name again, Molls?"

"Liam." Molly replied, quietly. Clearly embarrassed by the actions of her friend but used to it enough to let her continue.

"Liam! That's it!" Lily said. "Bless him, with his bleach blonde hair and fake designer clothes. I remember thinking, well, he's almost a man!" She then roared with laughter.

Mia could not help but look at her sister in disbelief, wanting to say something but determined to hold back for Molly's sake. Instead, she repeatedly thought: *'You're a knob, you're a knob, you're a knob,'* because Lily was.

When Lily went through to the kitchen for a top up of wine, Molly leaned in to apologise for her behaviour.

"It's fine." Mia said through her teeth, thinking of her sister and the perfect day she needed. Her bridesmaids fighting would not help.

Thankfully, Lily took a phone call in the kitchen, keeping her out of the room long enough for Mia to calm down slightly. The clock ticked on the mantel piece.

"Moll?" Mia said, looking to her big sister.

"Yeah?" Molly replied.

"I don't want to sound unsupportive or anything but are you sure this is what you want to do?" Mia asked. "Like, how do you know he is the right one?"

Molly thought for a moment.

"No, I'm sure." she said, nodding. "When I think ahead to babies, and adventures, and old age, it's William I want to be doing all that with."

Mia smiled, and looked adoringly at her sister, the sister she wished all the happiness in the world for. "I'm so happy for you."

Molly smiled back and they listened to the clock tick again.

"Should we go and have a dance?"

"You know I can't dance." Mia replied.

"No, but you can watch me." She grabbed her sister's wrist and pulled her through to the kitchen.

As Molly and Lily danced round to 'Girls Just Wanna Have Fun,' Mia checked her phone.

Though her Dad did not tend to send text messages, he sent one that night:

I love you, both. Tell her if you can. I understand if not. x

Mia could not help but bow her head in sadness as she read it. He was supposed to be there, watching his eldest daughter get married. To Mia, it felt as though the relationship would never repair; she could not see an end to the long-lasting feud.

**

Initially, the day began with a downpour. Molly panicked as soon as she woke up thinking it was a bad omen, foreshadowing how bleak her marriage was going to be. With the strong wind, the rain was almost sideways by 9am, though cleared up by 11am. Molly spent the first half an hour of her wedding day vomiting her nerves, and maybe some of the alcohol from the night before, into the toilet bowl. As the loving sister, Mia held her hair back and wiped her chin.

"I think I've seen you throw up more times than I have thrown up myself in my life." Mia said.

"What?" Molly scowled at her sister from her perch beside the toilet.

"Think about it." Mia said. "How many times did you crawl into the bathroom to vomit after a heavy night when you were a teenager? And there was poor innocent me trying to take a bath."

"You shouldn't have always been in the bath, then!" Molly let out a snotty laugh.

"Well, you should have learned to handle your drink earlier." Mia laughed and Molly shuffled back to slump against the wall. "I can't believe you're getting married today."

"I know." Molly breathed.

"Do you think you'll feel different, when you're married?"

"I don't know." Molly replied. "You'll have to ask me later, I suppose."

When Molly was done, Mia force fed her some toast, cleaned her face and sat her down in the chair for the makeup artists to do their thing. She was right to dread her own time in the chair; the woman was vicious when she did Mia's eyebrows. To stop herself from screaming out, Mia gripped her own thigh so hard, that it started to hurt too.

"Right, you're all done." The makeup artist announced.

"Oh, thank God." Mia breathed, launching herself away from the chair with a forced smile. Retightening her dressing gown, she ran up to the bathroom to see what they had done to her face. Her eyebrows were far too thin, and her eyes looked scary; she added some eyeliner to fill in unwanted gaps and accepted her look for the day. The hairdresser had done a lovely job on her hair, though.

Alone for the first time that morning, she stole the opportunity to check her phone.

[Jake] How's it all going?

[Mia] No tears yet. On track for now.

Jake was heading to the church with Fred; Mia was pleased she did not have to worry about him either sitting alone or being unwillingly scooped up by an over friendly family member. She sent him a quick dressing gown selfie, to show off her hair, then slid her phone back in her pocket.

When she emerged from the bathroom, Grandma and Molly called her into the bedroom; the rest of the bridesmaids were downstairs being attacked by the various artists. One did not manage to hold back her squeal of pain like Mia had and it echoed up the stairs. Mia ended up debating what would be worse, getting her eyebrows done again or being present for the conversation Molly and Grandma were having. Wishing she had an excuse to leave, Mia stood uncomfortably while they discussed wedding night underwear and garters. Mia wanted to fall through the floor. Instead, she hummed internally, studied the patterns on the ceiling and waited for it to end. It felt like it never would.

Much to Mia's relief, the conversation was over soon enough, and they began wrestling Molly into her wedding dress. Running up Molly's spine, there were forty buttons for Mia to work on while Grandma clipped on the jewellery and straightened the skirt. The photographer snapped away once she was covered enough to be decent.

When they had finished securing Molly in her dress, they stepped back to admire their work. The dress was a beautiful ivory with a flowing, A-line skirt covered in a light netting, that shimmered in the light. The body was mainly lace, sleeveless, with a Victoria style. It complimented Molly perfectly. Grandma had lent her feather earrings with a tinge of blue, for good luck.

"Oh, Molls, you look absolutely stunning." Mia said, staring at her older sister, eyes filled with love. "I'll be amazed if Will doesn't cry when he sees you."

"Darling, you look gorgeous." Grandma said, tearing up slightly with a wobble in her voice.

"Don't set me off!" Molly scolded, with a wobble too. "They'll have to re-do my make up."

By ignoring all personal space, the photographer managed to get photos of everything before they left the house. As she watched Molly and Grandma have their photo taken together, Mia felt a pang of sadness for her Dad, who should have been there. She hoped he was having a wonderful time in South Africa, playing with lions or doing something else both dangerous and adventurous.

"Right, I'll have the bride and the bridesmaids, now, please, ladies." The photographer said and Mia shuffled to where she was needed.

In total, there were five bridesmaids, including Mia. Before they even left Grandma's house, two of them had managed to annoy Mia, but she took a deep breath and refrained from throttling them.

When the 1932 Rolls Royce Landaulette arrived, Molly squeaked. Grandma piled into her car with the other four bridesmaids and set off fifteen minutes before Molly and Mia did, waving excitedly as they pulled away.

Half an hour away from Newcastle, nestled in the Beamish Valley, sat Beamish itself, the living museum of the north. With many historic buildings, its different villages and settings, the story of the north ever since the 1820's was told.

As a Human Resources Manager on site, William's job came with some added perks. Their wedding was to take place in the small Methodist church in the pit village, followed by the reception in the 1900's town. Redman Park, a small greenery with a bandstand at its heart, sat in the centre of the town and was cordoned off for the public for the day. A huge white marquee had been erected, ready for the party to arrive after the ceremony.

The church held sixty guests, so it was to be much more intimate than the reception, where nearly two hundred people had been invited.

"Mimi, I'm so scared." Molly whimpered, squeezing Mia's hand, as they passed Home Farm, the 1940's farm site, to the employee's entrance gates.

Mia squeezed her hand back. "Why are you scared?"

"I don't even know." Molly said. "There's so many people watching, I suppose."

"Molls, I'm going to be the big sister for a moment here." Mia said, sternly. "You're going to walk into that church and ignore absolutely everyone, you'll have a chance to see them all later. All you're going to focus on is the man waiting for you at the front, the man who loves you so much that he wants to spend the rest of his life with you. Okay?"

Molly nodded and managed a weak smile at her sister. In honesty, Mia was terrified herself, but it was not her time to be scared.

"Anyway, I'd be more scared of vomiting on your dress going along the windy roads." Mia said, with a cheeky grin.

"It's fine, I got it all up this morning."

"That's what you think." Mia said, holding a finger in the air. "But, there's still the toast!"

"Ahh!" Molly replied, comically hitting her forehead. "How could I forget?"

Both sisters giggled and smiled lovingly at one another, holding hands until they drew up outside the church. The driver hopped out to open the door for them and they emerged from the vehicle, into the sun, clutching their bouquets. Along the fence hung bannered flags of red, white and blue and the flowers bloomed in front of the stone brick.

"You ready?" Mia said, as Molly took a breath. She nodded. With her bridesmaids behind her, she marched, feigning confidence, into the church and down the aisle to a live version of 'Somewhere over the Rainbow;' William's younger brother sang and played the ukulele from the front. It was truly stunning. William turned to watch Molly walk down the aisle towards him, wiping away a tear at the sight of his gorgeous bride. Mia was pleased most of their makeup was waterproof, as she batted away tears herself.

The ceremony was beautiful. Grandma cried for most of it and Mia had to look away from her when she got up to do her reading: 1 Corinthians 13:4, 'Love is patient, love is kind…' Jake and Fred smiled and held thumbs up at her when she managed to say it all without a single mistake.

When they were ushered out of the church, two 1910 style London buses were waiting to take them to Redman Park. The bride and groom were last to arrive in the park, in a carriage drawn by two stunning shire horses. With the incredible weather and the unusual back drops, the wedding photographs were bound to be amazing.

Although not fully in keeping with the Victorian/Edwardian theme, they had hired two pizza trucks with ovens in the back of them to serve everyone. Soon, the tables were packed with satisfied guests and their empty pizza boxes. Light music was started by the DJ. Some of the games had been brought up from the school in the pit village for the children, and some adults, to play with on the grass. Hoop rolling was the obvious favourite, with most of the guests giving it a go at some point throughout the evening. The aim was to keep the metal hoop upright with the attached stick for as long as possible.

"How are you so good at this?" Jake asked, as Mia sprinted passed him with her hoop.

"How are you *not* good at this?" she laughed, racing Fred along the grass. "It's rolling a hoop with a stick!"

Even small children were running circles around him, much to Mia's amusement. Everyone seemed to be laughing and joking. There was so much happiness in one place, in the gorgeous setting on the remarkable summer's evening. They could not have asked for a better wedding. Jake laughed as Mia ran away from a bee, until it began to chase him, then the children laughed. Fred began teaching a little girl how to roll the hoop and she squealed with excitement when she managed. It was a day to be remembered.

"Now, everyone." came a booming microphone voice from inside the marquee. The music had stopped for this interruption. "If everyone can gather. I know there weren't going to be any speeches. But, as the best man, I had to say *something*."

William's oldest brother, Paul, was the opposite of the other two brothers. He reminded Mia of Farmer Boggis from Fantastic Mr Fox; he was enormous, with a smug face and a horrendous attitude towards anyone different from him. How they had come from the same family, Mia did not know. She made sure to have a drink before trekking inside.

As expected, his speech was dire. It was derogatory, cruel, sexist and simply not funny. It gained a few pity laughs from awkward members of the crowd. Paul did not seem to care; he enjoyed the sound of his own voice too much. When he ended his speech with a nod to Mia, she actively considered her ideal murder weapon.

"And Mia, you know what they say about the best man and the maid of honour," he said with a wink and she could not hide her disgusted face. "I'll see you at the bar."

"Well, on that note," the DJ said, clearly uncomfortable with the arrogant man that had stolen his microphone. "I think it's time we invite the new Mr and Mrs Roberts up for their first dance!"

Following Paul's speech, the first dance was exactly what everyone needed. Molly and William had aptly chosen Aerosmith's 'Don't wanna miss a thing,' one of their favourite songs. They had taken some dance lessons, so they impressed the crowd. They looked so happy and full of love; Mia could not help but wonder what adventures awaited them in married life. The applause echoed around the Beamish grounds when they kissed to end. Mia whooped and clapped as loud as she could then moved to the bar for drinks.

"I said I'd see you at the bar." Paul said, smacking Mia's backside as he appeared.

Fighting every urge in her body to slap him across the face, Mia still spun on the spot and grabbed the offending hand in a vice grip.

"Oh, steady on, love, you'll never get married with that attitude." Paul said with a sickening grin and turned to get himself a drink.

"Come on, bulldog." Jake whispered, as he and Fred appeared, leading her away. They clearly both wanted to beat him to a pulp too. She let them take her.

"I'll be right back." Mia said, excusing herself, and sweeping away.

Walking out of Redman Park, she crossed the cobbled road to the gap between the shops on the opposite side. It was early evening; the general public had been turfed out for the day, so she managed fifteen minutes alone. Ignoring the fact, she was in a beautiful bridesmaid dress, she made for the stables.

"What are you doing out here?" Jake asked; he had found her in the stables with the shire horses.

"I just needed a little breather from it all." Mia replied, tickling one horses' muzzle. "If one more person tells me it'll be me next or says something patronising, I'll send them headfirst into the cake."

"I'll send that Paul guy in with them." Jake laughed.

When she turned to him, she could not help but let a cheesy grin escape her. He looked incredibly handsome, with his crisp white shirt glowing in the fading light.

"You look beautiful." he said, allowing the horse to see him before stroking it. *Of course, he's good with horses*, she thought.

"...I don't think I've said that yet, today." he added.

"You don't look too shabby yourself." she replied, wrapping herself in his arms.

"Come on, let's go back. I think Fred's been captured by one of your aunties and might need rescuing."

Hand in hand, they crossed back over the cobbles to find Fred, whose Gramps had already saved him. He was sitting with Grandma and Gramps and welcomed seeing Mia and Jake, who took seats beside them. As dark began to fall, the fairy lights around the marquee really began to dazzle. Children had littered various layers of their clothing on the chairs so they could continue to run around on the grass. A woman passed by the table and Mia looked her up and down.

"Am I interrupting a good thought?" Molly asked, collapsing onto the chair beside her.

Mia shook her head and herself back into the room. "No, no, nothing important."

"I wondered if you could help me. I'm dying for a wee and I don't think I can manage on my own." Molly asked.

They swept back out of the gates and into the old tearooms where the toilets were.

"So, you two are cute together." Molly said, as she squatted, with her wedding dress hitched up around her neck.

"Yeah, he's a good egg." Mia smiled; she was leaning uncomfortably over Molly, holding most of her skirt in the air.

"And he's gorgeous." Molly said.

"Do I need to remind you that you have a ring on your finger?" Mia laughed.

"God, I do, don't I?" Molly replied, letting that fact sink in again. "I can't believe I have a husband!"

"I've got a brother-in-law, how weird is that?" Mia thought out loud.

After making sure Molly's dress was all back in place, they headed back to the party. Just as Mia was about to detour off from Molly, she heard someone collar the bride.

"I haven't seen your Mam around, Molly, is she here?" One of William's elderly aunts had asked the reasonable question, causing Molly to stutter and glow red.

"Molly?" Mia stepped in, claiming the attention of her grateful sister. "Fred needs you a moment, can I steal you?"

"Sorry, Nancy." Molly excused herself and let out a deep breath as she walked with Mia to the bar. "Thanks, Mi."

Mia breathed a sigh of relief, leaving Molly with William at the bar.

"You ok?" Fred asked, reading her face. "What happened?"

"William's Aunt Nancy asked Molly where Mam was." Mia said, quietly.

Fred made a face and so did Jake. Some people still were unaware of the change.

"You either need a drink or a dance." Jake said, smiling, as she dropped into a seat beside him. Maid of Honour duties were exhausting. She felt more like a firefighter.

"I'll get us some drinks." Fred said, pointing to the glasses. "Same again, mate?"

"Please." Jake replied, passing him the empties.

'I Wanna Dance with Somebody,' by Whitney Houston started playing.

"Come on." Jake said, patting her leg, and putting out his hand. "I'm going to dance with you at least once."

"Is it compulsory?" Mia groaned; her arms crossed over her chest as she refused to move from her seat.

"Get your arse up here and dance!" Jake said, starting to dance backwards.

Mia rolled her eyes, took the final shot of her drink for courage and dragged herself up to join him. Taking her hand, he spun her round on the spot and she tried to ignore others in the room who might be watching. She really was a terrible dancer. It was always her downfall in musical theatre productions.

"Since when do you know how to dance?" Mia asked, genuinely impressed at some of Jake's moves.

"Since always," Jake smiled, pulling her close. "You've just never had the chance to see properly."

"Well, I'm impressed." she grinned, allowing him to lead her around.

"I'm pleased I still surprise you." he grinned.

When the song ended, he twirled her one more time before an adoring look crossed over him.

"What?" she asked, with a curious look.

"I love you." he said, with a glint in his eye and a smile on his face.

Mouth of the Tyne, Anna Heslop

Chapter Fifteen

At 1a.m. the bar closed, and they were kicked out and dispersed. One of the trams took them to the main Beamish entrance, where they were met by a minibus to take them to Beamish Hall for the night. On the bus, Mia let her head rest on Jake's shoulder as they trundled along. It was only a short journey, which Mia was thankful for. She was ready for her bed. It had been an amazing, but tiring, day.

For an old building, Beamish Hall was exceptionally warm. On the way to their room, Mia caught sight of Molly practically carrying William to the bridal suite, they had come in the Rolls Royce. Evidently, a romantic end to their wedding was not going to happen. By the look of it, Molly was going to be spending her night checking her new husband was still breathing. She looked irritated. Mia held Jake back, so they did not get too close before the newlyweds disappeared into their room.

"I'm not as drunk as I expected to be." Mia said, as they reached their door.

"Interesting you say that…" Jake replied, wrapping his arms around her waist. They fell forward into the room once the door light turned green. "Holy hell, it's hot in here!"

Inside the room, it was even warmer, it was like the depths of the rainforest, swelteringly hot and sweaty. Though a fan sat in the corner, it was as weak as a cough when turned on, stirring the hot air around the room.

"God, I hope there's aircon." Jake said, desperately searching. Of course, with it being such an old building, there was no air con.

Not wasting anytime, Mia unzipped and whipped her dress over her head and darted into the bathroom to splash water on herself. The window was open a slither but would not budge any more than that. Underneath her bra was uncomfortably sweaty, and she just felt generally grim.

"Mi, can you help?" Jake shouted through to the bathroom.

"One minute." She dried her face and reapplied deodorant.

When she stepped out of the bathroom he was stood with his trousers around his ankles, tugging at the knotted tie still around his neck.

"You're so cute." Mia laughed, before going to his aid.

He ran his hands over her hips and began to draw her in, with a glint in his eye.

"I'm sorry, it's so hot, I don't think I can." she said, wiggling out of his grip. "I'm just going to jump in the shower."

Excusing herself, she waited until she was in the bathroom to fully undress and closed the door. She drew the curtain and started the shower from outside, letting it run while she leaned on the sink. *I didn't say it back, I can't believe I didn't say it back,* she thought. There he was, all six foot something of him, standing in front of her, declaring his love and she did not return the statement. Why could she not say it? Did she not feel it too? They had a great time together, they had common interests, the sex was good.

When she checked to see who was online, she saw a green icon next to Holly's name.

[Mia] Jake said: 'I love you' and I didn't say it back.

[Holly] Oh, shit, really? Why didn't you say it back? Too soon?

Mia could not find the answer. Leaving the question unanswered, she turned to the shower. Until she stood under the flowing water, allowing it to wash away the stresses of the day, she had not realised just how tired she was. Her skin sagged under all the excess make up and the pins in her hair were starting to cause a headache. By the time she had finished picking them off her head, she had a rather large pile next to the sink and had flooded the floor slightly.

When she thought about it, it had been a weird sort of day. Her emotions had really taken a kick:

- Thrilled for her sister

- Sad for her Dad

- Worried something would go wrong

- Happy to be with Fred and Jake

- Angry at Paul

- Shocked Jake had said what he said

The more she thought about it, the more her tiredness made sense; the adrenaline had kept her going for so long.

After overworking her brain in the shower, Mia messaged Holly back.

[Mia] Sorry, I jumped in the shower. I have no idea why I couldn't say it.

[Holly] Let's have a summit when you're home.

After scrunching as much water out of her hair as she could, she gave up and let it fall down her back. She towel dried her body and wandered out, to climb into bed beside Jake. He pulled her close to him from behind and lightly snored into her back; she had been in the bathroom longer than expected. Her mind whirred with no logical thought; no sense was produced, it just hummed all night, like a tired old computer on standby. She wished someone would tell her the answer but knew realistically no one else could.

**

Wedding breakfast was delicious; the remaining bridal party enjoyed it together. Out of the entire table, William looked the worst. His hangover had clearly hit with a vengeance. Molly kept stealing angry glances at him, which Mia pretended not to notice, though it was entertaining.

Making best use of the kitchen, Jake and Fred ordered full English breakfasts, which were enormous and smelled incredible. Mia had the slightly smaller version and added on omelette. It was so good she wanted to kidnap the chef to take home.

Molly chatted about her upcoming honeymoon. They were heading to The Maldives for three weeks and Mia could not have been more jealous. When she said her goodbyes to her sister and new brother-in-law, she reminded them to take plenty of photographs and to have an amazing time.

With all their bags playing Tetris in the boot, Mia climbed into Grandma's car with Grandma, Fred, Jake and Gramps. It was an uncomfortable journey, squashed in the back between Fred and Jake. She sometimes forgot just how big they were.

[Holly] You home yet, buggerlugs?

[Mia] Will be in about half an hour.

[Holly] Surf café?

[Mia] I'll be there when I can.

[Holly] Okies. I just walked in. Sian on shift so prepare for multiple opinions.

Grandma dropped Mia and Jake at Mia's flat before heading for the bakery.

"I think I'm gonna head straight off, is that okay?" Jake asked, lifting his bag over his shoulder. "I need to get sorted, then you can too."

"Yeah, that sounds like a good plan." Mia smiled; she fancied a nap rather than a trip to the Surf café.

"See you tomorrow?" Jake asked. Mia nodded and kissed him on the cheek. She was grateful he had not asked what was wrong; he was so kind. She waved him off, turned the key and started up the stairs to the flat.

Two hours later, Fred, Mia, Holly and Steph were all huddled round their drinks in the Surf café, while Sian served a customer.

"Right, we're all here now. What's going on?" Steph asked.

"Jake said he loved me."

"Oh my god." Steph squeaked and clapped with excitement. "That's great, right? What did you say?"

"Well, it obviously isn't great, or we wouldn't be having this conversation, knob head." Holly replied.

"Alright, no need for the sarcasm." Steph said, lifting her hands in surrender. "Why's that a bad thing?"

"I couldn't say it back." Mia said, glumly.

"Really?" Steph said, looking surprised. "I thought you two were in a really good place."

"Me too." Mia replied. "I think that's why it's scared me." Mia sighed. "I've done this with every other guy I've gone out with – pushed them away when things seem great. And most of those guys have been so lovely. Am I just too picky? Once the honeymoon phase is over, I'm out of there?"

Steph and Holly both frowned. Fred made a sympathetic face.

"Do you like him?" Holly asked. "Maybe he's just said it too soon?"

"Yeah, I like him." Mia replied. "But I don't know in what way. And I don't get it, because he's amazing. And if I can't love him, am I ever going to love anyone?"

"Right, first of all, take a breath and take a drink." Holly said, sliding her glass closer. "Then, I've got a question for you."

"Shoot." Mia said, after her sip.

"Do you want to rip his clothes off, or do you look at him more like a brother?" she asked.

Mia's heart sank, she knew her answer.

They bought her another beer and carried on as usual, letting her have her time.

"Excuse me a moment." Mia said, sliding off her chair and slipping outside.

Before long, Fred found her and perched on the fence at her side.

"Do you want to tell me what's going on?" He asked. "You were so happy yesterday."

"I just don't know what to say." Mia replied.

"Start at the beginning." he suggested.

"I don't even know where that is." Mia sighed, then cried, melting onto Fred's shoulder. "I just don't know what to do."

He pulled her in to a strong hug and let her cry.

"Mimi, what is going on? Did something happen at the wedding that I missed?" he asked, with a worried look.

She shook her head.

For a few moments, they sat in silence and Fred held her. Her thoughts were jumping back and forth – did she say something? Did she keep it to herself? Did she really feel that way? How could she even know? She thought about what Lily had said, she thought about the girl at the wedding who had caught her eye. She thought about how she felt when Maria had asked her if Sam was hot. She thought confusing thoughts about Sam.

Wiping the assorted wet from her face, she took a deep breath.

"Fred, I think I might be gay."

Fred let the seagulls talk for a moment or two, formulating an answer. Mia was terrified of his reaction.

"Okay." he said, nodding. "Are you okay?"

Mia laughed through the tears and snot. "Am I okay?"

"Well, I don't know what to say here, do I?" he laughed, nudging her.

She leaned her head on his shoulder. "Yes, Freddie, I'm okay, I think. Just trying to get my head around it."

"Is that the first time you've said it out loud?" he asked; she nodded.

"I'm proud of you, buddy." he said, resting his head on hers.

Halfway along Longsands, the patch of seaweed called the Nettley beds, poked above the ebbing tide.

"Can I ask something that isn't meant to sound insensitive?" he asked.

"Of course." she sniffed.

"How do you know?"

"How do you mean?" Mia asked.

"I mean, how do you know?" Fred asked, looking at her as though she might break. "Have you ever kissed a girl?"

"No." Mia replied. "But, didn't you like girls before you kissed one?"

"Oh, yeah, good point." Fred said. "Sorry, if it was a stupid question."

He put an arm around her and wordlessly said he loved her still. They watched people comb the beach. Four ships were lined up, waiting patiently to dock in the Tyne. Seagulls circled a couple enjoying their fish and chips on the sand. They made the mistake of throwing them one chip, which only made them more relentless in their swooping.

"Why don't you come to the shop a little earlier on Thursday night? I'm sure Gramps would love to have you for dinner."

Mia nodded. "That would be nice."

"Do you want to go back inside?" Fred asked, wiping her face with his sleeve.

"Yeah, I think I need to be with my friends." Mia sniffed. "I don't want to talk about it anymore."

"Do you want me to go in first and tell them not to talk about it anymore?" he asked. When she nodded, he gave her one last squeeze in a hug and wandered back inside on his mission.

Before following him, she checked her face in her phone camera and let the red puffiness die down slightly first. She took a deep breath and followed Fred's path back into her friends.

**

"You know, I've never actually been here." Jake said, feeding the sheep some more pellets.

"How?" Mia said. "You were raised in Newcastle, right?"

"I don't know." Jake shrugged. "I've just never come this way before."

After spending most of the previous evening sulking, she had decided to pack Monday with activity, to keep her mind, and Jake, busy. They had hopped on the metro to Chillingham road, where they zigzagged through the streets to Heaton Park, Armstrong Park and Jesmond Dene, the string of green parks in the heart of Newcastle. Nestled in the centre of Jesmond Dene, on the banks of the river, sat Pet's Corner, where they had stopped to feed some of the resident farm animals.

They walked miles, following the Ouseburn river out of the dene and towards Newcastle City centre.

"Quiz question for you, how many bridges are there over the Tyne?" he asked.

"I actually know this." Mia replied. "Seven wonders of the world, seven bridges over the Tyne." she replied.

"Which one is your favourite?" he asked, as they crossed over the swing bridge, the small red and white one wedged in between the larger bridges.

"Which is my favourite bridge?" she replied. "I don't think I've ever thought about that before."

They stopped halfway so she could decide.

"What's yours?" she asked, as they leaned on the railings, with the water flowing quickly beneath them.

"I think this one." he knocked on the metal frame. "It doesn't let its small size stop it; you know?"

"That's cute." she smiled. "My answer is probably dead boring, but I think it has to be the Tyne Bridge itself. I always know I'm home when I see it."

On the Gateshead side of the river, a collection of containers housed street food and new age bars. Everything seemed to be served on a slab of wood or in a jar, with paper straws, much to Mia's delight. She hated to think of the poor turtles when the plastic ended up in the sea. Under the canopy of one of the shacks, they chose a picnic bench, settling with their drinks and giant pizza slices.

As the sun lowered in the sky, Mia watched Jake eat his pizza, still internally battling with herself. She really did not want to hurt him but that seemed inevitable one way or another.

"You gonna eat that?" he asked, and she pushed it towards him.

"You have it." she smiled. He gladly accepted it.

**

Two hours before she was due at rehearsal, Mia left with her bag and started along the beach. With the tide out, she left no rockpool undiscovered, encouraging the sea air to blow her worries away. As she rounded Marconi point in Cullercoats, she happened across an old pipe end, following it along to the edge of the rocks. She was easily four hundred metres from the point end and there were no people in sight when 'Scream' by the High School Musical cast started playing.

In the most dramatic fashion she could muster, Mia stomped along the exposed rocks with her headphones in. The song lyrics spoke to her, and the emotions felt like they would burst from within her. It boiled her blood, drove her breath faster and tensed her muscles as she leapt between the rocks, turning the music louder. She punched the air and screeched along. It was incredible stress relief.

"AHHHHHHHHH!" she cried out to the sea, throwing her arms away from herself as she did so. It echoed over the water, out to the anchored ships, when the song came to an end.

"You alright, pet?" A fisherman popped his head up from less than ten metres away, having witnessed the whole meltdown. He was partially hidden behind a rock and she had missed his presence.

She nodded, desperately embarrassed that someone had seen her performance. As though thinking, he scrunched up his face, held a finger in the air and started digging in his cool box. Mia did not know whether to retreat or wait for his next move. She waited.

"Cheese or ham?" he asked, holding up two sandwiches wrapped in tin foil.

She smiled, chuckled, wiped away a spare tear and went over to join the kind stranger for his bait.

**

"Mia!" Angelika yelled. "Can I speak with you a minute?"

Mia sighed and stepped off the stage to cross paths with Angelika's wrath.

"Can I ask you a question?" Angelika asked.

"Yeah." Mia said.

"How long do we have before showtime?"

"Er – three weeks."

"Exactly." Angelika said. "So, I don't have time to molly coddle my star who should be up there shining without instruction!"

Mia's eyes started to fill again, which Angelika noticed.

"Take five everyone!" Angelika shouted to the cast, took Mia by the wrist and pulled her into the toilets.

"What's going on with you?" she asked.

"I'm sorry." Mia apologised, with a hang dog expression. "I'm just having a bit of a tough time at the moment – relationship trouble."

"Tell you what. Tonight, you are Elphaba. You are not Mia. You can be Mia afterwards when we go for a beer and drink all our troubles away, okay?"

"I can't tonight, but next week?" Mia suggested.

"I'll hold you to that." Angelika warned. "But, tonight, you are still Elphaba and you are my star. So, go up there and shine like one!"

After practice, Jake met her at the entrance to the theatre to walk her to his flat. With a bit of TLC, it would have been a nice place. But the landlord was rather inattentive and was poor at fixing it up. Every time she visited, she had to laugh at the layout of his room, it was like a teenage boy's room. Rather than having a normal double bed, it was one of the bunk bed double beds with a desk beneath it. The wardrobe stretched along one wall and the doors to it were all mirrors. A small futon chair occupied the rest of the space. Dumping her bag on the futon, she collapsed next to it, knackered. Jake set up Netflix and encouraged her to join him up the ladder, which she did.

They lay in bed with Mia as the little spoon and Jake as the big.

"Can we just snuggle?" Mia asked. "Is that okay?"

"Yeah, of course." He pulled her in close to his warm body and buried his face in between her shoulders.

Chapter Sixteen

On Tuesday morning, Mia woke up long before she was due to. Turning to face Jake, she watched him sleep for a little as he released tiny snores. Her brain would still not settle. She wished it was easy; she wished that she loved him so much it hurt. It *physically* hurt in her chest.

Creeping down the ladder was not easy; the bed was uncomfortably creaky, but she managed without waking him. She left Jake sleeping, got ready and darted off to work for a twelve-hour shift with Jay. It had the makings of a warm day; she could feel it in the air as she walked from Jake's to the beach. Summer always seemed to disappear too quickly. The nights were getting longer, the wind was slightly colder, and everyone was keen to cling onto the last of the nice weather where they could. For Mia, winter usually meant better surf and at least one good holiday out to visit her Dad around Christmas time, wherever he may be in the world at the time. Grandma's cooking was even more incredible than it normally was, and the Harry Potter display would be launched in November. There were lots of things to look forward to, but she did love summer. Especially being so close to the beach; it was the best place to live when the sun was shining.

As she approached from the north, she had the opportunity to walk the entire length of Tynemouth Longsands before arriving at the café. She was early, so took her time, enjoying not having to keep an

240

eye on Charlie or any wandering tennis balls. Every time they took him to the beach, he managed to both acquire and lose at least one tennis ball per walk.

She met with Jay at the base of the southern ramp and they hugged in greeting.

"Oh my gosh, your headscarf is gorgeous!" Mia said, admiring the latest in Jay's collection.

"Thank you." Jay grinned, giving it a pat. It was a dark blue like the night sky and was covered in tiny silver stars. She had the most amazing fashion sense.

As they stepped onto the decking, they were not the only ones in the vicinity. A local dog walker with her three Jack Russell Terriers sat at a table outside, waiting for the café to open. She looked exhausted, leaning back in the wicker chair and fanning herself with a bucket sun hat. All three dogs were overweight and looked as though they too would have appreciated a fanning. It was clear she spoiled them rotten.

"Thank goodness you girls are here! We walked a little far this morning!" she puffed in a soft Edinburgh accent. "We're all dying for a drink!"

Mia opened the door, Jay darted off to the coffee machine and Mia filled the water bowl for the grateful dogs

"Thank you, dears." she breathed, as Mia placed the bowl down for them. "I normally just bring them out in the pram, but the vet says they need to lose a little bit of weight!"

"Can I stroke them?" Mia asked, as the girls trotted closer.

"Why, of course! They're as soft as anything." The woman smiled. "This is Jemima, this is Jeannette, and this is Joyce."

Mia laughed as the dogs affectionately licked her fingers. "What unusual names."

"Well, I like my dogs to stand out, you know." she said. "I wouldn't want to call them something boring!"

Mia loved the thought of the woman shouting those names down the beach, though she could not imagine any of the three running far enough away to need to be called for.

"Run along, anyway, pet, I wouldn't want to keep you." The woman smiled. "I might catch you again."

Mia smiled, said goodbye and went straight inside to wash her hands.

"I don't know how you do that." Jay said, watching as the woman and her dogs left their stopping place. "That's my idea of hell out there."

"Oh, come on, they're harmless."

"Yeah, harmless until they bite your leg off." Jay groaned.

With only Jay around, Mia checked her phone when Jake messaged.

[Jake] You were away early this morning, missus. I missed waking up with you.

[Mia] Sorry, I didn't want to wake you! You looked so comfy.

[Jake] What time are you working tomorrow?

[Mia] In 9-3

[Jake] Fancy doing something after?

[Mia] Yeah, what you thinking?

[Jake] Oh, I have some ideas.

On Wednesday, the same lady returned with her dogs. Though still slightly out of breath, she was not as damaged and red-faced as the day before.

"You know, I might make a habit of this." she said, as Mia brought her a coffee. Mia smiled, said hello to the girls again and returned to work inside.

It was a relatively busy morning. Between flurries of customers, Jay had plenty to fill her in on throughout the course of the day. Her boyfriend's father had now accepted her as a future daughter-in-law, but his mother still had not. They had decided to play the waiting game, hoping it would not last too long. She asked more about Molly's wedding and Mia, in return, discussed Jay's hypothetical one.

"What would I wear?" Mia asked, refilling the paper straws. "A kameez or something? I wouldn't know where to start shopping."

"Oh, don't worry about that." Jay replied, making her nineteenth coffee of the morning. "I'll take you to get you sorted, maybe with a sari. It would be so much fun!"

"I, honestly, can't wait for your wedding." Mia replied, moving on to fold napkins around the cutlery.

"If it happens." Jay reminded.

"Well, let's say it does." Mia said.

"I hope you've got your dancing shoes ready." Jay grinned, beginning to turn her hands to dance.

Mia laughed, joining in. "Don't worry, you taught me well."

The year earlier, Jay had invited Mia and Steph to a Bollywood party. Her brother worked as a Bollywood producer and they were celebrating the success of the newest film, which turned out to be one of the highest grossing in Bollywood. Mia was so nervous about the dancing side, that Jay spent a whole evening with her teaching her how to dance for the party:

"Now, we'll use a song you're bound to know, but that will help when you're learning." Jay had said, turning the music louder to reveal Beyoncé and Shakira's 'Beautiful Liar.'

"Really?" Mia said, arms folded, not ready to embarrass herself in yet another style of dancing.

"Come on, it's easy." Jay replied, moving so smoothly and beautifully to the music. "Just try and copy what I'm doing."

Mia thought it would be better to have her first attempt in private than in front of a room full of strangers so gave it her best shot.

"That's it! See, not so hard is it? The trick is to relax. You can't dance well if you're stiff." Jay said, dancing circles around her.

Mia found she enjoyed it a lot more than English styles of dancing. Jay taught her some signature moves that were bound to see her safely through the party and coated her hands in beautiful henna for the occasion.

The party itself had been incredible fun. Everyone looked amazing to start; the food tables seemed to snake a never-ending path around the room and colour burst from every corner. The music was loud, the smiles were real and so much fun was had. Only, Mia wished she had been in Pakistani dress too, the fabrics and designs were stunning. Jay had helped them to navigate the food, encouraging them to try different dishes and steering them away from the painfully hot ones.

They reminisced as they worked. Changing the radio to BBC Asian Network, they also managed a few more dances during quieter periods.

After work, Jake was waiting for her outside the café, sitting in one of the chairs looking out to sea.

"Hey!" he said, getting up from his chair and greeting her with a kiss on her cheek.

"Hey!" she smiled and accepted it.

"I hope you're ready to get competitive." he said, rubbing his hands together.

"Oh dear, what have you planned?" she asked.

"You'll see." he replied, taking her hand. "You won't have to wait long."

They walked up the wooden stairs off the beach and crossed the road to Tynemouth park.

"God, I haven't been here for *years*!" Mia smiled, looking at the dinosaur themed mini golf course in front of her.

"Are you any good?" Jake asked.

"Oh, no!" Mia replied, shaking her head. "I am absolutely horrendous! Are you?"

"I'm middle ground." he said, gesturing like a seesaw with his hand.

As the dinosaurs roared, they moved around the course. Jake was much better than she was, but Mia knew the names of more dinosaurs than he did.

"It's highest score wins, right?" Mia asked, with a grin, swinging her club above her shoulder.

"You're such a sore loser." he laughed, shaking his head. "And I'm afraid you're losing, my dear, and quite badly."

"Alright." she huffed with acceptance. "You don't have to look so smug about it."

"Me? Smug?" he asked, from his perch on a boulder, where he stood, chest puffed out, like a victorious knight. "Whatever do you mean?"

She laughed and hit a ball in his direction; it missed like the rest of her shots.

Although Jake won the overall game, Mia, somehow, managed the trick shot at the end and won them free ice creams, which they gladly accepted.

By the time they were halfway to the flat, they were polished off.

"Hey, do you wanna?" he flicked his eyes towards the bed, upon realising they were alone in the flat.

"I would but I can't." she replied with a sad face.

"I thought you just had it?" he asked.

"It feels like it!" Mia replied. "But no, it's that time again."

"Damn, what bad timing." he groaned with a smile, pulling her into a hug. She took in his smell while she could; she was still weighing everything up. "It feels like we haven't had sex for ages."

It was true, the last time they slept together was before the wedding. She made an apologetic face and they debated over film choices instead.

**

When Mia arrived at the Bakery that Thursday evening, a beautiful dinner awaited her. The flat they lived in above the bakery was quite small, so dinner was laid out on the large wooden picnic table in the shop itself. Lighting was dimmed and the wood burner roared in the corner. Even though the shop was closed, the train line was still running, reliable as ever.

"Hi, Gramps." Mia said, swooping in to kiss him on the cheek.

"Hello, my darling, so nice to see you." he replied, with a smile that crinkled his warm face. "I'm so pleased you came."

"Me too." Mia smiled, eyeing the mountain of food in front of her. "Although, I don't know how much of this food I'll be able to fit in! It all looks amazing!"

"Oh, you'll find the room." he smiled. "You're looking far too skinny. Get some meat on the bones! I've got some cake for you to take home, as well."

Mia practically drooled on the floor. "Ah, I love your cake so much, thank you."

"Thank me later," he said. "Now, sit, sit, sit."

They took their seats and Gramps began taking the lids off the trays, unleashing even more delicious smells into the air. Mia's stomach growled loudly, eyeing the cheesy garlic bread nearest to her. Gramps had made a huge chicken pasta bake and prepared a large bowl of beetroot and walnut salad. Surrounding the mains, there were corns on the cob, breadsticks, potato gratin and chunky homemade salsa. Brownies were stacked on one side, angel cakes on the other. There were so many carbs on the table; Mia did not think her runs were long enough for the week to burn off how much she was going to eat. Following Gramp's lead, she began to tuck in.

"Did Molly and William get away alright?" Gramps asked, offering her some salsa.

"Yeah, they did." Mia replied, slicing into the pasta bake with a serving spoon.

"It's the Maldives they're gone to, right?" he asked, tearing the garlic bread.

"Yeah, I'm so jealous! She sent me some pictures when they arrived, and it looks gorgeous." Mia replied. "It's got a diving board on the balcony so they can jump straight into the sea from their room."

"I bet it's beautiful! They deserve a wonderful time." Gramps said. "I could do with a holiday. Your Grandma was telling me to book somewhere and just go."

"Why don't you?" Mia asked.

"It's hard to leave the shop." he replied, looking around the room. "There are always orders coming in. And it goes back to that old saying, if you want something done right, do it yourself." he sighed. "I suppose I could leave Freddie in charge, though."

"Oi, if you're off on holiday, Gramps, I want to be coming along as well." Fred said, with a full mouth.

"Me too, if you're offering." Mia laughed.

"When I win the lottery." Gramps smiled. "Now, stop talking and eat up before it goes cold."

They did as they were told and concentrated on their huge plates of food, with the only sounds being chewing and cutlery scraping on the crockery.

"So, Mimi, I can't wait to see your show." Gramps shouted through from the kitchen, somehow, he had disappeared to bring out even more food. Fred had barely said a word; his mouth was constantly full.

"Don't get your hopes up." she laughed. "Do you need me to get you tickets?"

"No, thanks, love." he said, emerging with steamy bowls of apple pie. It smelled delicious. "Your Grandma sorted me out."

"She did? That was nice of her." Mia replied, helping herself to more brownies and ice cream to accompany her pie.

"Ah, she's a good one, your Grandma." Gramps said with a wistful smile. "She looks after me, she does, pet. She's a lamb."

Mia gave Fred a confused look and he pretended not to see it.

**

[Jake] Just checking you're not lost.

[Mia] Picked up Charlie, on my way down now.

[Jake] What do you want to drink?

[Mia] Ooh, I really fancy a mojito, please.

Walking a little faster, Mia made it to the Surf café within ten minutes. Everything was set up for open mic night and a guitarist resembling Thor was impressing the audience with his pipes. Jake, Sian and Steph were already gathered around their favourite table, ready for Friday night. It was relatively busy, so Mia was grateful they had managed to arrive before her to get seats.

"Hey, you." She kissed Jake quickly on the cheek and took a seat, pointing to the spare cocktail. "Is this mine?"

"If you want it." he offered. "I can take it back if you'd prefer?"

"No, no." Mia said, taking hold of the glass. "It's good here, thank you."

She took a sip and it was delicious.

"Where's Dimitri? I thought he was joining tonight?" Sian asked in the direction of Jake and Steph.

"He's working late tonight." Steph said, rubbing her hands together. "I'm gonna head over to his after this, he's off tomorrow. I need to get me some."

"Mate, you are grim." Sian said, crumpling her face.

"Oh, shut up." Steph said, hitting her shoulder. "You say much worse than I do."

"Hardly." Sian argued, and Steph gave her a look as if to say 'really?'

"Are you guys getting up tonight?" Jake asked, pointing to the corner staging area with his beer bottle.

Mia looked at Steph. "I don't know, are we?"

"Why not?" Steph shrugged. "It's been a little while."

When the stage was free, and at Sian's request, Steph and Mia performed the acoustic version of 'Hey Ya!' by Outkast. Mia struggled not to shed a tear at the emotion in the room, with Jake watching her proudly, completely unaware of what was about to come. She loved him, she did. But, not in the way a girlfriend was supposed to love their boyfriend. Nothing had happened yet, and she already missed him.

When the song was over, instead of waiting at the table, Jake got up to meet her.

"Can I talk to you?" Jake said, taking her hand and leading her outside. They sat on the same fence line as Mia and Fred had. "Somethings wrong, what is it?"

Mia gulped; she could not bring herself to look at him. He took her hand. "You can tell me anything."

"There is something I need to tell you," Mia began. "But I'm scared to." The tears were creeping back. "And I don't think this is the place to talk about it."

"Should we go back to yours?" Jake asked, looking concerned; Mia nodded.

"Let me just text Steph." She said.

[Mia] Can one of you bring my bag home? I have keys.

[Sian] You okay, pal?

[Mia] Yeah, just heading back with Jake. Talk to you later.

[Steph] Love you.

They wandered up towards the flat, hand in hand.

"You can tell me anything, you know." Jake said, his sullen voice suggested he knew what was coming. "Take your time."

"I know I can. It's just finding the right words." Mia sighed; it was so hard to hurt him.

They kept walking.

"Are you breaking up with me?" Jake asked. He could not wait any longer.

"Yes." Mia sighed, still holding his hand. "But it's not that simple."

For the first time, Jake started to look angry, ripping his hand away from hers.

"Did you cheat on me?" he spat.

"No!" She said, holding her hands up in innocence. "No, nothing like that. I would never do that."

"Oh, sorry." he said, taking her hand again.

"Don't say sorry, you have nothing to say sorry for!" she took a deep breath and looked at her hands. It was better to just say it; to tell the truth. "Jake. I think I might be gay."

For a moment, the revelation settled in the air. "Okay." he paused, then let out a nervous chuckle. "I did not expect you to say that."

"Well, I didn't expect it to happen." she chuckled back with a small sob. "I'm so sorry, I don't want you to hate me."

"I don't hate you." Jake said. "I'm not going to lie and say this will be easy for me to walk away from, but I appreciate you telling me, honestly."

Mia sniffed and gave a weak smile.

"Come here, you." he said, unexpectedly pulling her into a bear hug.

**

"So, have you told anyone else yet?" Jake asked. He was lolled across her bed with his head on his hands. He was sad but the nice guy in him made him stay.

"Fred knows, but that's it." Mia replied. "I can't bring myself to tell anyone else."

"Not even Sian?" Jake asked. "I mean, she swings the same way."

"No, I don't know why." Mia said. "There's been a couple of times I could have told them, and I just chickened out."

They sat on Mia's bed, just talking, until Sian came home. Upon hearing them turning the key in the lock, she jumped up to shut her bedroom door. Jake looked at her, quizzical.

"I just can't deal with her right now." she whispered.

So she would not have to deal with anyone else for the rest of the night, Jake stayed until Sian had gone to bed, then left. He kissed her on the cheek and walked away from the scene of their broken relationship.

Chapter Seventeen

Unexpectedly, Steph joined Mia in the post break up pity party, except she was in the VIP section. Not long after 11pm, both Mia and Sian were woken up when a raging bull stormed into the apartment.

"AAAAAARGGGGGHHHH!" The noise erupted through the flat.

Mia nearly fell out of bed at the sound; Charlie flipped straight onto his feet in shock. Leaping out of bed, Mia threw on a t-shirt and dressing gown.

"What is happening?" Sian asked, rubbing her eyes and appearing at the bottom of the stairs as Mia opened her bedroom door.

In the living room, Steph had crumpled herself into a ball and was screaming and sobbing into a cushion. Charlie ran to her, then retreated nervously, unsure of what to do. Sian and Mia were just as apprehensive, looking at each other expectantly.

"Mate, are you okay?" Sian asked, tentatively as she and Mia crept closer. No reply.

"Well, she's obviously not." Mia half whispered; half mouthed.

"You try then." Sian hissed in a whisper too.

"Steph?" Mia asked. "What's wrong?"

Lifting Steph's shoulders slightly, Mia slipped in beside her and Sian covered the other side. Steph continued to cry hysterically. She was really howling, with full body shakes.

"Sian, get the good stuff." Mia said, nodding towards the door.

Disappearing into the kitchen with Charlie at her heels, Sian reappeared with a ginormous tub of Ben and Jerry's Phish food ice cream and three beers. They held her as she continued to cry, she was hysterical. The more she cried, the more she struggled to catch her breath. Mia's t-shirt was soaked in a matter of minutes.

After a while, with no sign of it slowing, Mia took charge.

"Right, Steph, look at me." Mia said and reluctantly Steph lifted her red face. "You're going to go upstairs, get ready for bed then come back down here straight away, okay?"

Steph nodded and dragged her heavy body off the sofa and up the stairs. They watched her go.

"Do you think he broke up with her?" Sian asked, quietly.

Mia shrugged. "I don't know, but it's probably a good guess. I've not seen her this upset before."

"Poor lass." Sian said. "Why don't you message Jake and see if he knows anything."

"Erm-yeah, I can do." Mia said, not feeling it was right to bring up her own difficulties at that time.

Nipping back into her room to grab her slippers, Mia was back on the sofa before Steph appeared again. She had calmed down slightly but the tears still stained her face.

"Come on, buddy." Mia said, patting the sofa beside her. "Come and tell us what happened."

As soon as she started talking again, the tears flowed with the words.

"So, I went around to Dimitri's and his room is on the ground floor." she sniffed, struggling to speak between sobs. Mia knew it well, it looked straight onto the street and was right beside the front door. "But he hadn't shut his curtains." She wailed loudly.

"I thought he was at work?" Sian asked and Mia glared at her when Steph cried even louder.

"He said he was, but he wasn't." she cried. "He had company. There were three of them in there."

Mia and Sian both sucked air through their teeth and winced. Deciding there was nothing helpful they could say to help the situation, they cracked open the beers and encouraged Steph to eat as much ice cream as she could manage.

Before long, between the three of them, they had managed to work through half a box of beer, with Steph also enjoying some gin on the side. Mia lit some candles on the fireplace in the kitchen when they migrated through. They dimmed the rest of the lights and Sian cranked up the volume on the speaker. It gradually got louder and louder as the drinks went down. Mia poured some Doritos into a bowl, covered them with cheese and melted it in the microwave. She then coated them with guacamole and tomato dip and placed them in the centre of the table.

"I miss everyone, do you guys ever just miss everyone?" Steph whined, hugging herself. "Like, Carol. Isn't Carol just an absolute legend?"

They cheers-ed to Carol being a legend and drank.

"Let's invite them round then." Sian said, wobbling on the spot. "Right now, let's be spontay-sponty- wow, that's hard to say when you're drunk, *spontaneous*."

"I'm on it." Mia trotted over to her phone, holding her glass higher than it ought to be.

[Mia] If anyone is awake, get your arse round here. Emergency cheer up sesh needed. Wear pyjamas and bring beer!

[Holly] What's going on?

[Mia] Drinking our sorrows. It's great.

[Holly] Dammit, I'm at work. Have fun!

"Holly's replied, but she's at work." Mia relayed.

"Booooo! Tell her to quit." Steph demanded.

[Mia] Steph says you should quit.

[Holly] Don't tempt me.

When Fred arrived, not long after 1am, all three girls were up on the kitchen counter singing '*I am Woman*' by Helen Ruddy, or more they were screeching it. Poor Charlie looked traumatised and welcomed Fred's arrival.

"Get your ass up here, Freddie!" Mia said, reaching a hand out to pull him up, nearly toppling off herself.

"Oh, dear!" Fred laughed, placing his six pack of diet coke on the counter to his left. "How much have you guys had?"

"Nowhere near enough." Steph slurred, as Sian propped her up.

"You know how you like the ladies?" Steph said, falling more on to Sian. "Maybe I like the ladies too, I've just never tried it."

"Right, I think you've had enough of that." Sian said, taking away her gin and handing it to Fred.

"Catch me, Freddie." Steph said, squatting down and leaping from the bench towards him. He managed to stop her from falling over but she landed so heavily, Mia thought she might have cracked the ceiling of the downstairs neighbours.

"Oops." she giggled and staggered towards the fridge.

Leaning over to push it closed again, Fred did his best to stop her. "Mmm, maybe you've had enough to drink."

"You know what I really want?" Steph said, scrunching her face in thought.

"Not until you tell me." Fred said.

"A McDonalds, I would kill for a chicken select right now." Steph moaned and ran her hands down her cheeks. "Let's go!"

"What, now?" Fred asked, pointing out the window to the darkness of the night.

"Yeah! Can we go? I *really* want a McDonalds, please, pretty please." Steph said, physically begging Fred. He looked at Mia and Sian, who gave a look of 'why not?'

"*Fine.*" Fred agreed; he had driven round so he could stop at the all-night garage first and was regretting his choice.

Much to Steph's delight, they drove up to the twenty-four-hour McDonalds at 1:30am. Sian briefly snoozed in the back and Fred kept turning around to check Steph had not vomited in his newly cleaned Corsa.

"We haven't done a night-time Macky's run for a while." Mia laughed; she had called shotgun so rode in the front seat.

"God, remember the time your Grandma thought you'd been kidnapped then we swanned in with Macky's at like four in the morning?" Fred replied, checking for cars at a roundabout.

"She was *not* happy." Mia remembered. "I think that's the only time she really shouted at me. I mean, she's told me off before but that was actual shouting."

"And your Grandma is scary without needing to shout!" Fred laughed.

"Tell me about it."

Going through the drive-thru was slightly difficult when Steph tried to shout her own order from the back seat of the car. Sian had to cover her mouth to force her into silence. They ordered a feast, with Fred pulling into the car park so they could enjoy it all. When there was a depletion in the ketchup supply, Steph clambered out of the car and, pretending to be a car herself, went through the empty drive-thru to get some more. Luckily, the McDonalds employees found her hilarious and passed over mountains of ketchup.

"I feel like parents." Mia smiled. Sian and Steph had both fallen asleep on route home.

"You can carry them to bed." Fred said quietly back.

When they pulled up outside the flat, Sian woke with a start, the same could not be said for Steph, who was reluctant to fully wake up or leave the car. Between the three of them, they managed to half wrestle, half carry her up the stairs to bed.

**

The next day, Mia lay in the bath, letting the bubbles swirl above her naked body. Luckily, her shift had been a short one that day; she had struggled to stay awake. It was the closest she had ever come to phoning in sick. As she soaked, her limbs felt heavier than normal, as though some unknown person had sewn tiny weighted beads to them without her knowledge. When she began to think about the weight of each breath, the panic set in, what if she forgot to breathe altogether? One day she would stop breathing altogether and that would be it. These thoughts were deeper than her bath water.

"Knock, knock." Sian said, tapping on the bathroom door. "Can I come in?"

"Yeah." Mia replied, making sure the bubbles were covering the vital places.

Sian crept in the door, closing it behind her and sinking to the floor.

"What can I do for you?" Mia asked.

"Do you want to talk about what happened to you last night?" Sian asked her with a raised eyebrow.

Internally, Mia began to panic, had Jake told her?

"What happened with you and Jake last night?" Sian asked.

"How do you know something happened?" Mia asked.

"Come on, you're my best mate." Sian said. "I knew something was wrong before you even left the Surf café. Especially after our conversation the other day."

Mia sunk further into the bathtub. "I don't know if I want to talk about it."

"Okay." Sian said, getting up and ready to leave. "Can I ask one thing though?"

Mia nodded.

"Are you two still together?" Sian asked.

"No, we aren't." Mia replied.

Sian pursed her lips and made a face. "I thought that might have happened. Well, you know where I am when you're ready to talk."

**

Initially, Mia thought she was handling the breakup well. Naturally, she was upset, but it did not really hit her until Monday. She had distracted herself by supporting Steph, who had been hit like a ton of bricks by what Dimitri had done. Instead of ceremoniously throwing all Dimitri's clothes out the window, as TV had taught them to do, she had made him his own shrine-like shelf. Only one t-shirt of his stayed off the shelf and that was because Steph had worn it for four days.

The trigger for Mia was finding one of Jake's t shirts mixed in with her own. She had just been for her fourth bath since the breakup when she found it.

When she lay on her bed, clutching it in one hand, she could not even be bothered to dry herself. Instead, she lay, staring into space until more tears began to fall. So many fell that there were too many to stop.

"Mi?" Sian knocked on the door and creaked it open. "Oh, Mi." she said, softly, creeping onto the bed and wrapping her friend in a hug.

"I'm sorry, I'm all wet."

"It's okay." Sian replied, still using her soft voice. "Girls don't usually apologise to me for that."

Mia could not help but chuckle through her snotty sobs. "You can't help yourself, can you?"

"I see an opportunity, I take it." she smiled, squeezing Mia tighter in a hug. "Do you want to talk to me?"

"I don't even know what to say." Mia cried. "I have no right to be upset. I did this. I'm the bad guy."

"Hey, hey," Sian soothed, stroking the hair from her face, away from the tears. "You're not the bad guy."

"I was the one who did the breaking up though." Mia sniffed.

"It doesn't make you a bad guy though. You can't help the way you feel or the way you don't, for that matter. At least you went about it in the nicest way you could, you didn't do it by text or cheat or anything."

"I just feel so bad."

"And you probably will for a little bit. Break ups are never nice." Sian said, hugging again. "But, if it's not right, it's not right. You can't force these things."

"I know you can't." Mia sobbed. "But he was perfect, and I miss him so much."

"Maybe, one day, you guys can be friends again." Sian replied with a smile. "He'll just need some time."

"Does that ever work?" Mia asked. "I thought once you broke up, that was it."

"I don't believe that." Sian replied. "You're both good people and if you care about each other enough a relationship can be adapted, if it's worth it."

Mia smiled; she hoped Jake would want to be friends someday, she really did. Feeling a little better, Mia took Sian's advice and enjoyed a nap before heading to rehearsal.

With only a few weeks left until *Wicked,* Mia took a deep breath before entering the theatre, doing her best to channel the advice Angelika had given her the week earlier. She had promised a pub trip afterwards too, so pasted a smile on her face, kept calm and carried on, in true British fashion.

Rehearsals were heating up even more but, Mia felt like crawling into a hole, not like standing in front of a full audience under a bright spotlight.

"Right, let's get the spotlight on you!" Angelika said, pretty much as soon as Mia walked through the door. It was blinding, but she pushed the emotions she was feeling into singing instead and delivered.

When she finished, Angelika gave her a standing ovation, throwing her seat back and applauding as loud as her hands would let her.

"Where did *that* come from?" Angelika beamed, looking like a proud parent while Mia's vocal cords recovered. "Ladies and gentleman, *this* is why she is our star! Brilliant, just brilliant, if you do that on opening night there won't be a dry eye in the house.

Excellent, take five, then get ready to come back and dazzle me again. Well done."

Mia nodded and gave a weak smile to excuse herself.

"Mimi!" Sam squeaked, bounding towards her and greeting her with a hug. "That was amazing! Seriously, you should have been where I was. I think you underestimate the power of your own voice."

Mia blushed. "Thanks."

"Don't look so embarrassed." she nudged her. "I tell you what, if the entire show is like that, we'll be having one hell of an afterparty!"

After rehearsal, they wandered down to the Spanish City in Whitley Bay. In 1910, it had opened as a smaller version of Blackpool's pleasure beach, eventually falling into disrepair after years of entertaining. Following its regeneration, a small microbrewery opened, alongside a fish and chip shop, tearoom and restaurant. They sat on old church pews, with a beer barrel as their table. There were at least ten of them, spreading over three barrel tables.

"So, how are the relationship troubles?" Angelika asked, as she delivered the pints to their new owners.

"Over with." Mia said, taking a sip.

"As in fixed? Or did you guys break up?" Angelika asked.

"We broke up." Mia said.

"Wait, you guys broke up?" Sam had left the other conversation to come into theirs. "Oh, I'm sorry to hear that."

"I'm not." Angelika said. "If it's not right, it's not right. Better to get out than get stuck in something that's not doing it for you."

Mia listened to her talk.

"It'll be rubbish for a bit." she continued, taking a sip of her drink. "But it always gets better."

Mia had a lot to think about; she woke up still tired every day. Her moods followed no rhyme or reason. Some days she woke up motivated, ready to better herself and embrace the good side of life, grateful for everything she did have. Other days, she was full of woe, struggling to exchange her sweatpants for jeans, feeling like brushing her teeth was an achievement in the morning.

The piano stool in Mia's room had become her anchor. Initially, she had tried to get in the water for a surf in attempt to clear her head, but she bumped into some of Jake's friends and it had not helped the situation. One had even tried hitting on her; at least it meant Jake had kept his word. He really was a good guy. *Damn, what's wrong with me? He's a great guy.* Mia had thought and the spiral of upset continued. Eventually, she had realised her safe space was at the keyboard, playing for hours on end. *Adele's* songs were particularly well played, 'Turning Tables' being a favourite. Like a misshapen shadow, Charlie alternated between following round Steph and Mia, cleverly sensing they were both facing emotional turmoil. He lay in the sunbeam beside the keyboard for hours while Mia played.

Occasionally, Sian would appear in her doorway. Mia would not turn but would continue to play. Eventually, her friend would sigh and walk away, clearly wondering what to do about her, desperate to help.

Still wanting to stick by her duties, Mia welcomed Fred on the Thursday night, as usual. The Lego tasks were getting more and more complex as time went on. They had moved on to creating the *Hogwarts Express* train and their collection was really growing. Mia was excited to see the completed product in November and was sure the public would be too once the theme was announced.

"I've got a bit of news for you." Fred said, not taking his eyes of the Lego pieces he was putting together. "And it could be taken either way, so I want you to see it as good news."

"Ri-ight." Mia replied, clicking two more pieces into place. "What's up?"

"Gramps, kind of, went on a date the other day." Fred continued. "With your Grandma."

"What?" Mia replied, unsure how to process the information.

"I mean, they only went to the theatre, I don't think it was anything weird." Fred said, fumbling a little with nerves in his words.

"I mean, it's a little weird if they're going out." Mia replied, still thinking.

"They're actually really quite sweet together." Fred said. "Gramps was in his best suit; I've never seen him so smart. And when your Grandma turned up, she giggled like a teenager."

Mia frowned at him. "Are you making this up? Like, is this a joke?"

"No, seriously."

"Why now though?" Mia asked. "They've known each other for years."

"Who knows." Fred shrugged. "I guess love works in mysterious ways."

"Love?" Mia asked. "How long has this been going on for?"

"Don't read too much into what I say." Fred said. "I don't know how long it's been going on for. I know Gramps didn't stay in my room at the wedding though."

"Sorry." Mia replied. "I guess it's hard to think my Grandma is getting more action than me." Mia sighed.

"Ew."

"I guess, at least they are happy." Mia shrugged. There was enough anger and upset in the world without her adding anymore to it. She decided to make a conscious effort to be happy for them, and to pretend they did nothing more than hug and occasionally hold hands.

Mouth of the Tyne, Anna Heslop

Chapter Eighteen

Wallowing is the right word to describe the actions of Steph and Mia over the coming week. They had spent so much time on the sofa they were starting to stew. Following the initial period of crying for Steph and indecisive emotions for Mia, they had moved on to lack of self-care and general grumpiness. Other than work, they seemed to simply exist in the flat. It had been four days since Mia had washed her hair and it was even longer for Steph. The coffee table was littered with their used dishes and plates, which was especially unusual for Steph, who was normally the quickest to clean. It was starting to smell.

Though Mia stood by her decision, she was still struggling with the complexities of it, and was yet to tell either of the girls the real reason behind the breakup. Each time she stopped herself from telling them, another bit of her self-esteem chipped away. Every time she came close, she managed to change the subject at the last minute.

"Weren't you guys watching this when I went out?" Sian asked, stepping into the living room. She had been to Morrisons alone to do the weekly shop on her way home from work.

"Yeah." Mia said, not looking away from the TV.

"We couldn't find the remote." Steph continued, staring at the screen.

"What so you've watched this how many times?" Sian frowned.

"I think this is the third now." Mia said.

"Maybe the fourth." Steph said, deadpan.

Sian looked as though she was about to say something but stopped herself and stomped upstairs to her room.

"I don't know why people recommend Bridget Jones' Diary after a break-up." Mia said, her voice slightly muffled as her cheek pressed into the sofa. "All it makes me think is that I'm going to die alone eaten by alsatians, I'll be that guy."

"What do you recommend instead?" Steph asked, still blindly staring at the television, her hair lolled in a messy bun on her head.

"Forgetting Sarah Marshall. Every time." Mia replied, growling in a stretch; Charlie mimicked her. "It's just more real and funny and includes two fingers up at the person who broke his heart."

"I've never seen it." Steph admitted, shrugging.

"Have you lived under a rock?" Mia replied, astonished, having watched it at least ten times solely the year it came out.

"We can watch that next." Steph said, waving her down. "Calm down."

They were snuggled on the sofa together under The Mother of All Blankets with Mia's legs draped over Steph. Bridget's friends were just about to drive to Paris in a Mini Cooper on the snowiest day of the year, so the film was nearly over. Neither girls were planning to move in the near future.

"Right, come on!" Sian clapped her hands together as she walked back into the living room and unplugged the television for effect.

"What?" Both Steph and Mia, unenthusiastically, lolled their heads in her direction.

"We're going to Holly's party. *All* of us. Get. Up." Sian tore The Mother of All Blankets off them. "You're not going to sit here and wallow in self-pity a moment longer."

They both groaned and tried to drag it back over them.

"I really don't feel like it." Steph whined, twisting her face.

"I'm serious!" Sian scolded, standing over them, hands on her hips. "Enough is enough. You're both going to get up, get washed, get dressed and get ready to get fucked up. The taxi is booked for 9:05."

She swept out of the room and up the stairs; the sound of running water could be heard. "Right, who's first? Shower's running so hurry up!"

They admitted defeat and, reluctantly, moved themselves from the living room.

**

It was hard to call Holly's house a house, when it was a garage with a bed in it. It was so incredibly Holly. The landlord was the owner of the rest of the house but had blocked his back door, so the back-garden path was reserved solely for the garage. Inside, the layout was unusual. The front door was on the far right, opening out on the kitchen/bathroom. A cupboard in the corner housed the toilet, but the see-through shower door opened out straight into the kitchen. Therefore, anyone taking a shower was in full view of the rest of the house occupants. It had one bedroom, which was the coldest room, as it still had the rolling door from its past life as a functioning garage. Holly and her friend, Kelly, both had a single bed in the room, like in an American College dorm, and had become far too familiar with each other. Luckily, the sofa was very comfortable, so they were able to leave each other to it if a guest was round. Kelly had a boyfriend, so Holly spent most of her nights on the sofa. Or, if she was working nights, they could alternate use of the bedroom.

Somehow, they had managed to squeeze around sixty guests in, even if they were packed in like sardines. Dotted amongst the crowd were some *very* attractive women, who were some of the dancers from Holly's work. Classic Rihanna was playing, 'Don't stop the music.'

"You guys came!" Holly fell out of the shower towards them, fully clothed.

"What were you doing in the shower?" Mia asked, catching Holly in a hug.

"I needed some water and couldn't get to the sink." Holly replied, as though that was perfectly normal. Mia chuckled at her friend; she loved drunk Holly.

"You're such a tit." Mia laughed.

"Oh, you just shh." Holly said, struggling to put a finger to her lips. "Go and get yourself a beer. The fridge is already full. Remember to replace the beer you take with a new one!"

Squeezing through the people to the fridge, they abandoned their beer and took some cold ones instead. Mia always found the initial moments at a party quite awkward – not knowing where to stand or sit, feeling in the way and unsure of who to talk to. They weaved back through to the bodies until they found a comfortable enough space near the washing machine.

"Do you actually know anyone here?" Mia asked, scanning the crowd.

"Not really, I think it's a load of her work people." Steph replied, sipping her drink. "And Sam?"

Mia looked over to see Sam in a cluster of women, waving enthusiastically in their direction, she waved back. *Why is she here? Why on earth is she here?* Mia thought. Every time she saw Sam, she felt rude, because she struggled to talk to her without tripping over her words.

"Hey!" Sam said, when she finally reached them. "What are you guys doing here?"

"Holly's a good mate of ours." Mia replied. "What are you doing here?"

"I came with my brother." Sam replied, rolling her. "But I think he found someone better to hang out with. I don't even know where he is, so I made new friends."

She waved at the circle she had just come from.

"What the hell are you doing over here?" Holly said, appearing and falling towards them again. "We're about to start ring of fire!"

They had no time to reply. Dragging them in a chain, Holly pulled them through the kitchen and to the oddly shaped living room. It was the smallest room, which was not hard considering there were only three proper rooms, and the floor was layered in the most bizarre places; the sofa had its own platform.

When they rounded the corner and saw most of the dancers congregated around the coffee table, Sian's eyes nearly popped out of her head.

Mia laughed and gave her a nudge, whispering: "Oi, mate, hide your hard on."

Sian exhaled, made a mental note to behave herself and took a seat on the floor beside Kelly.

"Oh, sorry." Steph said, apologising as she sat on the hand of her neighbour. Sam sat beside Mia.

"Don't worry about it." he said, with a large grin.

"Right, right, everyone, listen up." Kelly said, taking control of the crowd; Sian stared while trying not to. "International drinking rules are in place: No saying the word drink, no names, no swearing, no pointing, pinkies out and left-handed drinking, except for the lefties. Have I missed anything, Holls?"

"And no empty glasses!" Holly shouted and the room cheered. Kelly began to display the cards around the central pint glass.

"So, how do you play?" Sam whispered, leaning in close enough for Mia to smell her hair.

"Have you not played before?" Mia asked, with surprise.

"Not since, like, first year of uni." Sam replied, making a face.

"You pick a card then do what it says, pretty simple." Mia said. "Just don't break the circle or you'll have to down the dirty pint in the middle. Everyone gets to pour into it as well, so you really don't want to do that."

"Ew."

Towards the end, Steph came close to breaking the circle but was just safe. It turned out to be Holly who lost. When she had to down the central pint glass concoction, Mia was apprehensive. Holly was already legless; she could barely even sit still, spinning in a circle on the spot instead.

"Anyone for another?" Mia asked her immediate neighbours, as the game drew to a close. There were too many people playing for her to offer to everyone.

"I'll come with you." Sian said, downing the last of her drink.

"Can you get me a gin please?" Steph asked.

"I'll have anything but vodka." Holly slurred. Mia knew all too well that Holly and vodka did not agree; they had placed a ban for life on her after one fate filled night involving the spirit. It was the drink that turned Holly into an aggressive psychopath; she was usually so joyful.

Becoming less courteous as the night went on, Mia elbowed her way through the crowd to the fridge.

"God, Kelly is so fit." Sian said, appearing at Mia's side with the wandering bottle opener.

"What, Holly's flat mate?" Mia asked, taking it from her to pop the lids from their drinks. "And thanks."

"The very one." Sian said, looking back over her shoulder. "You're welcome."

"Do you ever go anywhere without creeping on someone?" Mia asked.

"I'm not creeping." Sian replied. "I've just made an observation."

"I bet you wouldn't kick her out of bed, though." Mia laughed.

"I bet you wouldn't either!" Sian said, staring from a distance. "Look at her!"

Mia moved her gaze from Kelly, granted she was attractive, to Steph, who was cosying up to the boy whose hand she had sat on.

Steph took the same hand and pulled him away from the circle. Sam watched them leave then made her way over to Mia and Sian.

"Well, Steph looks happy." Mia said to Sian, as Sam reached them. "What's up with you?"

Sam gestured to the corner where Steph had stopped with her young, rather gangly teenage love interest, to exchange saliva with him.

"Oh, that is brilliant." Sian laughed, leaving to take a photo of them.

"I think I *might* be sick." Sam groaned, before taking Mia's hand. "Come on, if this has to happen, I really don't want to watch it."

"What's wrong, like?" Mia asked, as she was whisked away, further into the crowded kitchen. Her hand felt sweaty as Sam held it.

Sam halted when they reached the bedroom door.

"That's my brother." Sam said, with an unimpressed look in her eyes. Mia laughed in her face, causing her to cross her arms across her chest.

"I'm sorry, but that's hilarious." she chuckled. "How old is he?"

"Eighteen."

"Oh my God, this gets better." Mia laughed.

"Thanks for helping." Sam said, sarcastically.

"Oh, come on." Mia smiled. "We can have Steph's life for this."

"Fair." she rolled her eyes. "I still don't want to watch it though."

"Do you want to go back in the living room?" Mia asked, wondering how to barge back through all the people without making some enemies.

"We can do, I think they just started truth or dare."

Dangerous, Mia thought, but allowed herself to be towed back over anyway.

For a party in a garage, the game was very organised. Someone had made prompt cards for the occasion, so the game never went stale. The worst Mia had to do was a body shot, so she got off very lightly. One guy had to strip completely naked, covering himself with only a party hat. To Mia's delight, Sam seemed a little horrified by the very naked man. She pretended it meant more than it did.

"Do you want another drink?" Sam asked, pointing to her empty bottle.

"Er, yeah, I'll come with you." Mia replied and they excused themselves from the spiralling game.

As they waited for the bottle opener to be passed their way, they stood, unsure of what to say in the limbo period. With the amount of people in the kitchen, they were being pushed closer together, until they were only inches from each other. Mia could study Sam's face in detail, she was so near to her – her recently shaped eyebrows, the freckles on her nose. The devil on her shoulder started singing 'Kiss the girl' from The Little Mermaid and she growled at it.

"Does this feel-" Mia started and thought she saw Sam lean in a little closer to hear her. "Like a fire hazard to you?"

Sam frowned and tilted her head slightly, obviously not expecting that sentence. "A fire hazard?"

"Yeah! I mean, there's just a lot of people here and only one exit." Mia stepped back a little, though the wall of bodies stopped her from moving too far, shaking her hands with an awkward tick. She knocked into a stranger, who was clearly struggling to stay upright.

As the stranger began to fall, Sam pulled Mia back towards her, out of harms' way. The stranger crashed to the floor and Mia found herself dangerously close to Sam.

"I'm sorry, I think I can hear Sian shouting for me." Mia said. Leaving Sam, she weaved through the warm bodies to the front door and out into open air, continuing through the smokers on the garden path and onto the street. As she reached it, Mia stumbled on the pavement and smacked to the ground like a sack of potatoes.

"Jesus, how wasted are you?" Sian asked, picking her up off the concrete, wiping stray gravel off her slightly bloodied knees. "You okay?"

"Yeah, yeah, I'm fine." Mia said. "I'm not even that drunk."

"You sure?" Sian asked. "I haven't seen you stack it for a while."

"Yeah, I just tripped on this." she said, kicking an uneven slab of pavement, releasing a growl of frustration.

Sian frowned at her friend, sat on the kerb and patted it for Mia to sit beside her.

"Mi, what's going on with you?" Sian asked, looking concerned. "You seem to have lost your Mia spark recently. Is it all this Jake stuff? I didn't think it would hit you as hard as it has."

"I didn't expect it to either, bud." Mia said, collapsing on the kerb next to her. "I'll be fine. I just need to sort my life out a little bit."

"Well, I'm always here for you. But I do miss my Mimi. I hope she comes back soon." Sian said.

Although her hard exterior suggested she was tough through and through, she was soft gooey caramel in the middle; she smiled and hugged her friend.

"Mimi, we need you!" Steph shouted; she had temporarily removed herself from Thomas' face to shout for Mia.

"What's going on?" Mia asked, stepping back into the garage.

"We think Holly is passed out in the toilet." she said, pointing at the closed door.

"Ri-ight." Mia said.

"Kelly says you can kick the door down." Steph replied, gesturing towards it.

"Why me?" Mia asked.

"Because Kelly said to so." Steph said, wrapping herself around Thomas again. Mia grimaced, then stepped forward to knock on the door.

"Holly?" she called. "Holls? Anyone home?"

No answer. Not even a groan. Mia looked at Sian, who shrugged. "Might as well. You wouldn't forgive yourself if she passed out and died, would you?"

"True." Mia said, facing the door again. She balanced herself, took a deep breath and booted the door, hard. It swung open straight away, narrowly missing Holly, who was passed out on the floor with her face on the toilet bowl.

"Wow," Sian said, as Holly snored from her post. "She's got class."

"Holly?" Mia said again, shaking her. "Holly, your Mam's here."

"I'm up, I'm up." Holly repeated. There was hair stuck to her face, just below her glazed over eyes.

"Come on, let's get you some water." Mia said, hauling her off the ground.

As Mia helped sober Holly up, she watched as her friends made the most of the party. Steph disappeared with Thomas, which was hilarious, and Sian, to Mia's surprise, was pulled out of the door by Kelly. It turns out they spent some time together in the back of Kelly's fiesta.

"I thought Kelly had a boyfriend?" Mia asked the half-conscious Holly.

"They're in an open relationship." Holly mumbled, as her head nodded and collided with the wall.

"You don't say." Mia said, checking her phone.

[Sian] Gone home with K. lol. See you in the morning.

[Mia] Gonna stay with Holly. Have fun. Use protection.

[Sian] Will do. Don't want no babies here.

Mia laughed, overly impressed.

"What are you laughing at?" Sam asked, dropping down onto the floor in front of her. The crowd had thinned, meaning there was a little more space to spread out.

"Sian went home with Kelly." Mia replied, trying to keep Sam in focus so there was only one of her.

"Really?" Sam slurred, swaying in her cross-legged position. "I'm jealous."

Mia looked confused. "You wanted to go home with Kelly?"

"No."

"You wanted to go home with Sian?" Mia asked.

"No."

"Then what?"

"It would just be nice to go home with *someone*." Sam pouted and Mia looked away from her.

"Oh."

Mia felt tension but was sure it was one-sided. The world was not that kind.

"How are you getting home?" she asked.

"I don't know." Sam replied, looking up at the ceiling. "My phone died, and Thomas is gone so I really need to figure out, you know, where I'm gonna stay."

"I'll order you an Uber." Mia smiled, ever helpful.

"Ah, ok, yeah, thanks." Sam replied, shuffling on the spot.

Mia tapped away on her phone.

"I've booked you an Uber for 3:05." Mia said, proudly.

"Thanks." Sam narrowed her eyes with a grin. "Why the :05?"

"Erm, it's just what we do." Mia replied, frowning. *Wasn't it?* she thought.

"But, why?" Sam chuckled, hugging her knees.

"Because, if you book it for, say, eleven, you're never ready, so you give yourself an extra five minutes." Mia wanted to stop every word as they tumbled out of her mouth.

"That may be the most ridiculously logical thing I've ever heard." Sam concluded. "And I love it."

At 3:05, on the dot, Mia stood outside waiting for the Uber driver with Sam.

"Bye, Mimi." Sam hugged her, slightly awkwardly, before jumping in the taxi and driving off with Saif.

As Mia waved to her the devil on Mia's shoulder returned: *You should have kissed her.*

"Shut up." Mia said.

**

When she woke up in the morning, in Kelly's bed, Mia was still chuckling at Sian's antics. A huge stain ran across the wall where, Mia assumed, someone had tripped and thrown their drink ahead of them and the light fixture was hanging down. At the foot of the bed, all the bottles for recycling were stacked high in boxes and there was cereal crunched into the carpet. The smell was overpowering, a mix of sick, sweat and vodka. Before going to bed, Mia had cleared a small patch of shelf to put her belongings on, so they were relatively safe. To the right of the shelf there was a foot shaped hole in the wall. There was no way they were getting their deposit back.

[Mia] I'm still so impressed. Hope you had a good night.

[Sian] It was so good. Currently making her breakfast.

Her phone made a 'whoop' noise as Sian sent a photo of the delicious food she was making.

[Mia] That looks incredible. Will you send some over?

[Sian] Get your ass home, there might be some left if you're quick.

[Mia] I don't think I'll be doing anything quick today.

[Sian] Is Holly alive yet?

[Mia] Nope. I've got a bin and water at the ready for her. No bacon though.

[Sian] That is going to be one painful hangover! Haha.

[Sian] Also, this came for you.

Another 'whoop,' another photo: it was a postcard from her Dad:

Hey love,

I hope you're keeping well and that the British weather isn't too shit for you at the moment. Still loving life out here right now, I've been working at a local dive school, all cash in hand, you know, so it's been great to pay the beer fund. I've met a great lass out here – name's Carina. She's from California. I'm thinking about heading over there for Christmas. If you want to join, let me know. I'm sure I can find the air fare for you if you want to come out. Would be great to see you. Love to you, Charlie and the girls.

Love, Dad x

As she day-dreamed about California, Holly groaned beside her.

"Morning, sunshine." Mia grinned, filming her friend as she emerged back into the world.

"What's going on?" Holly croaked. "What are you doing in Kelly's bed?"

"You're welcome." Mia replied. "I was making sure you didn't die in the night."

"Where's Kelly, like?" she asked.

"Enjoying Sian's company." Mia chuckled.

"Damn," Holly croaked, pushing herself into a more upright position. "That girl is good."

Once Holly was dressed, in an old tracksuit and a messy pineapple bun, they wandered out to the local Tesco Express, with its temptress of a bakery section. Unable to help herself, Mia picked out two pain au chocolate and placed them in a brown paper bag with the tongs. Without Sian's breakfast, hangovers were not the same, but the tasty pastry treat would make up for some of it.

Looking truly in pain, Holly stood perfectly still near the milk with her eyes closed.

"What's up with you?" Mia asked, stepping closer to her friend.

"I need to fart." Holly whispered, holding her beaten stomach, opening her eyes. "It feels like I'm going to burst."

"Can you wait until we're outside?"

"I don't think I can." They were in the back of the store. "I don't even think I can move."

"Well, stay away from me." Mia warned, moving back. Holly looked side to side then let it go. It was rancid.

"Eurgh! Jesus, Holls!" Mia squealed. "What have you been eating?! That's the worst smell I've ever smelled!"

"Shh, man!" Holly hissed, ushering her up the aisle. "Just walk."

They walked quickly up the long aisle, as a young child and his mother rounded the bend to where they had been. Upon smelling the horrific stench, the child promptly vomited on the shop floor, much to Holly's embarrassment. Steering Holly towards the self-checkout machines, Mia's eyes poured with tears. Once they were out of the shop, Mia laughed so hard it hurt her sides, her body straining to manage the level of laughter.

"I think that was the best thing I've ever seen." Mia said, wiping away the tears.

"I've never been so mortified in my entire life." Holly chuckled in disbelief.

"Even when I'm old and grey and not able to remember much, I'll still remember that." Mia laughed.

"Don't you dare tell anyone!" Holly warned.

"Mate, I'm telling everyone, I'm just sad I didn't get it on video." Mia howled.

Holly scowled.

Smiling sweetly, Mia handed a peace offering... "Pain au chocolate?" ...then kept on laughing.

Chapter Nineteen

Somewhere south of the river, one of the main roads was blocked following a seven-car pileup, Northumbria Police had busted a paedophile ring and one of the metro stations had suffered significantly at the hands of vandals. Destruction, misery, despair then the weather; Mia exchanged the News on TV for *The Simpsons* on her phone and settled in to watch another iconic episode.

Mia had accompanied Steph to the walk-in centre after her night with Thomas led to a water infection, alongside the regret. Because Mia had forgotten her headphones, she was having to watch on silent with subtitles, which meant she kept getting distracted.

There were retro posters on the wall, advising against various things like smoking and unprotected sex. When she noticed the large stonewall poster, she looked away quickly, as though someone may have noticed her reading it and made assumptions. '*God I'm pathetic.*' Mia thought, hanging her head in shame.

She thought about the irony of how a TV show you are watching can relate to the issues in real life so poignantly. The *Simpsons* episode she was watching contained a key story about gay marriage and how family members were struggling to accept the marriage. Mia thought about Molly. If her sister could not accept her Dad, how would she accept a gay sister too? Maybe it would push her over the edge.

"All done?" Mia asked, clapping her hands on her knees to stand, as Steph reappeared.

"Yeah," Steph said, holding up the white bag. "They've given me anti-biotics."

They pushed the door out of the waiting room and onto the street.

"Have you learned your lesson about sleeping with toy boys?" Mia asked.

"He's not exactly a toy boy." Steph defended herself as they turned back towards the metro station.

"He's eighteen!" Mia replied. "You're twenty-two. I mean, that's quite a jump."

"It wouldn't be such a big jump if we were, like, eighty-four and eighty-eight." she argued.

"Yeah, but you're not." Mia pointed out.

When they arrived at the station, the Metro was just pulling in.

"Come on, we can make it if we run." Mia said, sprinting for the bridge.

"Eurgh." Steph moaned and ran after her, to avoid waiting fifteen minutes for another Metro.

Out of breath and starting to see stars, they made it to their seats. Others in the carriage stared at them as they wheezed, with Steph squeezing her bag of antibiotics with every inhalation.

"We should have just waited." Steph coughed.

"I need to run more." Mia puffed.

As they recovered, they passed the Blue Reef Aquarium en route to Tynemouth. Between Cullercoats and Tynemouth was one of the prettiest views from the metro, looking out over the sea.

"What time are you at work?" Steph asked.

"I'm gonna have to head down when we get back." Mia made a face.

"I'm so pleased I'm off today." Steph sighed, sinking back on her seat.

"Rub it in, why don't you?" Mia replied.

"You've got three days off when we go to Edinburgh!" Steph said, raising her eyebrows.

"So do you." Mia laughed. "I'm just being lazy today. I fancy heading for a run then snuggling up with cake and chocolate."

"I might do just that, then I can properly rub it in."

"You're pure evil sometimes." Mia laughed.

They hopped off the metro at Tynemouth station and quickly nipped home. Steph walked halfway to work with Mia so she could buy her chocolate from the Co-op.

"Enjoy work." Steph said.

"Enjoy your chocolate, you bitch." Mia smiled and waved to her.

When Sian finished work, she skipped down the wooden steps to see Mia at Josie's.

"I've made a decision for you." Sian said, waltzing up to the bar as Mia displayed the fresh scones.

"Huh?" Mia said. "What are you talking about?"

"We need to get you set up on tinder." Sian said, thoughtfully.

"Er-no, I don't think so." Mia replied, shaking her head.

"Come on," Sian whined, sliding a hand on the counter towards her. "What's the harm in window shopping?"

"It's too soon."

"That's why it's window shopping and not actually dating anyone." Sian said. "You never know, you might see someone you really like the look of."

"I'm okay, bud." Mia said, rolling her eyes and stacking trays.

Sian was like a persistent child, carrying on the conversation until they got home. Luckily, Jay had not been at work or she would have joined in too.

"Fine!" Mia finally agreed. "You can set up a profile, but I get to check it all before you post it."

"That's fine by me." Sian ripped Mia's phone out of her hand and threw herself on the sofa to get to work.

"What kind of guy are you looking for?" Sian asked.

"I don't know." Mia replied, getting drawn into the conversation she had wanted to avoid.

"How can you not know?" Sian asked, tapping away on the phone. "What floats your boat in a guy? Brown hair? Blonde hair? Tall? Short? Muscly? Skinny? Beard? No beard?"

"Erm, I don't know." Mia said.

"Right, sit down and close your eyes." Sian said, and Mia did as she was told. "Now, I want you to picture your perfect guy."

Sam popped into her head. Every time Mia tried to banish her, she crept back in from the other side. *'Guys' sometimes meant 'girls,' right?* she thought.

"Okay?"

"Now, describe them to me." Sian ordered, waiting eagerly for the description.

Mia took a deep breath and kept her eyes closed. *Here goes*, she thought.

"What if none of that floats my boat?" Mia asked, she could feel her skin flushing and her breathing was quickening slightly, involuntarily.

"What do you mean?" Sian asked, still not looking up from the phone.

"I mean, what if no guys float my boat." Mia explained and, for the first time, Sian looked up at her with a confused frown but did not fill the space with another question. Mia kept her eyes tight shut. "What if I don't think I like guys anymore?"

Sian swung her legs off the sofa, put the phone down and clasped her hands together. "Erm-I would say that's completely fine, obviously."

She paused, clearly trying to find the correct words to continue with. "Do you mean in an asexual kind of way or in another way?"

"I think in a 'I think I'm gay' kind of way." Mia said. She had finally said it.

She opened one eye to look at Sian, who wore the expression of someone struggling to add some difficult math.

"That's great, bud." Sian said, with a soft smile.

"Are you shocked?" Mia asked, stealing another glance at Sian.

Sian let a laugh escape her. "Ha! Kind of, yeah, I'm just angrier at my own malfunctioning Gay-dar!"

Mia chuckled in response.

"Have you told anyone else yet?" Sian asked.

"Freddie knows. And I was honest with Jake when we broke up." Mia said, remembering the pain of hurting him.

"Well, I'm honoured I was third." Sian said.

**

With less than a week to go until their visit to Edinburgh, Mia was getting antsy in anticipation of her birthday weekend. When the whole gang got together there was always chaos in some form. Maria had done most of the planning; Holly and Sian had been banned from going anywhere near any of the plans. Sian favoured drinks in strip clubs and Holly had once accidently booked a room in a brothel instead of a hostel when they were travelling.

Originally, they were planning on having a party at their flat. But they wanted to go somewhere they would not have to worry about the noise level or the clean up afterwards. Also, Zoe had a habit of vomiting and had once vomited straight up a newly painted wall in Holly's old student flat.

Six days before they were due to leave, on the Saturday night, Carol and Maria were round at the flat. The girls had really taken to gathering in the kitchen, enjoying the fire, the music and the easy access to food. Carol had started making a packing list for everyone.

Steph had stayed in the living room, immersed in her laptop world, when Mia dropped in to check on her.

"Hey, bud, how you doing?" she asked, leaning on the door frame.

"Fine, yeah why?" Steph said, not looking up from her laptop.

"It's not like you to sit on your own in the living room while everyone else is in the kitchen." Mia replied.

"No, really, I'm fine." Steph said, clicking away. "I'm just busy."

"What are you doing?" Mia asked, cocking her head.

"Did I tell you a recently rediscovered SIMs?"

"No?" Mia said, flopping down next to her on the sofa to spy over her shoulder. "Was this before or after the Dimitri fiasco?" Mia asked. The roughest days had passed by enough for them to talk about it now.

"It was actually just before." Steph said. "I saw someone post about it on their Insta story and I dug my old one out. I forgot how addictive it was."

"Ooh, come on then, show me your family." Mia said, shuffling closer so she was snuggled into Steph's side.

"Well," Steph began. "I made me, you and Sian. And I did have Dimitri too."

"What do you mean you 'did have?" Mia asked. "I thought once you had them, you had them?"

"Oh no." Steph replied. "It's hard but you can kill them. I drowned him in the sea."

Mia gave Steph a slightly concerned side glance, thankful she meant in the game and not in real life.

"Are those jet skis?" Mia asked, pointing to the screen.

"Yeah, we have jet skis, a boat and a beach house." Steph replied then proceeded to talk Mia through the ins and outs of their entire SIMs lifestyle. Their virtual selves were living in the lap of luxury.

"Back in a minute, just taking Charlie for a wee!" Sian called, stepping out the front door.

"That sounds like a good plan." Carol said, nipping upstairs herself to the loo. Maria was the only one left in the kitchen when a blood curdling scream came through the wall.

"OH MY GOD! MIA! MIA!" Maria cried and Mia leapt off the sofa. "Mia! There's blood everywhere!"

"What's happened?" Mia shouted, running through as fast as her legs would carry her.

Maria was standing in the middle of the kitchen, clutching her left hand and staring at Mia in shock and fear. Carol came running down the stairs, fastening her trousers as she did so; Steph had thrown her laptop across the living room floor.

"What have you done?" Mia asked, stepping forward and lightly taking Maria's hand in hers.

"I was just chopping avocado and my hand slipped. The knife went through my finger."

True to Maria's story, there was a knife sized slice down her index finger, right to the bone.

"Let me have a look." Carol said, transforming into her former nursing self. "I think you're going to have to go to A and E."

"Will I need stitches?" Maria asked, looking sick.

"They should just glue it, don't worry." Carol said, turning to get her keys. "Come on, I'll drive you. I'll just have to drop you off though; the parking is terrible up there."

"Mimi, will you come too?" Maria asked. "I don't want to go in on my own."

"Of course."

Wrapping her hand in a tea towel, they made for the hospital. And, for the second time that week, Mia found herself in a waiting room.

"You know what I wish?" Maria said, clutching her hand.

"That you hadn't put a knife through your finger?" Mia said.

"Well, that," Maria sniffed. "But also, that I'd been cutting a less middle-class fruit. I mean, an avocado, come on."

They laughed, keeping spirits up until her skin could be glued back together.

**

After work on Sunday, while Mia was trying to decide what to do with her Monday off, Fred popped up on her phone screen.

[Fred] Fancy a road trip?

[Mia] Ooh, where you thinking?

[Fred] You free tonight/tomorrow?

[Mia] Of course.

[Fred] I'll pick you up at 8pm. Wear your walking boots and bring your camping stuff!

True to his word, Fred arrived at Mia's just before 8pm.

"This is all very exciting." Mia said, throwing her bag over her shoulder and onto the back seat.

"I thought we were due a spontaneous adventure." Fred smiled. "We've been far too boring in our routines lately."

"Am I allowed to know where we're going?" Mia asked, as they pulled out of the parking space.

"Not yet." he said.

Mia wiggled with excitement; she loved her adventures with Fred. They always ended up in random places, usually somewhere in Northumberland. More so when they were teenagers, they had a habit of getting in the car and seeing where they ended up. As long as they had told Grandma and Gramps, they were free to roam.

"If I pull up outside the Co-op, will you jump out and get the snacks for the road?" Fred asked, executing a jerky five-point turn in the street.

Mia nodded and dug around for her purse.

The goody bag she made consisted of four bottles of coke – two diet, two not, a tube of salt and vinegar pringles, chocolate buttons, some grapes and treats for Charlie. She also grabbed some bread, cheese and ham for sandwiches.

"Why the grapes?" Fred asked.

Mia shrugged. "I thought we could pretend to be healthy."

Driving west, they headed for Newcastle city centre and drove straight through it.

"Am I allowed to know where we are going *now*?" Mia asked. Charlie was strapped in the back seat, excited for the adventure ahead of them.

"I know you've been saying for ages that you wanted to go back to Sycamore Gap, so I thought we would finally go!" Fred said, with a smile.

"Oh my God! Yes!" Mia squealed.

Sycamore Gap was a section of Hadrian's Wall, the famous and historical Roman wall that ran from Bowness on Solway to Wallsend. In the gap between two hills, a beautiful Sycamore tree sat; hence the name. A state-of-the-art youth hostel and visitors centre stood nearby at Once Brewed. When Mia's Grandad had died, the family donated towards the centre in his name. When Fred and Mia were kids, they spent hours visiting English Heritage sites with their families and had particularly loved Roman history.

As they drove along the winding road towards the west, Fred blasted some old club anthems, favouring N-Dubz classics, and Mia broke into the pringles early.

Fred had booked a pitch at a hostel for the evening out in rural Northumberland; Once Brewed had no campsite. While the main hostel sat atop a hill, overlooking the stunning rolling fields and the Cheviot Hills, the camping ground was nestled in the wooded area down a steep path. A huge stone fire pit invited them over. They dropped their bags, tied Charlie to a tree and started setting up their small three-man tent. Upon finding the flattest patch of ground, they were satisfied and knocked the pegs into the ground.

"I love this so much!" Mia said, rummaging for a good stick to put her marshmallows on. She was impressed with the fire she had built, with the help of some fire lighters.

"Me too." Fred said, ripping into the marshmallow bag. "I thought it would do you some good."

Mia loved camping; she felt at home in the woods. The crunch of sticks and leaves under foot, the twitter of the birds, the mixed smell of the trees and vegetation; the fire dancing in the dark. The only downside was the stench of the fire that clung to their clothes when they retreated into the tent and their sleeping bags.

Just before midnight, Mia nipped out of the tent for a wee in the woods. Between a gap in the trees, she caught sight of a star shooting across the sky.

"Freddie!" Mia said. "Freddie! You need to come out and see the sky! It's amazing!"

Immediately, Fred began to rustle inside the tent and started unzipping the door.

"Wait! No! Wait a minute!" Mia shouted.

"Do you want me out there or not?" Fred asked.

"I do," Mia replied, redoing her trousers. "I just needed to finish weeing!"

Fred waited.

"Are you done yet?" he called.

"Hold your horses!" she shouted back, wiggling back into her trousers. "Right, you're safe!"

They wrapped up warm and wandered up the hill towards the picnic benches and viewing area. The only light was from their Maglite's – the tiny torches they were gifted as children from Mia's Dad. From their vantage point, they sat and admired the starry sky. Another three people from inside the hostel came out to join and look up at the majesty in front of them. Charlie, wondering why on earth they had left the tent in the middle of the night, curled up on the pebbled floor for a snooze. The sky was incredibly clear, with the rolling hills and green fields at its feet.

"Sometimes I forget how beautiful our world is." Mia breathed, hugging one leg on top of the bench.

"I think this is one of the best skies I've seen." Fred replied, craning his neck to explore the constellations above him.

"I wish I could feel this relaxed all the time." Mia said, appreciating how calm her body felt. "Thank you for bringing us back here."

"Any time." Fred smiled, and they snuggled together to admire the universe.

**

When they approached the gate, Fred clocked his eyes on the warning sign about snakes.

"Snakes? Are you kidding me?" he squeaked, pointing to the gate.

"How have you missed these signs before?" Mia asked. "There's always been snakes."

"Why am I just learning this now?" Fred asked, looking horrified.

"Because you're painfully unobservant?" Mia suggested. "Just tuck your trousers into your socks, you'll be fine. They normally run away from humans anyway."

"Oh, yeah, I'm sure that's true, snakes *run* away from humans." he mumbled, tucking in his trousers.

"You know what I mean."

Most of the mud was dried solid, making the gate entrances difficult to walk through. They kept Charlie on a lead, making the descents down each of the hills interesting.

"I swear, I'm gonna go arse over tits soon!" Mia said, as she struggled to stay upright with Charlie pulling on his lead. The three hills were very steep, with some stone steps helping under foot, but they made it to Sycamore Gap, digging out their sandwiches and remaining goody bag from the day before.

"Cheese or ham?" Mia asked, offering them to Fred. Charlie chomped away on his giant jumbone.

"You even have to ask?" Fred said, graciously taking the ham. "Thanks."

"You're welcome." Mia replied, biting into her cheese sandwich.

Chapter Twenty

After sorting her smoke-filled clothes from camping, Mia opened the doors in her room and sat in the sun shining through the balcony. Charlie took advantage too, lying in the space at Mia's feet. After their jaunt in the country, Mia felt so relaxed, like she had been sitting in a hot bath. She rolled up her sleeves in attempt to blur her solid tan lines and ended up dozing off for a short time, until Steph and Sian barged in the front door, looking slightly worse for wear.

"What the hell happened to you two?" Mia asked. Steph and Sian were crawling in the front door. Sian looked immensely pleased with herself, while Steph looked like she had seen a ghost.

"Oh, Mi, do we have a story for you." Sian said, throwing herself onto the sofa. "Literally get the popcorn and we'll tell you everything."

"Popcorn at this time of day?" Mia asked.

"You need it for this one." Sian said and Steph rolled her eyes.

"Okay, I'll get the popcorn, you guys go and get sorted." Mia said, moving through to the kitchen as the other two jogged up to their rooms.

By the time she had popped all the corns in the microwave, the other two had returned for story time. Mia loved it when Sian told the tales, she was such a good storyteller. The stories did not just have a start, middle and an end, but thousands of mini stories incorporated too.

"So, last night, we went along to the Wine Cellar." Sian began and Mia dropped a few popcorn clusters in her mouth. "Initially, we were only going in for one, but you know that never happens." Sian looked ecstatic; Steph looked mortified the tale was being retold.

"We ended up on a bar crawl and accidentally crashed a wake." Sian said, with a huge grin.

"You guys crashed a funeral?" Mia asked, grinning back.

"Not on purpose!" Steph defended their actions. "We didn't know it was a funeral."

"You still crashed a wake." Mia pointed out. "Did all the people in black not give it away?"

"Oh, wait, it gets better." Sian said. Her grin stretched from ear to ear. "So, anyway, we were at this wake and I start chatting to the bar maid. Very long story short, I ended up going with her to the flat above the bar for a little bit. Meanwhile, knobhead over here-"

"I'll take over from here." Steph cut in before Sian started making up her own version of the story. "I went outside to see if I could smoke in peace. I had some cigarettes but no lighter, so I went over to this couple to ask them if they had one."

Mia grinned wider, wondering where the story was leading from here.

"They were actually really cool. He was from Norway and she was from Ayre, up in Scotland. I just got chatting to them really, then one thing led to another and we ended up getting pretty drunk together.

When we ended the night, quite a way away from Tynemouth, they invited me to stay on their sofa."

Mia frowned. It was definitely a strange story but not as shocking as she expected.

Noticing her expression, Sian added: 'It gets better.' Steph glared at her.

"To put the cherry on top of the cake, I woke up this morning and I wasn't the only one in the living room. Guess who was sitting in the armchair opposite me eating his Weetabix." Steph said.

"Who?" Mia asked.

"Thomas."

"No-o!" Mia breathed. Sian nodded, looking exuberant.

"Yep." Steph said. "I went on the piss with Sam and Thomas' parents."

Mia and Sian roared with laughter, physically rolling in their seats.

"I swear, it gets better every single time I hear it." Sian said, wiping away a tear.

"Shut up, it was mortifying." Steph groaned, combing her fingers through her hair.

"What did Thomas say when you woke up?" Mia asked.

"Not much." Steph replied. "He went out pretty quickly."

"I'd love to have seen his reaction when he came downstairs and saw you asleep on the sofa." Sian said. "Was Sam there? I bet her reaction will be almost as good."

"God." Steph said, smacking her forehead. "I didn't even think about Sam. What the hell is she gonna say?"

"Probably nothing, to be honest." Sian said, suddenly dead pan.

"Yeah," Mia copied her expression. "I mean, you only shagged her brother and got drunk with her parents. What's weird about any of that?"

"I hate you both." Steph said, snatching the popcorn as they rolled around laughing again.

**

Most of the costumes were at the stage where they could be worn. On top of everything else, Carol was an amazing seamstress and had made all the costumes by hand. As showtime drew closer, she appeared more, sewing and stitching in between scenes, always beavering away to ensure everyone looked incredible. She had requested Mia to be fully painted that evening, to check how it looked with the costume.

"Wow, you really are *green*." Carol laughed, stepping back to admire her handy work.

Standing up and looking in the mirror, Mia saw herself fully as the Wicked Witch of the West for the first time.

"Woah! Look at my teeth! They look so white!" she stretched her mouth in her reflection. "Carol, this looks amazing, thank you." She skipped out of the bathroom, loving her costume.

"Right, everyone, we are getting really close to showtime now!" Angelika said commanding full attention. "I want to do a full run through, start to finish, no stops!"

Mia took a breath; the pressure was on.

"I'm going to keep a list of things that need improvement or that go wrong, and we'll have a debrief at the end. Any scenes that go wrong, we'll re-do them at the end."

A few times there were slight delays when people ran off the wrong side of the stage, when they needed to enter from the other side immediately after. A narrow corridor ran along the back of the stage, behind the scenery, and there were many uncomfortable encounters where they had to squeeze by each other. Though everything was hectic backstage, they tried their best to compose themselves on stage in front of Angelika; the more they got wrong, the more they would have to repeat and the later they would have to stay.

When Mia sung '*I'm not that girl,*' she poured her heart and soul into the song, stealing a glance at Sam mid-way through. Having the full costume made her feel more in tune with the character and seemed to give her more confidence.

During their 'interval' break, when Mia went to the toilet, she stood looking at it for a moment, wondering how she was going to touch things without getting it all green. In the end, the door handles, toilet flush and toilet roll all had smudges of green on them. She tried her best to wash them off, but it was a vicious circle. Eventually, when Sam came into the bathroom, she gave a hand with the cleaning process. Mia made a mental note not to allow her hands to be painted until actual show night from now on.

After they performed the whole show, Angelika only made them repeat two scenes, neither required Mia to push her vocal cords too hard. When they were released, Carol was ready for them. She stood backstage, by her clothes rail, ready to catch everyone's costumes, attaching their names before they were hung up. Most of the cast darted off to the pub as quick as they could, leaving only a handful in the theatre. Mia trudged back to the bathroom to start the task of cleaning herself.

Initially, Mia tried to wipe the paint off with makeup wipes, but it just seemed to smudge it more into her skin. Stripping down to her bra, she scrubbed with a flannel and soap, struggling to reach the back of her neck.

"Do you need a hand?" Sam offered; Mia had not realised she was leaning in the doorway and jumped.

"Jeez, you gave me a fright!" Mia breathed, clutching her partially green chest.

"Come here, give me some wipes." Sam laughed, and Mia was very aware she was half in her underwear. She breathed in slightly and moved her arm back, taking a sneaky look to check she had shaved her underarms; she had. "I'm sorry, but you look pretty ridiculous right now."

"What do you mean?" Mia feigned horror. "I was just about to walk home looking like this."

"I mean, if anyone was going to pull off this look it would be you." Sam said. "Do you have a bobble?"

"Yeah." Mia replied, handing her one.

"Kneel down, you're too tall up there." Sam said, and Mia did as she was told. Sam ran her hands under Mia's hair, bringing it all to lie down her back. "Wow, your hair is so long."

"Yeah." Mia chuckled, nervously. "I really need it cut."

"No, you don't, it's gorgeous." she said, admiring the golden sheet that fell in front of her. Once she was done, Sam tied Mia's hair in a bun and began clearing the green paint from Mia's neck, leaning so close Mia could feel her breath. Mia had some strong words to say to the butterflies in her stomach.

"What are you up to this week?" Mia asked. If she talked, it was a distraction.

"Oh, you know, this and that." she mumbled. "Work as usual, heading out with some mates on Friday, I've got a judo competition on Saturday."

"Judo?" Mia asked, clearing the paint around her eyes. "I didn't know you did judo. How long have you done that?"

"Oh, I've been doing it for years." Sam replied. "I'm not very good, but I love it."

"My mate does it too, she loves it, Jubeda Makhdoom?" Mia said.

"No way, you know Jay?" Sam gasped. "She's an absolute legend! Like, I wish I was half as good as she is."

"Yeah, we work together, she's mint!" Mia agreed.

"She just set up a new initiative, did you see it?" Sam asked. "Trying to get more women, particularly Muslim women into sport. How cool is that?"

"Like you said: *legend.*"

<u>Chapter Twenty-One</u>

For the weekend they were away, Fred's Gramps had agreed to have Charlie. They had a black Labrador themselves called Geordie, whom Charlie adored, so Gramps was happy to have two companions for the weekend. Before leaving the flat, Mia made the mistake of winding Charlie up about where they were going. He wiggled so much that she could barely get his lead on him.

"Bye, boy." Sian and Steph both cooed over him as they said their goodbyes. Mia had packed him a small bag and Sian tucked his favourite monkey toy on top of it.

It was a beautiful evening. When Mia set off, she walked down to the river's edge rather than directly towards Tynemouth Front Street. As she looked out over the sea, the local dolphin pod danced beyond the piers, enjoying the small waves trailing behind the pilot vessel. Charlie dragged her along, desperately pulling her towards the sea.

"No, boy, we aren't swimming today." she said, giving his head a stroke.

As she walked past the walls of St George's Church, Mia looked over them into the garden. A public footpath ran through the grounds and she diverted off to take it. When she reached the open door, something compelled her to go inside. She tied Charlie up to the bench in the front garden and stepped inside. Other than a pigeon flying between the rafters, she was the only one in there.

The interior was stunning. Huge stained-glass windows decorated the walls and were visible through immaculate stone arches. It could easily seat three hundred people with perfectly varnished wooden pews stretching the length of the church.

She had never really been a religious person. Her Grandma had encouraged her to go to church on the key dates in the calendar like Easter and for a Christmas carol service, but her Dad was a strong atheist. Walking down the marble aisle, she admired the beautiful building, hoping the pigeon would not poo on her as it flew around. In the far-right corner, there was a black metal stand for lighting candles, and she lit one, making a small donation for the notion, then took a seat in the second row of pews. Her mind wandered. She had always pictured getting married in a church like St George's. But maybe now she never could. Was it a choice? Had she not been attracted to men in the past? Or was that what was always wrong with the relationships? If hell was real, would she go there?

Leaving her candle behind, she walked out the church and back to a waiting Charlie. He wiggled with excitement and put a smile back on her face. They turned along the seafront, walking until they crossed the beautiful smell of the bakery. Holding Charlie on a short lead, she knocked and walked in to meet Fred.

"Happy Birthday Eve!" Mia cried out to Fred, pulling him into a hug.

"Happy Birthday Eve, Eve to you!" Fred said back, lifting her up in the embrace.

"Is your liver ready for the weekend?" Mia asked, stepping back from the hug.

Fred looked to consider for a moment. "I hope so. I'm stocked up on insulin, just in case."

"That's good." Mia said. "You dying would really put a downer on the weekend."

That night, they had chosen to have their Harry Potter building session in the bakery while Fred's Gramps tried out some new recipes on them. Sitting at the picnic table, they worked, while Gramps walked in and out with new treats for them.

"Freddie, I think I have a crush." Mia said, trying to put together one of the windows on the castle.

"Oh?" Fred replied, concentrating on another window. "On who?"

"You remember Sam?" Mia asked.

"Oh, yeah. She does theatre stuff with you, right?" Fred said, flicking through the instruction book.

"Yeah, that's her." Mia said.

"Is she gay?" Fred asked.

"No, definitely not." Mia replied, making a face.

"Well, that's not a great crush to have then, is it?" Fred said.

"I mean, I don't really know many gay people, only Sian but she's like my sister, there's nothing there at all." Mia replied. "Also, I don't think you can steer the crush boat towards certain people."

"No, but you can window shop a little and see what's out there." Fred replied. "You're not gonna look for meat in the vegetable section, are you?"

"What the hell are you on about?" Mia asked, frowning.

"I just mean, why not try and find a girl you like who has a chance of liking you back?" Fred asked. "Then, who knows? You could maybe even go on a date?"

"Oh no, I'm not ready for that." Mia said, shaking her head.

"Maybe not now, but you might be eventually." Fred pointed out. Mia squirmed.

"Have you had any luck on Tinder?" Fred asked, searching through the spare pieces.

"I haven't really looked on it to be honest." Mia said.

"Didn't Sian set it up for you?" Fred asked.

"Yeah, she did." Mia replied. "But I don't know, I'm just not really sure if I could go on a date with a girl. Like, what do you do? I don't know this game. I only know the boy game. I've pretty much got that down to a T."

"Practice makes perfect I suppose." Fred shrugged. "What was your first date with a guy? I bet that didn't go perfectly first time."

"Oh God, yeah it was awkward as hell." Mia remembered. "We went to the cinema, which was nice, but he went to kiss me, and he poked me in the eye with his nose."

"How have you not told me that before?" Fred laughed.

"I don't know." Mia replied. "I like to keep you in the dark about some things."

"Ahh, that is my downfall. You know everything." Fred said.

"Anyway, let's have a look at your phone."

They took a short pause to flick through her Tinder app.

"You've got a match!" Fred said.

"How do you know?" she asked, scooting closer to him.

"Because it says, you dinosaur." he rolled his eyes at her. "She's cute."

She looked over his shoulder. *Yeah, she is.* she thought.

"Why don't you message her back?" Fred suggested.

"No, I wouldn't know what to say." Mia said, taking her phone back and stowing it away in her back pocket. He decided not to push her anymore about it.

"What about you and Sam?" Fred asked. "Could there be anything there?"

"I wish." she sighed. "But I'm nine thousand percent sure she's straight."

"Are you sure? Or is it just a feeling you have?"

"Just a feeling, I guess." she mumbled.

"Well, maybe you're wrong." he shrugged, and her mind began to wander back to the places it went at night.

**

A mere few hours before they were due to go, Mia's duffel bag lay empty on the floor beside her bed. A mountain of clothes was piled on top of her duvet as she tried to decide what to take with her. In true Steph form, she was packed, organised and with her bags at the front door; Sian had to be convinced to take more than just a clean shirt, a change of underwear and a toothbrush.

"What more do I need?" She asked, adamant she had covered all bases.

"Maybe something to sleep in?" Steph suggested.

"What's wrong with sleeping in boxers?" Sian asked.

"Do you really want to sleep topless in a shared room with Carol and Fred?" Steph said.

"Oh, come on, Carol's an ex-nurse, she's seen tits before, and I'd hope Fred has." Sian replied.

"At least take an extra t-shirt, maybe two so you have a different outfit for the second night." Steph was starting to mother her.

"Here's an idea. Why don't you just pack for me?" Sian asked. "Then you're happy and I can go and do a beer run."

"Fine by me." Steph replied with a shrug. So, as Steph packed for her, Sian dragged Mia to the Co-op for some boxes of beer.

By 3pm, they were outside the flat with bags and beer playing Tetris again with their belongings. Piling into two rusty old Hyundai's, one Holly's, one Carol's, they started their journey up to Edinburgh. It was a little over one hundred miles from Tynemouth to the Scottish capital; Holly had prepared a mixed playlist especially for the drive. Fred and Sian had already cracked open beers before they crossed into Northumberland, possibly to deal with the terrible mix of music playing; Holly was an unexpected opera fan.

"Can we please, please, please change the music?" Sian begged, covering her ears in the back seat.

"Driver chooses, sorry." Holly replied, with a flip of her middle finger.

"Yeah, well, I'd like to see you fight me." Sian said, ripping the chord out of Holly's phone and replacing it with her own.

"Hey!" Holly shouted.

"I'm sorry, I just couldn't listen to anymore opera." Sian replied. They continued up the road to the sounds of Smash Mouth with 'All Star.' Holly was even more cautious with her driving when they crossed the border, Scotland seemed to have a speed camera every four miles.

"Did that one just flash?" Holly asked as they passed a camera.

"I think it did." Mia said, pointlessly turning around to look back towards the camera.

"But I was doing fifty-eight and it's a sixty!" Holly said. "God, I cannot get another speeding fine. I've already done the bloody speed awareness course."

"I'm sure it'll be fine, maybe it was a test." Mia replied, trying to reassure Holly, who stressed all the way to the city centre.

They parked a mere five-minute walk from where they were staying. The city was still beautifully decorated following the Edinburgh Military Tattoo, which ended the week before, but it was packed with tourists still for the bank holiday weekend. Deep in the heart of the Old Town, halfway up one of the winding, cobbled streets, sat The One Edinburgh Hostel. It was a place for people all over the world. A huge map stretched across the wall in the entrance and people could place a flag on the map to show where they were from. When they stumbled through the narrow doorway in reception, a young, bespectacled hipster greeted them warmly. He looked like a thinner, less dishevelled version of *Harry Potter* and his accent was somewhere between Canadian and Dutch.

"Hello! Welcome to The One Edinburgh Hostel." he sang, clapping his hands together merrily. "Are you all checking in?"

"No, we-" Sian began but Carol gave her a nudge before she could continue her sarcasm.

They were shown to one of the largest rooms in the hostel that contained six beds, with two bunk beds and two singles; it had a sliding wooden door leading off to a small toilet. Holly and Mia were staying in the small private room next door with the double bed. As the two snoring members of the group, they had been exiled. The larger room had a small kitchenette and Carol began cooking almost immediately, stating how they needed to line their stomachs. Nobody argued. As she bustled around, refusing any help, they poured over their slim outfit choices and lazily played *Psych!* on their phones.

"I packed last night, and I still don't know what I want to wear?" Mia grumbled, hands on hips as she studied her options.

"What are your choices?" Holly asked, throwing herself onto the bed.

"This, this or this." Mia said, pointing to each outfit laid out individually.

"I'd go with this one for tonight." Holly said. "You'll probably be drunker tomorrow, so I'd get the white outfit out of the way before then."

"Good plan." Mia agreed, storing the other two outfits.

"God, I'm shattered." Holly said, stretching out on the bed. "That drive took it out of me more than a thought it would."

"You need a beer." Mia said, tearing into the box at the foot of the bed and throwing her a bottle. "It'll be a little warm but get it down you!"

Holly did as she was told, and Mia opened one for herself then slunk through to the kitchen to put the rest in the fridge, leaning around Carol as she began cooking.

"Right, everyone, grab a bowl!" Carol chimed when dinner was ready. Fred was by her side in an instant – before the word 'bowl' had left Carol's lips.

"Don's a lucky man, C." Fred grinned, gladly accepting his food.

"It's only pasta." Carol replied. "And he knows how lucky he is."

Dinner being served was like another scene out of Cheaper by the Dozen with so many mouths to feed. An assembly line was set up, with Carol serving the pasta and the bowls being passed along, until everyone had food in front of them.

"Thanks, Carol." was mumbled around the room.

Another assembly line formed to wash, dry and put away the dishes before everyone temporarily dispersed.

While Carol and Sian napped and others showered, Mia enjoyed the outdoor space with Holly, Maria and some cold beers. The ordinarily whitewashed wall had been coated in spray painted art, reaching up to the top windows of the hostel.

"I think this is one of the nicest hostels we've been to." Holly said, looking up at their surroundings.

They were sitting on the picnic benches on the decking out the back of the hostel. Old trees and buildings entwined above them; branches were littered with fairy lights.

"Yeah, it's a bit nicer than that place we stayed at in Germany. Do you remember?"

"Where we refused to pay extra for the bedding?" Holly laughed. "Thank God we'd brought blankets with us."

"Dad, actually, sent me another postcard the other day." Mia said, taking a swig. "He's thinking of heading over to California with his new girlfriend. Fancy it? We haven't adventured for a while."

"Yes! Oh my God, yes. When?!" Holly said, leaping to life.

"Alright, chill out." Mia laughed. "I think he's heading over for Christmas, but I don't know how long he's staying. I think he'll be quite flexible."

"Well, I'm keen for whatever and whenever." Holly said, lying back on the bench.

"When are you jetting off again?" Mia asked Maria.

"In a couple of weeks, I can't wait." she smiled. Her older sister, Cora, lived in Japan, working as a teacher.

"How long are you going for?" Holly asked from her perch.

"Three weeks." Maria squeaked. "I can't wait to see Tokyo!"

"Argh," Holly groaned. "I'm literally so jealous."

Later in the evening, they were deep in the depths of Hostel, in the basement. It had been transformed into a bar, aptly nicknamed 'The Rave Cave,' with sticky floors and cheap beer. With it being buried underground, there were no neighbours to consider when choosing the volume. Every inch of the thick walls was covered in scribbles and graffiti. A parting arch way split the bar in half. At the far side of the room, nestled in the small space, was a specially modified beer pong table, still coated in the stains of previous victories. A Portuguese stag party were playing terribly. In the corner by the door, sitting on the surrounding benches, the girls and Fred were playing a drinking game of Giant Jenga. It was so tall they had been given builders hats for their own safety.

Maria pulled a brick out: "Drink three fingers if you've had sex in a car."

Three of them drank.

Sian was next to go: "Categories. Okay – sex positions."

Carol groaned. "I don't know all the names."

"It's fine, Carol, if you don't know the name just act it out." Sian said with a wink.

"Oh, stop it." Carol laughed, tapping Sian's leg. "Behave yourself."

"Don't worry, Carol, that's exactly what I came to do." Sian grinned.

Poor Fred lost the round when he struggled to follow Holly's 'The Plough.'

"What even is 'The Plough?" he asked. "I think you made that one up."

"I didn't!" Holly protested, clapping her drink down. "Mia, come on, I need your help."

Mia obliged, playing the part of the man while they acted it out, obviously, fully clothed.

"See." Holly said. "The Plough."

"Ok, you got me." Fred laughed, putting his hands up in defeat.

"Who's next?" Zoe asked, bouncing on her seat.

"Steph, it's you." Mia pointed to the tower and Steph carefully chose her brick.

"Never have I ever – full circle." Steph read, placing it on the top.

"Ok, never have I ever had sex with my kids in the same room." Carol drank.

"Carol!" Sian gasped, throwing a hand over her mouth. "You absolute minx!"

"Oh, come on, Steph, that was mean." Carol scolded and Steph giggled.

"Fine, never have I ever had sex on a friend's bed." Carol said, looking smug as Steph drank.

"Who's?!" The circle echoed.

"Oh, does no one else know this?" Carol asked. Steph flushed scarlet and shook her head. "Oops, my mistake."

"Come on, who's was it?" Sian and Zoe prodded her wherever they could reach.

"Sorry, Mimi, it was yours." Steph, guiltily, admitted.

"What?! When?!" Mia asked, with her jaw hanging down. "What the hell?"

"I'm sorry, Mi." Steph whined, half guilty, half trying not to laugh as Sian howled beside her. "Just, your bedroom is so much closer to the front door."

"Did you at least change the sheets?"

Steph looked even guiltier. "Well, no, then you would have known I'd been in there."

"Ew, dude, no!"

The rest of the group were crying with laughter.

**

No one would have suspected that Steph's stomach had been lined; she was paralytic. She leaned forward and attempted to tap the top of Holly's bottle with her own, so it would overflow. Instead, she succeeded in knocking it clean out of her hands, only for it to smash on the floor.

"Mate! Come on, that was full!" Holly whined with a scowl.

"Sorry, I'll get you another." Steph apologised, standing up and swiftly tripping over her own feet. Mia only just caught her before she hit the floor.

"You sit still, I'll get you one." Mia said, rising to head for the bar; Fred followed her.

"Are you having a good birthday?" she asked.

"Yeah, you know I don't like the fuss though." he replied.

"I know you don't, but you can still have fun."

"And I am." he sipped his beer. "But I'll be happier when the torch passes to you."

Carol made until just before eleven before turning in while the others booked a taxi to the clubs for five past. As they climbed the stairs out of 'The Rave Cave,' Steph ping ponged off every wall.

"Do you think she'll manage to get out?" Maria looked mildly concerned.

"She'll be fine!" Sian replied, smacking Steph on the back and almost knocking her flying.

Mia caught her before she hit the ground.

"Act sober!" Mia hissed, pulling Steph towards the car.

They made their way to a pub first, to decide where they wanted to go. They had prematurely climbed into a taxi then realised that none of them knew Edinburgh night life at all. With pints, they piled into a booth together and began researching on their phones.

As their screens flicked to midnight, Holly appeared with a tray of shots.

"Happy Birthday, you massive cock!" she called, dishing out the drinks. "Welcome to the club 22."

"Tequila, really?" Mia said, twisting her face.

"Just shut up and drink it." Holly said. "Cheers!"

And they all drank, trying to hide how much the tequila burned their throats.

In true Sian form, she took control of the night and led them to a place Mia thought sounded like a strip club. It was on one of the main streets, where Edinburgh Castle could watch over their wrongdoings.

"This is my kind of place!" Sian said, rubbing her hands together as they walked in. Two girls were kissing while sharing a stool to one side and two boys were kissing on the opposing side. The walls were lined with old arcade games. A disused waltzer car was set up as a table and a machine on the wall dispensed single cigarettes for £1 each. Record covers spattered the ceiling as a mismatched jigsaw and a fairground horse was acting as the prime photo spot near the bar.

"Could you be any gay-er?" Holly laughed, as Sian scanned the room, like a lion surveying a herd of antelope before pouncing.

"Watch me." Sian tipped an imaginary hat in Holly's direction and made for the bar.

"What is she like?" Holly smirked, watching Sian saunter off.

"Hey, do you have a mirror in your pocket?" Sian asked her first potential lady-friend, who immediately grabbed her jeans to check.

"No, why?"

"Because I can see me in your pants." Sian said.

Mia laughed as she dug out her purse.

"Can you get me a drink?" she said to Holly, handing her a £20 note. "Get yourself something too."

"It's your birthday, you can't buy!" Holly said, trying to hand it back.

"Don't be daft, I need a wee, just take the money."

"*Fine.* What do you want?" Holly raised her voice to be heard. The DJ was shouting out to the club.

"Anything." Mia said, excusing herself to the loo.

Leaving Holly with the money turned out to be a mistake. When Mia returned, still sober enough to know how disgusting the toilets were, Holly sat at one of the waltzer tables with twenty Jager bombs in front of her.

"Dude, what the hell?" Mia said, eyeing the army of drinks.

"They were only a pound each!" she looked incredibly pleased with herself.

"So, you had to buy twenty?" Mia conveyed her shock with her hands.

"Mi, they were a *pound*."

Mia gave in and dropped down next to her. "Okay, fair, that is a bargain."

Everyone else refused to get involved. Instead, they circled the table while Holly and Mia drank every one. After ten each, they were both bouncing off the walls due to so much red bull energy drink.

"Hey, Fred, Fred, Fred, hey, hey, Fred." Mia poked him with every word.

"Ouch!" he snapped, imprisoning her finger in his fist. "What?"

"Can we – can – can we go and dance?" Mia stammered. Her eyes and face twitched from the excess caffeine.

"Go on, go dance, I'll watch." he said. Mia pulled a grumpy face as the song changed.

"Oh my God! Freddie, come on!" she grabbed his hand and pulled. Upon hearing the song, he laughed and gave in. They danced like their lives depended on it to Queen's 'Don't Stop Me Now,' followed by banger after banger. The whole gang danced until sweat was pouring off them; the atmosphere was infectious.

"God, I'm boiling!" Mia panted, fanning herself, after a solid hour of jumping around.

"Me, too." Maria said. "Do you wanna go outside for a bit?"

Mia nodded and allowed Maria to take her hand.

"Ahhhh!" Mia breathed as they stepped into the cold. "That's so much better."

"Do you want a cigarette?" Maria offered, taking a seat in a doorway outside the club.

Mia started doing star jumps. "No, I couldn't do star jumps as well if my lungs didn't work." she said. The Jager bombs were still whizzing around her body.

"Fair enough." Maria laughed, lighting hers.

She took a drag or two and shivered slightly as the wind blew past. Mia continued to star jump.

"Mimi, I've got something I need to tell you." Maria said.

"Oh, yeah?"

"Yeah." Maria scrunched up her face to look at her. "And I'm scared to tell you because I love you so much and I don't want you to hate me."

"Why would I hate you? I wouldn't hate you. I love you to pieces." Mia said, she had alternated to skipping on the spot. It sounded exactly like what she had said to Jake when they broke up, except she was too hyper to really register.

"Mi, can you stop skipping for like two minutes?" Maria said, growing impatient. "I'm trying to tell you something."

Making the face of an angry child, Mia dropped down onto her haunches.

"Better?" she asked.

"Much." she replied, then took a deep breath. "I've sort of started going out with Jake."

"Okay." Mia said, rocking back and forth; Maria narrowed her eyes. "Did you hear what I said?"

"You're going out with Jake."

Maria waited for the reaction. Mia could not find the right words or emotions; she did not really know what she was thinking. Was she angry? Was she happy? Was she completely unfazed? She probably should have been something, but her body was enjoying too much of a buzz to care.

"I'm sorry!" Maria looked very upset and began to tear up. "I didn't plan for this to happen. We just started talking and it turns out we've got a lot in common. Then he asked me out and I said yes and and and…" she trailed off, waiting for Mia to say something.

"Are you happy?" Mia asked and Maria wiped her nose with her arm.

"Yeah." Maria nodded. "Yeah, I am."

"Well, why didn't you invite him?" Mia suddenly burst out with. She was very drunk.

"Wait – what?" Maria said. "Invite him to your birthday weekend?"

"Send him a message, invite him up for tomorrow night." Mia instructed.

"Are you serious?" Maria asked.

"Yeah, why not?" Mia said, her attention turning to a feather that floated by. "If you're seeing him, you should have fun with him, right?"

"Right…"

**

Back at the hostel, Mia was hunched over another bowl of Carol's pasta. They had not been able to find an open takeaway on the way home, much to her disappointment. Even trusty Old McDonalds was closed by the time they left the club. With her vision blurring in and out, Mia concentrated hard on staying upright and not spilling the food on the floor. Holly was warming a bowl for herself while Maria washed up. Carol was flat out on her bottom bunk and they were trying hard not to wake her, which was all going well until Sian had gone to go to bed. As she mounted the ladder to climb onto the top bunk, Steph, who was occupying the lower bunk, sat up, smiled at Sian and vomited through her teeth.

Sian released the highest noise Mia had ever heard come from her mouth. Instead of rushing to help, Mia kept eating her pasta, slow on the uptake. Meanwhile Carol, who was definitely awake, catapulted out of bed and threw an empty bowl underneath Steph to catch most of the vomit.

"Sian, get me another bowl." Carol instructed, and Maria passed her one.

Realising what was happening, Mia's chuckle developed into a full-blown laughing fit as she and Holly rolled round on the floor. They were no use to anyone.

As Carol stripped the bed, Sian marched Steph across the hall to the bathroom to wash the vomit out of her hair.

Once they had collected themselves and still sniggering, Holly and Mia snuck out of the room before they were given a job to do.

Mouth of the Tyne, Anna Heslop

Chapter Twenty-Two

Waking up the next morning wedged in between Sian and Holly was not what Mia had expected. Lots of details from the night before were hazy and she had done the classic Mia drunk trait of banishing her t-shirt. Being in the middle of her two friends, she awkwardly stretched trying not to wake them up however, quickly developed a horrible cramp in her lower left leg. In pain, she launched herself forward off her bed, still topless, and began dancing around the room, gripping her calf and producing loud 'Ow's. The cramp was the most painful, followed by jumping around without a bra.

Sian was clutching her stomach and trying to breathe again, and Holly was rubbing her head. They had both been injured during the occurrence, as Mia had hit the bed either side of her to get up – hitting where they both were.

"What the hell is going on?" Holly huffed, still rubbing her forehead. "At what point was it necessary to use my face as a launch pad?"

"I've got a cramp." It was soothing now so she began stretching her leg out and calming down.

"How horrible for you!" Sian coughed. "That wasn't the wakeup call I wanted."

"Sorry." Mia sighed as her cramp disappeared. Neither seemed phased by her toplessness; it was too common following a night out. Hearing the kerfuffle, Maria and Zoe burst into the bedroom with a yelled chorus of 'Happy Birthday!' and jumped on the bed.

"Thanks, guys." Mia smiled, covering herself the best she could and wiggling into one of Holly's nearby t-shirts.

They threw present bags in her direction and Fred shouted through from the kitchen. "What do you want for breakfast, Mimi?"

When she traipsed through to the other room, laden with presents, Fred placed a full plate on the bench for her to collect.

"Happy birthday, Mi." Carol smiled, pulling her into a hug. "I only got you something small, but I hope you like it."

"Carol, you didn't need to get me anything!" Mia said.

"Well, like I say, it's only small." Carol replied.

The present was beautiful wrapped in eco-friendly paper, tied up with a thin piece of brown string and accompanied by hand made card:

To Mia,

Happy Birthday. Have a wonderful day. You deserve the best this world has to offer.

Much Love Carol and Don x

The present itself was a small easel with a stunning painting on it of Longsands Beach. It would take pride of place on her bedside table.

"Oh, thank you, Carol. I love it so much." Mia smiled, hugging her again.

The presents were all simple, sweet and personal. Mia hated opening presents in front of people, thinking her reaction, no matter how hard she tried, was never good enough to do such lovely presents justice.

Fred had bought her a new pen knife with the words 'keep off my piano' inscribed on the side.

"Thanks, Freddie." She hugged him, before gathering all the thoughtful gifts together into one present bag. They enjoyed a beautiful cooked breakfast and slowly got themselves dressed and ready for the events of the day. With only one bathroom between eight of them, it took longer than it should have done.

In true Carol form, she had prepared an activity for them to keep them entertained in the day.

"You're such a Mum, Carol." Sian laughed, giving her a nudge.

"You love it." Carol smiled back. "I hope everyone is ready for a scavenger hunt!"

There were mixed reactions rippling through the group. Carol ignored any grumblings and waited while they split in half.

"Do we have our teams?" Carol asked, clutching the instruction sheets she was yet to reveal, and there was nodding in response: Fred, Zoe, Mia and Holly vs Maria, Steph and Sian. "Right, is everyone ready to go?" More nodding. "Off we go then."

They all left together and headed for the castle. Edinburgh castle sat atop castle rock, meaning they had an uphill walk to reach it from the hostel. The main seating areas from the Tattoo were still being taken down when they arrived.

"Now, when I give you your paper, you have one hour to complete as much of the list as possible. It works in a points system. It's a photo competition, so you need to take a different photo for each bullet point. You can't have one photo covering two bullet points, for example." Carol said, handing out the lists. "I'm going to go and look round the castle and will meet you back here in an hour."

Unfurling their lists, they began reading.

Carol's Edinburgh Photograph Scavenger Hunt:

(Number of points awarded for each photograph)

1 point:

- A bus schedule
- A shopping trolley
- A bicycle
- Something tartan

2 points:

- A business card
- A shopping bag
- Front page of a local newspaper
- Selfie with a box of cereal
- A bear
- Hard Rock café
- A sightseeing bus

3 points:

- Selfie with a bald man
- Entire team reading
- Entire team drinking from same drink
- Entire team with a police officer
- Entire team throwing coins into a fountain
- Someone dressed like Harry Potter
- Cow
- A museum

5 points:

- Entire team in the smallest possible place
- Entire team jumping on cobbles
- Cat café
- Greyfriar's Bobby statue

"Let's start with the 5 pointers and work backwards." Mia planned. "Someone google where Greyfriars Bobby is from here."

"I'm on it." Fred said, clicking away. "It's about half a mile that way." he pointed, and they started to jog down the hill. "The Museum of Scotland is near there too so we can stop on the way." For most of the pictures, they were red faced and slightly sweaty from running in the baking heat.

"I thought it was meant to rain a lot in Scotland." Zoe said, the reddest of them all. Thinking it would be cold and wet the full weekend, she had only packed warm clothing.

"Not all the time though, Zo." Mia replied. "I did try to tell you." It felt like they did not stop running for the first half an hour other than to snap the photographs. At Cowgate, they managed to find a statue of a cow split in half, seeming like it was jumping threw the walls of a pub, and snapped the cat café near the old Grassmarket.

"Why is this city so hilly?" Zoe wheezed, as they sprinted ahead of her.

"Do you want a piggyback?" Fred offered and she laughed; he took to pulling her by the hand instead up the steeper hills.

When they stopped on the Royal Mile, the stretch of pedestrian road running up to the castle, they managed to get a selfie with a bald man, who then took a picture of them all jumping on the cobbles. As they reviewed their photos, a group of strangers, all dressed in yellow, suddenly surrounded them and began to sing.

"What's happening?" Fred said, looking around at the circle he was trapped in.

Holly laughed and began to dance. "It's one of those silent disco tours."

They ended up enjoying a verse and a chorus with the flash mob singing Walk the Moon's 'Shut Up and Dance,' before they started running again.

"Come on!" Holly shouted. "We've only got three minutes to get back!"

"You go! I'll catch up!" Zoe shouted back. While Holly ran on ahead, Mia stopped to help Fred pull Zoe faster. They just made it back to Carol in time, with Zoe collapsing into a heap on the floor at her feet.

"I'm loving the commitment." Carol chuckled.

"Never." Zoe panted, waving her hand. "Never put me on a team with Holly again that involves any sort of exercise."

When Carol added up the scores, they were neck and neck until the photo of the entire team in the smallest possible place. While Sian's team had crammed into a narrow alleyway, Mia and company had all squashed into a red phone box and managed to close the door. This stole them the crown.

"Yes!!" Holly and Mia celebrated.

"See, Zoe, it was worth it." Holly said, clapping her on the back.

"What do we win?"

"Bragging rights." Carol replied.

Holly looked as though she might complain then shrugged, turning to rub it in Sian's face instead.

At lunchtime, they retreated to the back of an old pub on The Royal Mile. Though it looked full at first glance, the waitress led them through to the secluded room. It was as though it had been reserved specifically. Mia ordered a deliciously calorific baked camembert, with a sliced cobb loaf, salad and a pint. She adored being surrounded by her happy friends and shared a short video of them all just chatting and eating on her Instagram story.

"Well done to the winners." Sian said, bitterly accepting her defeat and raising her pint glass. "Even though I think it was rigged."

**

Pre pre-drinks started in the hostel room that night. At lunchtime, Steph had ordered they all be ready to go by 8pm for the quiz she had prepared; dress code: shit shirts. Once she had straightened her own hair, Maria turned into a hair dressing station for everyone else, though disappeared briefly when Jake arrived at the hostel. Mia completely forgot she had invited him until Maria ran down to greet him.

"Happy birthday, Mi." he said, stepping into the room, apprehensively. Since they had broken up, he had allowed his beard to grow out more and it tickled when he hugged her. "I got you a little something, but I'll let you open it later."

He held it up to show her and leaned it against the wall. She smiled, sat back down and shook her head to disperse the forming thoughts. "So, ladies and gentlemen." Steph began, standing in front of them all in her Quiz Master glory, trying to absorb all the attention rather than allow an atmosphere. "I hope you're all ready for the Mia centric quiz I have prepared for you all. Jake, you've got about two minutes to put your shit shirt on before I begin. Everyone else, get your pens and paper!"

They hung off various bunk beds, in their shit shirts with Carol made snacks, waiting to get painfully competitive with each other for the second time that day. Sian squeezed Mia's knee in a comforting gesture.

"Now, for this quiz, there are twenty-two questions, one related to every year since Mia was born." Steph instructed. "I need three teams."

Fred and Mia paired up and were horrendously bad at the quiz, coming last in every round except the google earth round, where Steph had taken screen shots of famous landmarks and had them guess what they were.

"I don't even know what the Kremlin looks like normally, never mind from space!" Sian protested.

Carol and Holly won, with Holly parading her prize Toblerone bar in Sian's face, basking in her second triumph of the day. Meanwhile Steph excused herself from the room and Maria scuttled to the light switch. The room went dark.

"Now, Fred, I know you don't like the fuss, but you are being included for the singing." Carol said, as Steph re-entered the room with one of Gramps' best creations yet. It was one of the best cakes Mia had ever seen. It had immaculately laid green icing on three quarters of the cake, with the remaining quarter blue like the sea. On the green section, Gramps had built an edible version of Tynemouth Priory and Castle ruins, with tiny sculptures of Fred, Mia and Charlie sitting on a bench at its feet. Small waves were etched into the 'sea' where dolphin fins poked out of the blue. Though Fred had originally planned to make one himself, Gramps had denied him the honour.

"Happy birthday to you, happy birthday to you, happy birthday Fred and Mi-a, happy birthday to you." They all sang as the candles flickered on the cake.

"Ready?" Mia asked Fred and he nodded, with them blowing them out in one go together.

"Now, Sian did want to put forty-four candles on, but I said that might be a fire hazard!" Carol chuckled. "Now, move in together so I can take a picture!"

Holding her phone high and concentrating so hard she stuck out her tongue, Carol took a photo that Mia knew would make her wall.

"Wait, Carol, you need to get in too." Mia said.

"No, no, I'm okay." It's a lovely one of you lot." Carol waved her down.

"Here, Carol, I'll take it." Jake offered and Mia smiled in thanks.

"Smile!" Jake said, and he clicked the screen. "Beautiful!"

Before long, they were back in the rave cave again, huddled together playing another game of giant drinking Jenga, though they had a brief interval to dance around to Taylor Swift's '22.'

Still suffering from the night before, Steph was holding back slightly and had planned to carry everyone else home that evening, should they need it. Mia could already feel herself getting drunker than the night before, even though she was pretty drunk then. Everyone had wanted to buy her a birthday drink and the shots kept appearing as if by magic. Before Jenga, they had been roped into a game of beer pong and the other team were excellent. Mia was struggling to see or walk straight, and they had not yet left the hostel.

When it was Holly's turn, she slid the block out with ease and read it. "Oh, Gawd." she said, turning it round for the group to see, 'Kiss the person to your left.'

Maria laughed. "That's the second time, you've got to use tongues now!"

Mia gave a slightly alarmed look at Fred. She had no feelings for Holly, she was like her sister, but it was still the first time she was going to kiss a girl.

As Holly stepped closer, Mia could not help but be nervous.

"Oi, oi!" Sian called, as they moved closer to each other. *This is weird. So weird.* Mia thought. But there was no backing out of a dare.

Taking the lead in the situation, Holly grabbed Mia's face and pulled them together, sealing it with the kiss. It felt weird, but only because it was Holly and not because she was a girl. When they pulled apart,

Mia found herself a little awe struck, but Fred kindly pulled her back to her seat quick enough.

The night became very fragmented. One minute she was playing Jenga, the next she was in a taxi, then she was dancing in a club, then she was on bar counter. Though she managed to stay upright, there were a few close calls where her friends needed to catch her. The drinks kept flowing and she kept drinking them. Whatever was given to her went straight down the hatch.

As her birthday disappeared with midnight, she sat on a wooden planter at the back of a club in the smoking area, sipping another double vodka and coke. When Maria took her hand and pulled her to the toilet, she ping-ponged off the walls heading down the stairs and made friends with passing strangers. Every minute required a running commentary, even as she was weeing.

"Oh my gosh!" she stuttered loudly from her cubicle. "This toilet seat is sooooo cold!"

As she sat, staring at the back of the toilet door, making faces to herself, she realised how drunk she was.

"Mimi, let me in." Maria knocked on the door, so Mia opened it, still squatting over the metal toilet bowl. "What's taking you so long?"

"Hey!" Mia swayed in a circle, still sitting down, then answered in a regal voice. "I am not slow! You, my dear, are simply too quick for me!"

"Oh God," Maria laughed, as Holly appeared. "You're hammered!"

"What are you two doing?" Holly asked and Maria pointed at Mia.

"Check out Little Miss Lightweight over here." Maria laughed, but looked fondly at Mia, who was batting the toilet roll like a cat hitting a wool ball.

"It's been a while since we carried her home, ey?" Holly said, nipping into the next cubicle.

"Aww, she was so cute back then." Maria cooed. "Remember, she was so sweet and innocent until we corrupted her."

"You mean she hadn't lived yet!" Holly laughed. "Look at her now!"

"I am." Maria said with raised eyebrows as Mia struggled to dress herself again. "Thank God she found us."

When the hand drier would not work, Mia punched it, then momentarily passed out with her head on it. From then, as she found her second wind, keeping track of Mia, for Maria and Holly, was like trying to hold onto soap in a shower. Eventually, Maria passed her duties onto Steph as she slunk away with Jake.

Everyone was a lot drunker than the night before, but the drinks kept coming. During one song, Sian got overexcited and started to strip, swinging her shirt above her head as she danced. Mia joined in, with Fred laughing but desperately trying to cover their modesty.

When Mia caught sight of Jake and Maria together, she stopped dancing and frowned, still unsure of what she was feeling. Managing to temporarily lose her babysitters, she escaped up the stairs and outside, where it was cool enough to help clear her head. She crossed her arms and found herself in another doorway.

Her phone pinged.

[Sam] Happy Birthday! (Sorry it's late) Are you having fun?

[Mia] Thank you and yes. You should have come too. I miss you.

[Sam] I miss you too buddy.

Buddy. Mia re-read it with a twist of her face. *Buddy.* What was she even doing lusting after Sam? She was never going to take any notice of her, never feel the same way about her. *Eurgh.* She just wanted to yell at the world and the alcohol was not helping.

"Hey, do you have a light?" A guy asked, standing above her. He had a kind, slightly weather-beaten face, with black hair that seemed to flop in any direction it wanted to.

"No, sorry." she shook her head.

"You okay?" he asked, cocking his head, his Kiwi accent shining through. "I don't often see pretty girls moping around in doorways on their own. You guys normally travel in herds, don't you?"

She looked up at him with a soft smile. "Herds? We aren't cattle."

"You know what I mean." he replied, placing a cigarette in his mouth. "Packs, clouders, murders, all of the above."

"We aren't wolves, cats or crows either." Mia argued, with a flick of her eyebrow.

"I'm impressed." he said, putting his hand out, offered a greeting and to pull her to her feet. "Hunter."

She took it. "Mia."

**

With no Fred or Sian or even Jake to knock some sense into her, it went ahead. By coincidence, Hunter was staying in The One Edinburgh Hostel too, but he led Mia past her room and up to his in the loft of the hostel. Across the ceiling, the wooden beams of the building zigzagged, with towels and various pieces of clothing hanging from them. It was clearly a room for longer staying guests. It still housed eight beds, but they were all singles and spaced out more from each other in the larger space. Considering the time of night, the room was practically empty. One other person occupied a bed in the far corner of the room, but they were asleep, so they had to be quiet. Mia's stomach was doing flips; her decision making was not at its strongest.

They started to kiss and scrambled awkwardly on to the mattress of the single bed; it squeaked loudly.

No matter how drunk she was, she was always super careful. Grandma would have a flip if she had a baby out of wedlock; she also did not want one anytime soon.

"Do you have a condom?" Mia asked, squirming internally. She hated asking but it was being asked.

"Er-no." he said, looking sheepish. "Does it matter?"

"Erm-yeah." Mia replied, frowning.

"I don't have any diseases, if that's what you're worried about." he said.

"I'd just rather not risk anything." Mia whispered.

"Oh, well," he said. "We can still do other stuff."

They started kissing again, allowing their hands to wander and roam free.

"Are you sure you don't want to go further?" he asked, dancing his fingers on her bare stomach.

"Yeah, I'm sure." Mia had sobered up a lot. Instead of enjoying the hook up, she had spent most of the time thinking. "Actually, I'm tired now, I'm gonna go to bed. Tonight, was - fun."

She kissed him on the cheek, gathered her clothes and, leaving him slightly dumbstruck, made for the exit.

"What, you guys are done already?" A voice came from the far side of the room. "It was just getting good."

Shuddering, scowling and overall grumping with herself, Mia dressed in the hallway and retreated to her own bed. Wanting to avoid questions, Mia made straight for hers and Holly's bedroom, bursting straight through the door.

"Oh my God!" she squealed, closing the door as quick as she could, having interrupted Jake and Maria doing God knows what. "I'm sorry!"

Massaging her temples with her fingers, she took a breath and moved into the other room, giving a sleeping Holly a hard jab in the ribs.

"Ouch!" Holly yelped, waking suddenly. "What the hell was that for?"

It was pitch black so Mia could not see who was home and who was yet to return from the streets of Edinburgh.

"Why aren't you next door?" Mia hissed, pointing at the door.

"I let Maria have it." Holly groaned then realisation dawned. "Oh shit, did you go in?"

"Yes, I went in!" Mia snapped, rubbing her head, the hangover was already making itself known.

"Ahh, crap, sorry man." Holly winced.

"It doesn't matter just budge over, let me in." Mia demanded, shoving her over and climbing in beside her.

"What happened with you anyway?" Holly asked.

"I'll tell you in the morning." Mia grumbled, having already closed her eyes to sleep.

They snuggled in the single bed as the door creaked open. Maria and Jake were occupied next door, Carol, Sian and Steph were all asleep.

"Shh!" Zoe said into the darkness, as she crept to the far bunk bed. "Let's go in my bed."

Enough light was coming through the curtains for Holly and Mia to exchange a look, facing each other. Holly held a finger to her lips while they listened.

"Who's she with?" Mia mouthed, and Holly indicated for silence more aggressively.

Zoe and her acquaintance climbed onto the bottom bunk and under the covers; Steph was inches away from them and Fred's bed was above them.

"Shh," Zoe giggled. "You'll wake Steph!"

The acquaintance giggled back, and they started kissing. The bed creaked as they rolled around and there was a lot of shhing.

"Oh my God, she's with *Fred*!" Holly hissed.

Mouth of the Tyne, Anna Heslop

Chapter Twenty-Three

Opening her eyes, the next morning felt like a chore. Builders were drilling holes in the floor of her brain. The hangover and shame were skipping hand in hand. Not long after she had peeled her eyes open, she covered them again with an open palm and groaned to the room, alerting Holly to her consciousness. The only thing she was proud of from the night before was that she had kept her top on in her sleep.

"Morning, buggerlugs." Holly croaked with a stretch. "Glad to see you survived the night."

"Just." Mia groaned back, turning on her front to hug her pillow. Her hair stuck to her head and her eyelashes were tangled together uncomfortably.

"Look." Holly whispered, pointing to Zoe's bed. Fred lay on his back, shirtless and snoring slightly, while Zoe spooned his side and hugged his chest.

"I can't believe that happened." Mia whispered back with a look of shock. "It's pretty cute, like."

"Yeah, it is." Holly replied, with an evil grin. "We can still rip them to pieces over it though."

Mia chuckled. They were the only ones awake in the room so continued to speak quietly.

"So, what happened with you last night?" Holly asked, pulling the duvet so it covered her legs.

"I went home with someone." Mia admitted, looking down at the pillow.

"You what?" Holly asked, making a face. "How did I manage to miss that?"

"Yeah." Mia sighed, sucking air in through her teeth.

"Who did you go with?"

"Just this guy." Mia replied, flicking her eyes to the ceiling. "He's staying in one of the rooms upstairs."

"Which guy?" she frowned, thinking back to the night before. "Did we see him in the rave cave?"

"I don't think so. He's called Hunter, he's from New Zealand."

"Bloody hell, add a Kiwi to your map." Holly laughed. "Magic vagina strikes again, ey?"

The 'Magic Vagina' was the lovely name Holly had created back when they were travelling together. It developed when Holly realised Mia seemed to be successful with anyone she lusted after. In Holly's eyes, it had a 100% success rate. Then again, Holly did not know about Sam.

"I wish it would use its powers for good and not for evil." Mia croaked back.

"Ooh, that bad, huh?" Holly replied, running a hand threw her hair. "What happened?"

"It was just weird, you know." Mia said, punching her pillow to puff it up. "We didn't have any protection, so we didn't have sex-"

"Good lass." Holly interjected with a congratulatory nod.

"But it was just a bit awkward *and* we had a creepy guy awake and watching us."

"Ew, why didn't you stop?" Holly asked, twisting her face.

"Well, I didn't know he was watching until the end!" Mia said, rolling her eyes. "It's not like I invited him to."

Holly shuddered. "Men are grim sometimes."

Mia nodded in agreement.

"How are you about the whole Jake and Maria thing, anyway?" Holly asked, leaning on her hand on one side and tilted her head slightly, as if trying to coax out the truth.

"Honestly, I'm happy they're happy." Mia said, looking away. Fred knew. Jake knew. Sian knew. The more people she told the more real it became. The less chance of going back there was.

"Really?" Holly asked, lying back with her arms crossed behind her head. "You're a better person than me. I don't think I could be okay with a mate going with one of my ex's."

"I mean, there is something weird about it." Mia said, trying to choose her words carefully. "I think it would be different though if he had, like, broken my heart. But I did the ending so I'm good, I think. I'm gonna go with good, even if I have to convince myself a little more."

They lay in bed, chatting and generally putting the world to rights until Carol came shuffling in. She had been outside, enjoying a morning cuppa and knitting on the decking in the sunshine. Ever the early bird, she would usually rise at 5am and be out for a morning swim most days.

"Up you get! We need to be out by 10!" she said, in a voice far too cheery for a hangover morning and they both groaned. Yes, they were awake, but they were not ready to get up.

Kick out time at the hostel felt early at 10am. Carol was certainly the mother of the group even more that day, turfing everyone out of bed, making sure they were packed and away, so they did not have to pay extra. She had them cleaning the kitchen, stripping their beds, doing the dishes and generally making sure the place was nicer than when they found it.

"It's a good rule to live by!" she pointed out as she sprayed Dettol on the benches.

"It's a hostel, Carol." Holly groaned. "I think we just cleaned it for the first time since it opened."

"Then we've definitely left it cleaner than we found it!" Carol sang, stuffing all the dirty bed sheets into one duvet cover.

"If someone could carry me, it would be much appreciated." Sian grumbled, letting her feet fall heavily as she clomped down the stairs. To say she was not a morning person would be an understatement.

Fred, subtly, helped Zoe with her bag. No one had asked them about the night before, yet. Perhaps only Holly and Mia had seen.

They hauled their bags back to the cars, packed them then decided to follow their stomachs. By the time Fred had rolled out of Zoe's bed, he had not had time to make another spread of beautiful breakfast. Dragging their sorry bodies through town, they found a quaint little coffee shop, on a winding street just off The Royal Mile. It offered an appealing breakfast and they marched inside to fill their stomachs. On the ground floor, there were only five tables, and all were full. Various adverts littered the front window and plants grew inside wherever they were able to.

A narrow, metal, winding staircase led them down to the floor below, which looked like it had been carved into castle rock itself. It was clear the owner was enthusiastic about art, every uneven, rocky crevice was filled. Magnificent paintings, mainly depicting luscious countryside, hung on every wall. It was an oddly shaped room, almost round. When Mia was a child, her Dad used to read her a series of books about The Faraway Tree. A character called Moonface lived in the tree, therefore, his home was curved. All his furniture needed to be curved too to fit the shape of the room. It reminded Mia of Moonface's house.

Scraping their chairs back, they took their seats and buried their faces in the menus.

"Will someone please just pick for me? It's too early to read." Sian yawned without covering her mouth.

"Mate, did you ever brush your teeth this morning?" Maria wafted the smell away from her.

"A coffee will cover that, don't worry." she replied, smacking her lips. "And maybe a bacon sandwich too."

There were plenty of looks being thrown throughout at breakfast. Fred and Zoe were very sheepish with each other about the night before and Maria and Jake kept throwing nervous looks at Mia, unsure of how to interact with each other.

Carol led the conversation that morning as the others slowly woke up. Zoe was best at mirroring her liveliness and Mia overheard Carol discussing the plans for her scout group with her. They had been off for the full summer but were regrouping in the September and jumping straight into their Lifesaver Activity Badge. Carol planned to take them down to the local lifeboat station so the scouts could learn about saving lives at sea. While she talked, Mia thought about how refreshing a dip in the sea would be that morning. She swore by it being the best hangover cure and daydreamed of a hungover surf, that and eating Weetabix Minis.

When breakfast arrived, Mia drooled a little bit before tucking into it. She had ordered a breakfast bun – sausage, bacon and fried egg swimming in tomato ketchup. Because the chef had not popped the yolk, it burst when Mia bit into it, spilling the yellow goo all over her hands. It was the messiest and most delicious sandwich Mia had ever eaten.

"Are you enjoying that?" Carol asked, laughing at the mess she had made.

Mia nodded, with a huge smile and a mouth full.

To burn off their breakfast, they decided to take a walk up Calton Hill. It was a small hill hike in the heart of the city. On top of the hill sat a large and unfinished stone monument next to a contemporary art gallery. With the combination of nice weather and it being Bank Holiday Sunday, plenty of other people had shared their idea.

"Hey." Fred puffed, catching up with Mia. "What the hell happened with you last night? I lost you."

"Me?" Mia replied. "What happened with *you* last night?"

Fred looked stunned and stuttered, clearly not expecting that response. "What do you mean?"

"I know you got with Zoe last night." Mia revealed, cocking an eyebrow.

"Why would you think that?" Fred asked, trying to act confused. Mia could see the cogs turning in his brain as he thought.

"Dude, I *saw* you." Mia said with a grin.

"Oh." he replied, pursing his guilty lips. "Wait, where were you?"

"I was in Holly's bed." she said, nonchalantly.

"What? Did you and Holly-?" he whipped his head round.

"What? No! No!" Mia pulled a face and waved her hands. "Maria and Jake were in our room, so I ended up piling in with Holls."

"I was gonna say, what a birthday for you." Fred laughed, his breath quickening as they reached the summit.

"Anyway, stop avoid my question, you." Mia said, elbowing him. "How did you and Zoe happen?"

Fred checked no one else was near to them then suddenly went giddy. "I don't really know, to be honest. It just, sort of, happened. No one else was around and she suddenly just kissed me, out of nowhere."

"So, she made the first move?" Mia kept her voice down.

"Yeah." he nodded.

"Did you guys sleep together?" Mia asked.

"No, we didn't." he replied. "I thought you knew everything from that bit anyway if you were only the next bed over?"

"I wasn't actively listening to that bit, Freddie." she rolled her eyes. "Once I knew it was you, I stopped listening pretty quickly and blocked my ears."

"Ahh, okay, well, I'm pleased you did." Fred looked elated. "There was quite a lot to hear."

"Ew, dude, no." Mia gave him a shove. "I'm happy for you and I want to know bits, but not the icky, sticky bits."

Fred laughed and they continued their ascent.

From the monument, the views were stunning. South Queensferry was clearly visible with the bridges lining up in perfect formation. With the river and sea, the country and the sea, the view was breath taking.

"Did you know that until 2011, the Forth Road Bridge was being painted constantly?" Mia said, pointing to the bridges.

"What?" Sian asked, climbing onto a small stone square to pose for a picture.

"Every time they finished one end, they needed to start again on the other." Mia replied.

"We haven't had 'fun facts with Mia' for a while." Steph said, clapping an arm around her shoulder.

They climbed onto the monument itself, taking a group photo that resembled an album cover. Jake took the picture, not wanting to intrude on another one. He and Mia had still barely spoken. She really was not angry with him; she just did not know what to say to him. If anything, she was quite jealous. Jealous that they suited each other and seemed to like each other so much. She was jealous of

Maria for liking him the traditional way. Even when the others climbed down, Mia stayed atop the monument, swinging her legs in quiet contemplation, allowing the breeze to blow through her hair. It always seemed to help.

Holding hands, Maria and Jake wandered away to the best grassy viewpoint together; Mia watched.

"How far away are you right now?" Sian woke her from her trance and followed her eye line to see what she had been looking at. Jake scooped Maria up under her arms and spun her round as she laughed.

"Why did you tell him to come if it was just going to upset you?" Sian asked, dropping down next to her.

"I didn't think it would bother me as much as it does." Mia replied. "And I wasn't exactly thinking properly with drunk brain."

"Did you tell Maria why you really broke up with him?" Sian asked, squinting in the sunlight.

"No." Mia said, lifting her knee up to her chest as she sat. "Three people knowing is enough for now."

"You know, it's hard to believe sometimes, but the people who love you will still love you." Sian said and Mia twitched the corner of her mouth.

"Come here." Sian said, pulling her into a head lock. "I can't wait till you're over the shit bit and I can take you out to enjoy the dark side properly. You can learn from the best."

Mia laughed and shoved her off. "I'm not taking any advice from you."

"I'm not talking about advice. I'm talking about actual lessons." Sian smiled. "They make you pass a test before you receive the newsletter."

"You're an ass." Mia laughed, nudging her.

"Yeah I am." Sian replied. "Anyway, stop torturing yourself and come play with us."

Treading carefully so not to fall, they climbed down from the monument and wandered over to where the main cluster of the group was gathered.

"How long do you reckon before you can drive?" Carol asked, laying her coat on the grass to sit on; in contrast, Holly plonked herself down in the dust.

"I won't risk it until at least five." Holly said, leaning back on her hands.

"What do you want to do this afternoon, then, Mi?" Carol asked as Mia and Sian joined them.

"I don't know." Mia said, thinking. "Let's see where the afternoon takes us?"

Much to Zoe's dismay, they returned to castle hill to visit Camera Obscura, stopping briefly at the large department store, Jenners, where Steph and Mia played a game of 'Where's Miranda?' without their costumes. The staff were less than impressed. In Camera Obscura, they took the most photos in the illusion where one person looked much larger than the other. The illusions had them entertained for almost two hours. At the very top of the building sat the 'camera' itself, which, using mirrors, could explore the live goings on of the capital city below. As they sat in the darkened room, the guide zoomed the camera in to the castle keep, where a man proposed to his boyfriend. The whole room melted.

Not long before home time, they stopped in an Irish pub for wood fired pizza and filled themselves for the final time. Mia looked round her friends, wanting to say how grateful she was for them and for such a nice weekend, but she did not know where to start.

**

On the journey home, Mia was trying her best to stay awake for Holly's sake. If it was possible, her hangover had gotten worse hour by hour throughout the day. The three in the back had no stamina and were fast asleep before they had reached Dunbar. When they passed the speed camera that had flashed Holly on the way up, she slowed down to half the speed limit just in case.

Holly dropped them all at the bakery and beeped twice as she drove away.

"Gramps?" Fred called, pushing open the door to the café, only to be greeted by Charlie.

He was so excited to see them, jumping up excitedly at them as soon as they entered the shop.

"Hey, boy! Hey! Who's a good boy?" Mia and Sian were on the floor playing with him in seconds.

"Does he look fatter to you?" Mia asked, eyeing his size.

"After two days?" Steph replied.

"I know it's only been two days, but Gramps always feeds him so much!" Mia laughed. "I'm surprised Fred isn't morbidly obese."

"I'm not *morbidly*, but this belly comes from somewhere." Fred said, lifting his t-shirt and clapping his hand on his stomach.

"I don't hear you saying no to my pies and cakes very often, lad!" Gramps said, appearing from the kitchen. A trademark flour dusting coated his left cheek as he cleared his hands with a tea towel.

"Who could say no to you, Gramps?" Fred smiled. "I got you something by the way."

Digging in his pocket, Fred pulled out a small and battered copy of The Adventures of Sherlock Holmes, gifting it to Gramps.

"Oh, thanks, lad." Gramps said, taking a seat on the picnic bench and starting to flick through the pages. Leaving the girls, Charlie sat himself down against Gramps' leg and looked up at him for affection.

"Has he behaved himself?" Mia asked, leaning to ruffle Charlie's ears.

"He's been as good as gold." Gramps said. "Leave him anytime. The customers love him. He was fawned over yesterday. Geordie doesn't really bother himself with the customers anymore."

"Oh. And thank you so much for the cake." Mia said, throwing her arms around Gramps. "It was the best cake I've ever seen or tasted."

"You're welcome." he laughed, accepting her hug. "You've got another one coming your way on Tuesday mind."

"Tuesday?" Mia asked, wondering if she had forgotten something important.

"Your Grandma asked me if I could put a tea on so we could have a little family birthday celebration for you both, just small, you know." Gramps replied.

"That sounds lovely." Mia smiled. "Let me know what time."

"Will do." Gramps replied, then looked around at the room.

"Anyway, did you guys have a good time?"

"It was great." Fred replied. "I want to sleep for a week now though."

"I've got too much work for you to do that." Gramps said, and Fred gave an overexaggerated groan.

With a final thank you to Gramps, they clipped Charlie's lead on him and started home with their bags.

Charlie charged in the front door and sniffed every inch of the apartment. He took a huge drink and dribbled water from his chin and ears all over the kitchen floor.

Instead of unpacking, Mia dropped her bag and lay straight on her bed. Though she had to unpack, do her washing, shower and make some sort of dinner, she could not be bothered. Instead, she ate some leftover cake and crawled back to her room without brushing her teeth.

Even though she was off work on the Monday, she climbed into bed early to recover from the weekend's events. When he was finished nosing around, Charlie pushed open her bedroom door, jumped on the bed and snuggled in for the night. She pulled him in as her little spoon and was soon snoring into his fur.

Mouth of the Tyne, Anna Heslop

Chapter Twenty-Four

On Monday morning, Mia made the decision to get her life in check. In the night, she had dreamed about Sam again and was debating whether to continue a text conversation off the back of Saturday night. She was stuck in the limbo of feelings, not wanting a relationship to define her life but feeling incomplete without one. She wanted to be a strong independent woman who needed no one else in order to be happy.

At twenty-two, she would be single, happy and proud of it, most of the time. The decision was made.

Selecting her female empowerment playlist and starting with Beyoncé's 'Run the World,' she set about making her very generic list:

- Lose weight
- Be successful in new job
- Book a trip
- Be happy with self

Standing in front of her mirror in her sports bra, shorts and slippers, she breathed out and took a photo. In the bathroom, she reluctantly stood on the scales and weighed herself: 12.5 stone. Mentally making her goal 11.5 stone, she downloaded necessary fitness apps and decided to keep going until she achieved her aim. Nestling her headphones in her ears, she set out on a walk with Charlie. By the time they were home, they had walked almost ten kilometres.

Feeling refreshed and, embarrassingly, a little achy she sat on her bed and began unpacking for the weekend, when she came across the unopened gift from Jake. It was wrapped in Star Wars themed paper, decorated with stormtroopers and tied together with a neat red ribbon. When she tore it open, she was slightly confused to see a Wicked score book inside. Many times, Jake had sat on her bed while she played from the copy, he knew she already owned. Maybe he thought she needed an upgraded version, without the tea stains and crumples. Though, when she opened the front page, she saw the real gift. It was hand signed by the original cast, included Idina Menzel, who Mia absolutely adored. A small card fell out from between the pages:

To Mia,

Happy Birthday. I hope Idina sprinkled a bit of her stardust on this book for luck, not that you need it. Keep dazzling the world.

Love Jake x

**

Everyone was in good spirits when she arrived at rehearsal, the rippling nerves turned to murmuring excitement for the evening. They all sat on the stage, like school children in assembly, waiting for their instructions from Angelika.

"And how was your weekend?" Sam asked, appearing by jumping on her shoulders and bouncing down beside her. "By your texting, I'd say you had a good one?"

Mia laughed and pushed some stray hair behind her ear. "Yeah, it was good, thanks. It took some recovery this morning mind. I slept

in quite late and I don't know if I want to drink again before
Christmas."

"Well, you can get that mentality out of your head right now." Sam
warned.

"Why?" Mia asked, frowning but was interrupted before she
received her answer.

"Right, everyone." Angelika clapped to encourage silence and Sam
tapped a finger on her lips to quieten Mia.

As expected so close to showtime, Angelika wanted another full run
through. She strongly disagreed with the notion of only one dress
rehearsal, meaning they had a minimum of four. It did help with
cementing the scenes and lines to memory. The only scene Mia was
still encountering some difficulty with was the 'Defying Gravity'
one where she was hoisted in the air with her broomstick.

The scene was just before the interval, so the curtain dropped when
Mia was still suspended in mid-air. Usually they aimed to bring her
back to earth as soon as possible.

"Er, guys?" she called, still hanging from the rafters. They had
lowered her slightly but stopped about five metres before she
touched the ground.

"Sorry, Mi!" One of them called from out of sight, not sounding
overly concerned. "It seems to be stuck."

Mia hung, facing the closed curtain, wondering what to do with
herself. She could hear shuffling and footsteps on the other side and
questioned what was happening. All of a sudden, the piano started
back up and the curtain drew back revealing the cast and crew,

singing 'Happy Birthday;' Sam appeared with a cake. With the whole cast singing to her from the stage below, she could not stop herself from crying a green tear.

They lowered her down so she could blow out her candles and everyone cheered when she blew them all out in one go.

"Can we tuck in now, Mi? We've been drooling over it for the last two hours." One of the older cast members laughed.

The atmosphere among the cast and crew was infectious with the combination of the upcoming show and Mia's birthday and a good bunch of them headed out to Tynemouth. Even though she had her fill of alcohol over the weekend, they made sure she had another birthday drink or two with them.

They needed three taxis to get them all along to the bars, where they congregated in Spurn's Lighthouse, nicknamed The Spurn, a small bar serving local beer and ales with a band in the corner. The owner, Dutchy, was an ex-trawlerman and was good friends with Gramps. He always poured them extra measures and made excellent recommendations.

When they left, there were five of them heading back to Whitley Bay in a taxi, but no large taxis available.

"Can I stay at yours tonight?" Sam asked, trying to solve the problem.

"Erm-yeah, of course." Mia replied, stuttering.

The others squashed into a taxi together, waving as they pulled away.

"Sorry, I just thought that saved paying for two taxis, are you sure it's okay?" Sam asked, looking guilty.

"Yeah, of course, you're more than welcome." Mia replied.

Smiling, Sam skipped forward and linked her arm.

"Hey, Mi." Sian shouted from the living room and Charlie ran through to greet them. Upon hearing Sam cooing over the dog, Sian leaned forward in the chair to see who accompanied Mia home. "Hee-ey, Sa-am."

"Hey, how you doing?" Sam said, smiling as she took her shoes off.

"Good thanks, yeah, you?" Sian asked, trying hard to conceal her grin.

"Yeah, not too shabby, thanks!" Sam replied, then turned to Mia. "Where's your loo?"

"Upstairs and straight on to the big bathroom." Mia said.

"You've got more than one bathroom?" Sam asked, stepping onto the first stair.

"There's another tiny one in a cupboard off to the left." Mia said.

"Didn't realise I was in a mansion." Sam said with a wink, then jogged upstairs, with Mia watching her go.

"Oi!" Sian aggressively whispered to catch Mia's attention. "Come here!"

"What?" Mia hissed, stepping closer. Their conversation continued in hushed tones.

"What's she doing here?" Sian asked, pointing to the stairs, as though Mia would not know who she was talking about.

"She didn't want to get a taxi home on her own." Mia replied.

"Oh, yeah, whatever." Sian scoffed; her eyes lit up. "Are you gonna bang her?"

"No!" Mia said.

"Why not?" Sian asked, grinning like the Cheshire cat. It was all so exciting for her.

"I don't even know where to start! It's just not going to happen!" Mia hissed.

Sian let out a short laugh and took a sip of her drink as Sam reappeared.

"Can I borrow something to sleep in?" Sam asked with a smile.

"Yeah, of course." Mia replied, ushering Sam towards her bedroom.

"Hang on, Mi." Sian stopped her, getting up off the sofa. "Sam, you're more of a similar size to me. You can borrow some of my clothes."

"Thanks." Sam followed her upstairs and Mia collapsed onto the sofa with Charlie. When they returned, Mia had to clench her teeth together to stop her tongue from lolling out of her mouth.

Sian had lent her the shortest shorts and the tightest, lowest strap top and looked incredibly happy with herself.

"Well, I'm exhausted, I think I'll go to bed." Sian said then mouthed. "You're welcome." Mia scowled at her. "Night, guys."

"Night." Sam smiled and waved.

"I think I'm gonna head to bed too." Mia yawned and stood up. "Let me just get you a blanket. Do you think you'll be warm enough?"

Sam looked perplexed. "Can I not just sleep in with you?" she asked.

"Erm-yeah." Mia replied. "Of course, you can."

They moved through to the bedroom together with Charlie at their heels. Mia's heart was racing, and she worried she might forget how to form a proper sentence.

"What side of the bed do you sleep on?" Sam asked, standing at the bed side, waiting to take direction from Mia.

"Erm – normally the left." Mia said. "I don't mind though; I can sleep on either side!"

"I normally sleep on the right." Sam smiled. "It's like it was meant to be."

Mia gave a nervous laugh and excused herself from the room.

While she was in the bathroom, Mia's thoughts were scattered and bouncing off every wall. How often did you have to share a bed with your crush? A room, yes, maybe even an awkward car journey but very rarely a bed. Did she wear a bra, or did she go braless? Did she launch herself out of bed as soon as she woke up to go and brush her teeth? What if she snored? Or kicked? Or cried? Or took her top off? She had had a few drinks after all.

When Mia climbed into bed, she lay as close to the edge as she possibly could, not slipping off her bra until she was under the duvet.

"Mimi?" Sam asked, as Mia subtly dropped her bra onto the floor.

"Yeah?" she replied.

"Are you nervous?" Sam danced her fingers on her chest.

"Nervous?" Mia asked, quietly gulping to herself. "Why would I be nervous?"

"You know." Sam said, letting her words hang.

"I do?" Mia asked, she felt suddenly sweaty.

"Yeah." Sam said, quietly "Because the show is getting so close now."

"Oh, right, yeah. A little bit, I suppose."

Mia could not help her mind from wandering. She imagined what would happen if Sam was gay and she had the confidence to make a move. The more she thought, the more she blushed, as though embarrassed in case Sam could hear her thoughts. She was desperate to turn the light off, to hide her red face, but the lamp was on Sam's side of the bed. Even thinking of it as 'Sam's side of the bed' made her tingly.

"Can you get the light?" Mia asked, pointing to the lamp.

"Yeah, of course." Sam said, flicking the switch. "Night, Mi."

"Night."

Mia did not sleep. Instead she lay, staring at the ceiling until about 5am, when her eyelids finally succumbed to the tiredness.

**

"Morning, sunshine." Sian sang from the kitchen; she was wrapped in her polka dot dressing gown cooking bacon and eggs. "Eggs?"

"Please." Mia croaked and stretched herself awake on the sofa; Steph was cuddled in the armchair with Charlie, who was wiggling his way over now Mia was awake.

"Hey, Sam, what are you doing here?" Steph asked, as a dishevelled Sam wandered into the living room.

Sian narrowed her eyes, looking suspiciously between Sam and Mia, quietly.

"Mi and I just ended up in Tynemouth last night after rehearsal and I didn't want to pay for a taxi home." Sam replied; she was wearing Mia's dressing gown.

Sian kept eyeing them and giving them glances right up until Sam left.

When she did leave, Mia took to sorting her room and was so occupied doing so that she had not noticed Sian leaning in her doorway.

"Ok, I have to ask," Sian began, and Mia jumped, clutching at her heart.

"Jesus, you scared me." Mia hissed. "Don't you knock?"

"The door was open." Sian shrugged then walked in to sit on the bed, she rolled onto her stomach and kicked her legs up behind her. "Anyway, stop avoiding my question."

"I'm not avoiding anything." Mia replied, anxiously thinking how she *could* avoid any forthcoming questions, so took to facing away and sorting her sock drawer.

Sian was staring at her, intensely, with her head propped up on her arms. "What's going on with you two?"

Mia unpaired and repaired two grey, ankle socks. "I don't know what you're talking about."

"Yes, you do." Sian said, bluntly, looking smug.

"I really don't." Mia tried to act nonchalant by shrugging and avoiding Sian's gaze.

Sian raised her eyebrows. "Come on, do you think I was born yesterday? I know a morning after when I see one. She was wearing your dressing gown."

Mia chose not to reply. Sian studied her face then pressed on.

"Did you sleep with her?" Sian asked.

"No!" Mia spun round.

"Did you share a bed?" Sian asked.

"Well, yeah we did." Mia replied.

"Did you kiss?" Sian asked.

"No, nothing happened. Nothing at all." Mia said, adamantly, and Sian leaned forward to prod her in the back.

"Why not?" Sian whined, disappointed.

"What do you mean 'why not?" Mia asked, frowning and shuffling further away from Sian. "Sam is straight, how many times?"

"Oh, come on." Sian threw her hands in the air as she scoffed. "She is sending vibes all over the shop right now."

"Is she? Or did she just see a simple solution to a taxi related problem?" Mia replied.

Sian gave her a look.

"I'm just saying." Sian said, holding her hands up. "I wouldn't rule anything out. Everyone's a little bit gay."

**

When she arrived at Gramps' in the evening for their birthday tea, she was still thinking about what Sian had said. Surely not everyone was a little gay. She could not imagine Molly ever being even a little bit gay. It was the first time she had seen her sister or her brother-in-law since they had returned from their honeymoon and, in all honesty, she was finding them a bit too much to handle. It was as if they were keen to have children as soon as nature would allow them to and they could not keep their hands off one another. Thankfully, Gramps and Grandma were more reserved in their relationship.

"Oh, you have outdone yourself with this one, Gramps." Fred physically applauded when Gramps walked in with his latest creation: a two-tiered Hadrian's Wall themed birthday cake. The wall itself ran around the first tier, with Fred, Mia and Charlie on top of the cake, sitting by a campfire outside their tent.

"You need to go on the Great British Bake Off or something." Mia said, standing to appreciate the full view of the cake. "I've never seen cakes like yours."

Gramps stood a little taller; it was certainly a cake to be proud of. Only mildly concerned at how much she was ruining her 'lose weight' goal after only one day, Mia tucked in, melting at its deliciousness.

"So, Mi," Grandma began, slicing the knife more into the beautiful cake. "Are you excited to start your job?"

"I think so." Mia said, wiping some jam from the corner of her mouth.

"When do you start, pet?" Gramps asked, accepting his slice.

"30th September." she replied before taking another irresistible bite.

"Oh, not long now!" he said, with an excited smile.

In reality, Mia had been so occupied with everything she had put off preparing for her new job. She and Steph had trekked into Newcastle to buy smart and proper 'work' clothes one evening after work, she had signed her contract and that was about it. Steph was starting a graduate scheme and Mia was entering the charity sector through Surfers Against Sewage. It was a dream job in the fundraising department, but it required kicking her brain into gear.

Their tea ended early. Molly and William could not seem to contain themselves anymore and dashed off as soon as they were free. Fred and Mia both tried to hide their horrified faces when Gramps suggested Grandma sleepover. Mia thanked Gramps for the delicious meal, hugged them all and started home. Fred ended up escaping too, planning to drive out to Costco to have an excuse to flee.

"You can just come to mine, you know?" Mia offered as they reached his car.

"I think I might later, thanks." Fred replied, unlocking it. "I need to do this shopping run anyway but I'll buzz you later."

With Sian out on a date and Steph at work, Mia was on track for a few hours alone with Charlie. She walked in the front door, threw her bag into her room and kicked her shoes into the allocated spot. It was not until she flopped onto her bed that she realised Charlie was nowhere to be seen. Usually, he was straight to the door to greet them.

"Charlie?" she called; no response. "Charlie?"

When no response came a second time, she pushed off the bed and began to explore the flat, shouting as she went.

There he was, lying on his side on Sian's bed.

"Hey, boy." she said, softly, gently sitting down next to him. "What are you doing up here?"

Without lifting his head in her direction, he looked at her. His breathing was laboured, and his tongue lolled; he needed urgent medical attention.

Running back downstairs to grab her phone, she started calling round straight away, desperately trying to find an available friend who had a car. Fred was not picking up his phone, he would be halfway to Gateshead anyway. No answer from Holly, Maria or Carol.

In desperation, she made the call.

"Hi," It was the first time they had properly spoken one to one since the breakup. "I'm so sorry to call, but I don't know who else can help. It's Charlie."

"What's up?" Jake asked, immediate concern jumping into his voice.

"There's something wrong with him. It's like he can't breathe." As she described his poorly condition, she began to sob. "He's just really not well."

"Okay. Google where the emergency vets is, and I'll be round as soon as I can. Can you do that?" he asked; she could hear him getting ready as they spoke.

When Jake messaged to say he was outside, Mia carefully scooped Charlie up and carried him down to the awaiting car. Upon seeing Jake, Charlie lazily wagged his tail.

"Nice to see you, too, boy." Jake said, giving him a sympathetic pat. Luckily, the emergency vet was less than two miles away.

"I'll wait out here till you're done." Jake said, as she left the car and she smiled, meekly.

When the veterinary assistant opened the door, he did so with a reassuring smile.

"Ah, this little fella must be Charlie?" he said, and Mia nodded.

In the assessment room, she lay him gently on the surface of the table for the vet to check him over.

"Ah ha! I see the problem." The vet said, after she checked in his mouth. "I'm just going to give him an anti-sickness injection."

After the injection, she tilted Charlie's head back, as Mia held him. From his throat, the vet began to pull out a string of wool. As Mia watched in amazement, the vet pulled and pulled until a significant amount of wool sat in a pile on the table in front of Charlie.

When she paid, Mia was still in shock at how much had been pulled out of Charlie, but so thankful he was okay.

Still carrying the exhausted little dog, Mia trekked back out to the car.

"What's up with him?" Jake asked.

"Genius here decided it was a good idea to eat the bathmat." Mia replied.

Jake had to laugh.

"Thanks for bringing us." Mia said, stroking Charlie's head. "And - thanks for the present. I love it. I love it so much. You didn't have to do that."

"Hey, just because we aren't together anymore doesn't mean I don't want you to be happy." Jake said, indicating left out of the street. "And I thought that would make you pretty happy."

"You're right, it did." she smiled, continuing to stroke Charlie. With the panic over, they drove back to Mia's flat, with Mia deciding to ask about the elephant in the room.

"How are you and Maria?" Mia asked, awkwardly.

"Are you only asking to be polite?" he said.

"No, I want to know." she replied.

"We're good, we're really good." he cracked a half smile at the thought of her.

"Are you happy?"

"I am."

And Mia found herself genuinely happy for them.

Chapter Twenty-Five

With show week fast approaching, Mia did not have much time to think or worry about anything else. Any thought space was taken up practicing lines or worrying about staging, sets or costumes. Her inner ears remained green for almost a week. All the vital people had their tickets and were showing a mixed range of support. In true Zoe fashion, she was extremely excited and thought the show would be wonderful no matter what. Sian and Holly had stated frequently that they planned to make a tally chart of mistakes made throughout the night. Nerves were showing in other cast members and silly mistakes were being made in the final rehearsals; Angelika looked as though she might explode with her favourite catchphrase of the moment being: 'I need a drink.'

With the height of tourist season coming to an end, the café was quieter than it had been, but Jay helped keep Mia occupied. The mop handles became their microphones and they did their own renditions of various songs. Jay made Mia practice all her songs for the show in the 1-2-1 situation.

All the local children were back at school, bringing the routine back into the weekdays. At 3pm each day, streams of children from the nearby schools would flood out of the gates, usually heading straight for the beach to enjoy the last few weeks of sun with their friends. The cold winter wind was starting to creep in, threatening the start of the indefinite cold weather.

Mia had used the partial balcony in her room daily and kicked herself for not having used it more, earlier in the summer. The family on the corner had two young girls, who were out in the garden playing most days. They even turned it into their own campsite one night, with four of them plus the dog piling into a small tent. Mia could normally hear them playing.

The cast performed their final dress rehearsal two days before opening night, so they could rest a little in between.

"Can you believe we go live in two days?" Sam asked, adjusting the microphones. She never let the cast members put them on themselves, claiming to know the perfect place to clip them. "How nervous are you? On a scale of 1 to 10?"

"I'd go for an 8." Mia replied, contradicting her ever present butterflies. "I'm nervous, but I'm still waiting for the bone shaking panic to set in."

"If I had your talent, I would never be nervous." Sam smiled, straightening up and dusting off her knees. "I'd just get up, belt out the songs and wait for the applause to roll in!"

The final dress rehearsal was the first performance to go mistake free and Angelika cried with relief.

"Amazing!" Angelika clapped, then pulled herself together. "If you do it just like that in two days' time, I'll proudly call you my cast! Now, over the next two days – rest, relax and remember your lines! I'll see you all at 3pm on Friday!"

They were dismissed; Carol gave Mia a lift home and promised to pop round the following night to see them all.

Around 10pm, Sian banged on the bathroom door with a closed fist. "Mate, I love you, but if I hear 'Defying Gravity' one more time, I'm gonna throw you out the window."

"Sorry!" Mia shouted back, changing the record on her singing voice.

**

The evening before opening night, Mia grabbed her surfboard and jogged down to the coast. With September in full swing, the autumn swell had returned, bringing clean sets and banishing tourists. The beach belonged to the locals again. As she sat out back, waiting for the perfect wave to carry her in, she ran her *Wicked* lines in her head, trying not to let her thoughts stray away to anywhere more dangerous. Staying away from the other surfers as much as she could gave her the chance to mutter some of her lines to herself and practice. Being in the water always helped clear her head. There was something about sitting in the water, staring at the beautiful coastline before her. It was so calming. A perfect set would roll in, she would have a play, then it would flatten off again to give them a break.

As the sun began to set, she kept a look out for her final wave, riding it in as the horizon swallowed up the sun. She traipsed reluctantly out of the water and to the spot under the boardwalk where she hid her rucksack.

[Steph] We're in the Surf café, if you want to join. Whole gang, even Charlie. x

Carrying her surfboard up the beach, she snuck behind the lifeguard shed to get changed into shorts and t-shirt. The smell of wetsuit still clung to her, but she was heading to the best place to be accepted for it. Leaving her board in the board rack at the door, she waved at Sian, who brought an Amstel to the table for her.

"Good surf?" Steph asked, brushing some crumbs off the tabletop.

"So clean." Mia said, exhaling loudly. "Exactly what I needed."

"Well, don't get too comfortable there," Sian said, pointing to the corner stage. "You're up next."

"Nah, you guys have got enough of me singing this week." Mia said, reaching for the skies in a stretch.

"You can't have too much of a good thing." Sian replied, nudging her, then rising from her seat.

"I think that was almost a compliment." Mia said, taking a swig.

Sian took the reins and the microphone from the previous performer.

"Now, surfers and surfettes," she commanded the room and they turned to watch her. "For most of you this girl needs no introduction. But, for those of you who don't know, I introduce you to the star of the local upcoming production of Wicked, my best friend, Mia Moore!"

With a few encouraging shoves from Fred and Holly, she got to her feet to take the stage, dragging Steph with her.

"I'm sorry we are so unprepared." Mia said into the microphone.

"We were told about this around thirty seconds ago."

Low chuckles murmured through the crowd as Mia and Steph decided on a song, settling on 'Go Your Own Way' by Fleetwood Mac. Collectively, *Rumours* was the flat's favourite album. Through the blinding light, Mia could just make out Carol tapping her foot to the beat.

Everyone applauded when they finished.

"And just another reminder everyone." Sian said, claiming the microphone once again. "Mia is starring in Wicked tomorrow night. If anyone wants tickets, there are some available to buy at the bar."

They applauded again and Mia, thoroughly embarrassed by her friend, took her seat once again. As a full group of eight – Carol, Zoe, Holly, Mia, Fred, Steph, Maria and Sian, they spent the evening enjoying each other's company, laughing hard and eating far too much. Mia experienced another moment where she leaned back from it all, appreciating what and who she had. Her friendships made her so grateful and full of cheesy, mushy love.

**

When she woke the next day, Mia was terrified. Her night's sleep had been horrendous, she had tossed and turned all night with worry. So many people she knew were going to be there watching, there to notice if she messed something up. Even Sandeep and Aanya were coming, Gramps had sold them tickets himself.

Wrapping herself in her dressing gown, she shuffled through to the kitchen, poured some breakfast and turned *Friends* on in the living room. Charlie huddled in next to her, sensing her fear and trying his best to offer comfort. Each time she stopped stroking him, he hit her with his paw.

"Are you going to help at all, or are you going to sit there like a nervous lemon all day?" Steph asked, shooing Mia's legs onto the sofa as she hoovered.

"Why would a lemon be nervous?" Mia asked, shovelling in the last mouthful of cereal.

"Because it lived in a kitchen surrounded by knives?" Steph said, as though the answer was an obvious one.

"Ah, touche." Mia replied, saluting Steph with her spoon.

"*Anyway,* are you going to help me set up or are you just going to act like a plum?" Steph said, hands on her hips.

"What's with all the fruit references?" Mia asked, avoiding the real question.

"MIA!" Steph growled.

"Alright, I'll help." Mia huffed, dragging herself on to her feet. "What do you want me to do?"

"You can start by taking Charlie for a walk and really wearing him out." Steph said, pointing to Charlie, who was wiggling excitedly at the sound of the word 'walk.' "But, don't get him wet! I don't need him dragging sea, salt, and goodness knows what else through the house when he gets back."

Mia saluted again to the others, got washed and dressed and set out with the happy little spaniel.

They were hosting the after- after party for whomever was still standing following the after party in the green room. The green room was only open for an hour or so after the performance ended, so they always needed somewhere else to continue. Sam and Steph had cooked up the plan without Mia's knowledge initially, forgetting to tell her until the drinking games started arriving to the house in amazon orders.

Sian's new soundbar was ready and waiting under the windowsill; the fridge was filled with nibbles and beer in preparation. Warning notes had already been slipped under the doors of the neighbours, along with an invite to the afterparty. A huge banner reading 'You Were Wicked!' was already hung across the kitchen.

"That's a bit premature, isn't it?" Mia asked, holding one end and reading it for the first time. "What if we make a complete belly flop of it?"

"Then I'll get a marker pen and changed it to say 'weren't." Sian said with a smirk.

**

"How's everyone feeling?" Carol asked, her voice chiming as she waltzed into the dressing room. Mia managed a nervous smile back to her; she thought if she opened her mouth, she may vomit. How Broadway actors did it she would never know.

Sensing Mia's nerves, Carol made a beeline for her.

"You'll be *fine*." Carol said, squeezing Mia's shoulders. "As soon as you've said your first line, you'll be grand."

"What if I forget that first one?" Mia asked, drumming her fingers on the desk.

"You won't."

"What if I fall over on stage?" Mia asked, switching to biting her nails.

"You won't."

"What if-"

"You won't!" Carol looked serious, taking Mia's hand away from her mouth. "You're going to smash this."

Mia smiled meekly, again.

Each time Mia poked her head around the side of the stage, she saw someone else she recognised. Grandma, Gramps, William and Molly were among the first to turn up, closely followed by Sandeep and Aanya. The girls almost had their own row near the back, with Don Boon, Carol's husband, joining them not long before the curtains lifted. Zoe and Fred came in together, looking very cosy, much to Mia's delight, closely followed by Maria and Jake.

In between her spying, Mia gave herself panicked looks in the dressing room mirrors. When she first arrived that evening, her hands were so shaky, she doubted whether she would be able to help paint her face properly. Luckily, other than some black liner around her eyes, the rest of her exposed body parts were solid green. She had gone to the theatre well before 3pm to start the layers of sponging required to turn her green. Her black wig was pinned to her head with what felt like thousands of hair slides and hair sprayed around the edges to stop strands of blonde falling out. As she paced, she twirled the end of the black plait in her fingers, trying to control her breathing rate.

Hoping it would help, she sat back in her dressing room chair again, re-reading her first line repeatedly. Sam appeared in the mirror behind her.

"Are you ready?" she asked, dipping her head to look Mia's reflection in the eyes.

"No." Mia said, glumly. She felt it was the most nervous she had been in her life.

"Oh, you'll be great." Sam said, throwing her arms around Mia's neck, then jumping back from the paint.

"Thanks." Mia spun around to meet her face properly, noticing the dash of paint that had rubbed off. "Oh, you've got a bit of green on your cheek, just there."

Mia pointed to the patch but stopped herself from touching Sam's cheek centimetres before she did; she could feel herself flushing under the makeup.

"Oops." Sam said, leaning over her to reach the mirror. "Thanks." Scrubbing her face, she managed to remove the smudge, stretching dangerously close to Mia as she did so.

"If you get nervous, just look at me!" Sam smiled, stepping back. "Then, you don't have to look at the audience."

Mia smiled at the kind gesture but thought about how looking at Sam would make her the most nervous she could be. She was already thankful her boner was invisible.

"Right, everyone." Angelika called over the dressing room speakers. "Fifteen minutes 'til curtains up!"

Tensing even more in her chair, Mia gripped the arms. If her knuckles had not been green, they would have been white.

"Oh, crap, I've got to go." Sam said, looking at the door. And, because she could touch nowhere else without stealing more green paint, Sam pecked a kiss on Mia's lips. "Mi, you're going to kill this."

Mia's eyes nearly popped out of their skull at the sudden, unexpected gesture.

"I'll see you at the after party." Sam said with a wink, darting off to her decks.

As Mia heard the orchestra start up, her stomach tingled with excitement, for more than one reason. The feel of the music had her heart beating faster with adrenaline and the shock of the kiss had helped to disperse her nerves. She stood in the wings, waiting for the spotlights Sam shone to be filled. The scenery was lit, with the huge map of Oz illuminated for the audience, and the dragon began to shake.

"*Good news, she's dead!*" The chorus sang; the show had started. With the map lifted, the huge clock dominated the stage behind the cast. Watching everyone throw themselves around with such energy and dazzle the audience in the first scene the way they did put Mia on the highest of highs. Although, during Mia's first scene, her knees were shaking so much she thought she was going to crumble. Carol was right though, as soon as she managed her first line and first scene, she was in the flow.

There were only a few mistakes. At one-point, Glinda the Good walked on stage before the scenery had changed so stopped, said 'whoopsie, take two' and walked back off but she got several laughs. When the curtain dropped at half time and the audience leapt up to buy their ice creams, Mia was lowered from her suspension back to the stage. Carol came running out, tears coating her face, and threw her arms around Mia.

"You were amazing! Oh, my gosh. I couldn't help but cry!" Carol's face was streaming with tears and she dabbed it with a tissue under her glasses.

"Don't speak too soon, Carol." Mia laughed, allowing the stagehands to disconnect her wires. "We're only halfway through."

"I know but that scene." Carol had pride in her face. "That scene was just so powerful."

Towards the end of the show, Mia began to wish it would never end. The elation was incredible. Everyone was on fire, truly enjoying every second of performing. In the audience, Mia's friends and family were winning the competition to be the loudest and led the standing ovations.

As the final applause took place, Mia received the loudest cheers for her individual bow. She was overwhelmed by the evening and cemented the memory in her brain. Squinting through the lights, Mia saw Sam, up in her tower, smiling proudly at Mia and blowing her a kiss. With a grin back, crystal clear against her green skin, Mia caught it, swiftly. Although the spotlight was still on her, no one shared the private moment but them. And though Mia knew it was still nothing but platonic for Sam, or so she thought, she blushed like a schoolgirl under her layers of green.

The End.

Printed in Great Britain
by Amazon

57666891R00221